"DO YOU KN
YOURSELF IN SUCH COM

"Of course." Tess raised her chin, but did not lean toward him to make her point. She did not want to chance bumping into Heddy's cage, which was next to her feet. If Cameron had been curious why she had brought it here instead of leaving it with the other bags in the cart that followed the carriage, he had not asked. "Do not write me off as a hopeless bumpkin."

"Knowing the rules is not the same as knowing how to comport oneself when one is faced with a challenge among the Polite World."

She clenched her hands together, glad her gloves hid how her knuckles must be bleaching with her fury. "I promise you I shall do nothing to embarrass you, Cameron, such as flirting with the Prince Regent."

"Are you always so outspoken?"

"I am always this *honest.*"

"A perilous trait in London."

She laughed. "Then I must risk that peril, because honesty is a habit I do not wish to lose."

Cameron shifted on the seat, sliding his arm behind her. Again, as when they had spoken last night in the library, he did not touch her. She was glad, because she was unsettled even when he was this close. If he let his fingers drop to curve along her shoulder, she doubted she would be able to form a single logical thought . . .

Also look for these Zebra romances by Jo Ann Ferguson

HIS
UNEXPECTED
BRIDE

Jo Ann Ferguson

ZEBRA BOOKS
Kensington Publishing Corp.
http://www.kensingtonbooks.com

For Francesca
who understands the magic

One

He had to be dreaming.

Cameron Hawksmoor tried to make his eyes focus, but everything was blurred. Just as in his dreams.

But why was he dreaming of a delicately carved tester bed with curtains of pale rose chintz? That was not a man's dream. A man did not let his nightly fantasies take him to a room shadowed by drapes pulled closed over tall windows. Certainly not windows with brocade draperies of a deeper rose than the bed curtains. A man dreamed of tawdry taverns or dangerous roads through a mist-shrouded wood or a lusty maid who regarded him with an inviting smile as she slid her hand across his chest and . . .

Cameron choked back a gasp as his thoughts seemed to come to life. Raising his head, which ached as if he had struck it against a tree—*twice*—he saw slender fingers resting over his bare chest. He tilted his head to follow the arm, covered in white fabric that glowed too brightly in the dim light. With a moan, he sank back into the pillows and put his hand to his head.

It was not his habit to give a bottle a black eye, but from the way his skull resonated and even his slightest breath seemed to resonate like a bunch of fives against his face, he knew he must have done so last night. Even more uncustomary was the fact that, in a drunken stupor, he had brought some woman to his bed. He was not his brother, who seemed to believe it was a man's duty to bed every woman who happened to cross his path. He had been true to Pamela until he had arranged for her to find another protector before he left London last time for the Continent.

Dear Pamela. Cameron let his thoughts linger on her a moment as he envisioned the lovely woman who had been his mistress before he went to do his duty for England and join in the battle against Napoleon. Now he was back from the Continent, and he was ready to enjoy the pleasures he had fought so hard to preserve. Not, however, with sweet Pamela, whose flashing dark eyes and hair as golden as the summer sun and whose voluptuous form had captivated him from the first time he had seen her. Upon leaving, he had not wanted to hold her to a promise to wait faithfully for him. She had no interest in marrying, and neither did he. The arrangement had been perfect for both of them until he could not ignore the call to defend the Crown. He wondered if she still was with Stedley. Most likely, for the man had plenty of blunt to lavish on Pamela, who did have a weakness for pretty things.

The woman's fingers shifted on his chest, as ethereal as the passage of a lark over a meadow. Although his thoughts were filled with Pamela now, that must not have been the case last night when he brought this serving wench to his bed. He hoped she would be understanding about how he had downed too much of Masterson's brandy. Some small token would be sure to please her and enable him to disassociate himself from this unexpected complication.

He did not have to worry about distressing his host. Bernard Masterson had been jovial last night, if Cameron could trust his frayed memories. Masterson was not a member of the *ton* because he was the younger son of a younger son, but he set a good table and had an excellent cellar and had been a great friend of Cameron's late father. Once the two men had belonged to the same club, but Cameron seemed to remember they had had a falling out. Why could he recall his father grumbling about that when he could not remember the face of the woman in his bed?

Her fingers edged along him again as the wench murmured something in her sleep. Her provocative touch suggested she was not truly slumbering, but was teasing him, urging him to take his pleasure with her once again. Again? Blast it! How much had he drunk that he could not recall her before waking by her side?

With the dusk cloaking the bed and the pain riveting his head, he could not clear his eyes to see her well. He leaned toward her. Sweet fragrance wafted from her, and, fearing he was a leather-head, but knowing it was far too late for second thoughts when the wench was curled up by his side, he tipped her face up. He stared at her soft lips and watched them part in the moment before his mouth claimed them. His fingers swept up through auburn hair spread across her pillow and his. He must have been deeply foxed to forget the luscious taste of these lips. He should—

Cameron yelped as her slender fingers struck his face, sending renewed agony ricocheting through his head. Pulling back, he leaned on one elbow and cradled his forehead in his hand. He grasped the woman's arm with his other hand, crushing the fine linen and lace on her sleeve.

Linen? Lace?

"Who in hell are you?" Releasing her, he pushed himself up to sit against the headboard of the bed. Some carving jabbed his back, but he did not move, waiting for the room to settle itself before his stomach revolted.

The sour aftertaste of brandy tainted his mouth. He ignored the disgusting flavor. He knew he had downed too much of it. What he did not know was why Masterson's serving wenches wore lace as fine as a lady's.

"What are *you* doing here?" she retorted.

He groaned. Not only did her clothing copy a lady's, but her voice was quality. A serving wench might be satisfied with a token, but an upper maid would demand much more. He was not interested in obtaining a new mistress. He wanted to think only of the one he had left behind two years ago.

When he grumbled an oath, the woman gasped, "My lord, please remember yourself!"

"I wish I could. I wish I could recall anything that has happened in the past twelve hours. I . . ." His voice trailed away as the truth of her identity finally penetrated his brain. He forced his eyes to focus. No, it was impossible!

But there was no mistaking the face so colorless that her green eyes shown like twin emeralds framed by the auburn fire of her hair. With lace curving up beneath her chin and linen dropping over her as she sat facing him, he was not treated to the view of her lithe curves he had admired yesterday when his host introduced him to his daughter.

Daughter!

What was Tess Masterson doing in his bed?

"I have asked you once, and I will ask again before I have no choice but to ring for a footman," she said. "What are you doing in my bed, Lord Hawksmoor?"

"Quiet!" He touched his throbbing head. His mind was still working too slowly. He never had had such a bout with brandy, even when he had quaffed too much the night of his father's funeral to ease his grief. "By the elevens, have some pity on a man who is suffering from megrims."

"A headache is no excuse for you being *here!*" She started to push past him, then pulled back, an expression of horror on her face. She must crawl over him to get past him, he realized, because the bed was not in the center of the room, but pushed against a wall.

"Be quiet," he ordered again. "No, rather, give me an explanation of what in the blazes is going on. You can start with why you are in here in the room your father granted me for my use during my visit here."

"I think not. This cannot go on a moment longer."

"Miss Masterson . . ." How much more ridiculous could this become! No, not ridiculous, for he would have ruined the young woman's reputation if it became known she had been sleeping beside him.

His mouth straightened. Was that her plan? To sneak into his room and then cry out she had been compromised? He had heard of such things, but had not guessed he, Cameron Hawksmoor, would become a victim of such a scheme.

"Get out of my bed!" She shoved against his legs, pushing them over the edge of the mattress.

When they hit the floor, another peal of pain rang in his head. He was about to snarl at her, but stared down at his legs. He was wearing his cream breeches and one shoe. The other lay beside a small table covered with a tatted doily. Atop it, a small cage was covered with a cloth. A bird? If so, he did not intend to remove the fabric. A bird singing would add to the ache in his head.

Exasperation filled him as he stood. He wobbled the single step toward the glass over a washstand. That distance was almost too much. The washstand nearly toppled as he grasped it, trying to keep himself on his feet. Putting his nose close to the glass, he stared at his face and tousled black hair as if he had never seen them before. The reflection was his. If this was still a dream, he looked blasted pitiful instead of being the hero of his own nightly imaginings. Splashing water onto his face, he wiped it vigorously with a cloth hanging by the bowl. A mistake, for more pain followed.

"My lord," came the vexed voice from the bed, "I do not know why you would believe I gave you leave to run tame through my chambers."

"Your chambers?"

"Yes." She crossed her arms over her breasts, which were tantalizingly shadowed by her nightdress. "Are you still so fuddled that you fail to recognize this is not a guest room?"

"I find I have little interest in looking about at the furniture when you offer such a tempting sight."

Red flashed up her face as she grasped a blanket and, tugging it out from where it had been tucked in, threw it over her shoulders. "Forgive me for keeping you from making other observations, my lord. I am not accustomed to having profligates in my private chambers. If you will indulge me and look around, you will see I am quite correct when I say these are *my* rooms."

Her very serenity added to Cameron's irritation. Taking a deep breath, he dared to lurch back to where she sat with the blanket now pulled nearly to her chin. He leaned his hands on the bed before he could fall on his face, but he glowered at her. "If you think to force me into the parson's mousetrap with such a show of blemished honor, Miss Masterson, I urge you to rethink your scheme."

"Scheme?" Her eyes grew wide. "I have asked you to leave, my lord. Will you do so, or must I—"

"Must you what? Scream? That would bring the very servants you have ready to *intrude* upon us, wouldn't it?"

"You are mad!"

His reply was halted by what he was startled to see. Remnants of passion shone in her eyes. Mayhap he was insane, but he was certain of one thing. She had softened in his arms for the length of a pair of heartbeats before her hand had smacked his face with every bit of her feigned indignity. His fingers tingled as he remembered how silken that unruly fall of auburn hair had been.

He reached out, and she edged away. Slapping at his hand, she said, "Begone, I tell you!"

"Give me a chance to get my head settled on my shoulders."

"You can do that elsewhere."

"I can do what I wish where I wish."

She frowned. "What stuff and nonsense are you spouting? Begone, or I shall—"

He was not sure if he was more determined to keep her from shrieking and creating a scene or if he simply could not restrain his curiosity to rediscover the flavor of her lips. Before he could decide, he had grasped her by the shoulders, pulled her up to her knees, and captured her mouth. She struggled to escape him, but he enfolded her to him. With her arms caught beneath the blanket, she could not free her hand to strike his face. The breath she had pulled in for a scream shuddered out of her in a sigh. Her lips quivered in the moment before he claimed them again while his fingers swept up through her hair.

He shifted to kneel beside her on the bed. Before he could, good sense clouted him even more viciously than her hand had. Was he bereft of his mind? This woman, no matter how lovely she might be, was not his to tumble. Her father was his host.

Shoving her back gently, for 'twas his own head that needed to be banged against the wall and have some sense knocked into it, he turned away. He was gasping for breath as if he had run from one end of a line of battlefield infantry to the other. Forcing himself to regain his calm took more strength than he had expected, but he was able to face her with a cool smile as he said, "That, Miss Masterson, is what I could do . . . if I wanted to."

"You are loathsome!"

"Mayhap you should have considered that before you invited me to share your bed."

Tess Masterson stared at the man standing beside her bed as if he had every right to be here. *Her bed!* Sweet heavens, how was she going to extract herself from this muddle with her reputation intact? She had not guessed when Lord Hawksmoor and his friend, Eustace Knox, had presented themselves at her father's door yesterday afternoon that before a single day had passed, Lord Hawksmoor would ruin her.

And himself as well, for the marquess barely resembled the man who had arrived here yesterday. Instead of being in prime twig, as he had been in spite of his long journey from a friend's house near Norwich, he was as wrinkled as a washerwoman's washboard. One stocking was torn and drooping, and he still had not put on his other shoe.

Yet his features remained compelling . . . and dangerous. That was the word Jenette had used to describe him yesterday, and Tess suspected her French abigail had much more knowledge in those matters than Tess did. Jenette was correct, because, beneath his dark hair, there was a small scar over his right eyebrow, just at the very place where he easily could have been struck by a rapier or a ball in a duel. The taut line of Lord Hawksmoor's jaw, now clenched with the pain he was struggling to hide, was softened only by a cleft in his chin. The rest of his face matched his name, because he had a strong, aquiline nose that would befit a bird of prey, and his startlingly blue eyes offered a challenge only a fool would confront.

Tess could not afford to be want-witted now. She must think with caution and with lucidity how to extract herself from this unexpected situation.

The first thing must be to convince Lord Hawksmoor

she needed his help instead of his kisses. *His delicious kisses*. She silenced the part of her mind that had whispered those perfidious words. He might be a dashing blade, but she would be dashed before she allowed him to compromise her. She refused to believe it was too late to save her honor.

Resettling the blanket over her shoulders, because it had slipped when he had pulled her to his hard chest, she said quietly, "I can assure you, my lord, I did not invite you here."

"Then why I am here?"

"That is a question you should be able to answer better than I. You were the one who intruded into my private chambers. I did not invite you here. Whatever you may think of me, my lord, I am not a harlot." She blinked back tears. Dash it! She did not want to surrender to weeping now. It would solve nothing. "Oh, Papa will be shattered I am ruined."

He ran his hand against his unshaven chin. "By the elevens, if you are being honest with me now, then I have made a horrible mistake."

"I am being honest, and you have made a horrible mistake. Not one mistake, my lord, but two, for you were wrong to come in here, and you are even more in error to linger."

"Miss Masterson," he asked, his voice now as hushed as hers, "where does your abigail sleep?"

"Beyond my dressing room."

"Is your dressing room behind that door?" He pointed to a closed door that was half-hidden by the drapes covering the window farthest from the bed.

She nodded, and her hair fell forward. As she brushed it back, she was caught by his gaze. She could not disregard the longing in his eyes. His fingers rose toward her, but he only ran them along her hair.

"Stop that!" She wanted to cry out her dismay, but on

that one thing he was correct. Her cries of resistance might be the very thing that brought someone into the room.

Lord Hawksmoor drew back his hand and regarded it with puzzlement, as if he could not guess why it had touched her. "Forgive me, Miss Masterson."

"I believe you have much to ask forgiveness for, my lord. Will you please leave?"

"As soon as I can be assured I will not be seen."

She nodded, knowing that to do anything out of hand now would guarantee her downfall. They must take care.

"Does your abigail come in to check you during the night?" Lord Hawksmoor asked.

"Of course not!" She rose to her knees, her indignation refusing to allow her to sit. "My father has never had any cause to distrust me."

"Good." He smiled. "Let us keep it that way."

"What do you mean?"

"What I mean is we should pledge to act as if last night never happened. It was an error, which I regret deeply, Miss Masterson, but your reputation should not be besmirched when you did nothing worse than sleep in your own bed." He frowned, then winced, and she knew his head must be hurting dreadfully. That was the price he would have to pay for drinking himself into such oblivion he had crawled into her bed without realizing she was already there. "What I do not understand is how I got here. As I recall, the guest rooms are in another wing from the family's quarters."

"They are."

He bent to pick up his shoe, then grasped the tester pole. Leaning his head against it, he moaned. "By the elevens, my head is going to explode."

Taking pity on him was an instantaneous response, for she had heard Papa complain several times about the agony that followed a night of revelry. Even though she should despise Lord Hawksmoor for creating this unbelievable situation, Tess slipped off the bed and put her arm around him, steering him to the chaise longue by the window. He leaned back on it with a groan.

"Thank you," he whispered. "You are being kinder than I should expect you to be."

"I know." She dipped a cloth in the tepid water in the ewer next to her dressing table and settled it on his forehead. "My lord, if you are to sneak out of here, you must be able to walk without bumping into every piece of furniture. That is the quickest way to announce where you have been."

"You seem to have more knowledge about a man creeping out of a lady's bedchambers than I had anticipated."

Tess rolled her eyes. How could Lord Hawksmoor be jesting *now?* Or was he joking? She frowned. "If you would pause to think, you would know I am basing my comments on nothing more than good sense. You must not call any attention to yourself as you slip away."

"I will need directions to return to my own bedroom, for I fear I have no idea where it is in relationship to this room."

"Is that what happened? Did you get turned around in the corridors?"

He started to shake his head, then flinched again. "The devil take this head!"

"Please, my lord, watch your language."

Opening one eye, he looked up at her. "I can reassure you what I said was far less crude than what I was thinking."

"What you should be thinking of now is how you will get back to your rooms."

"And how I can find out what caused me to end up here last night." Sagging into the pink cushions on the chaise longue, he said, "I recall nothing after I finished playing cards with your father and Eustace, just as some other chap came to call."

She sat on the stool facing the chaise longue. "What other man?"

"A very thin man who was a full head taller than your father. What hair he had left was iron gray, and his clothes were simple and dark." He pulled the cloth down over his eyes. "I do not recall anything much of his face."

"You are describing Dr. Tucker, who is the vicar at the church in the village." She jumped to her feet, suddenly fearful. "Why did he call at such a late hour? Was something wrong?"

Lord Hawksmoor grumbled, "I do not recall, and I do not, at the moment, care. Don't we have enough wrong now to keep our anxiety focused on the problem at hand?"

"A problem that will be solved if you would skulk out of here. The reason Dr. Tucker called . . ." She heard a distant clock chime the hour. Sweet heavens, it was already mid-morning. By this hour, Jenette should have come into the room to bring breakfast. If her abigail had entered and seen Lord Hawksmoor—no, it was too appalling even to consider, but every passing minute increased the chance of Jenette walking in here.

Lord Hawksmoor must have taken note of the chiming as well. "It is time for me to try to be on my way."

"First, let me take that cloth."

He peeled it from his forehead and dropped it toward her hand. It missed and fell to the floor. With a grimace, she bent to retrieve it. She straightened, but faltered when she could not ignore his gaze sweeping along her with the unrestrained hunger that had been on his lips when he had pulled her into his arms.

Going to the ewer, she hung the cloth beside it. She clutched onto the dressing table with both hands. No other man's stare had ever unnerved her like this. When they had been introduced yesterday, she had not been so disconcerted, although she had noticed his good looks and charming smile. Had his kiss awakened something within her that she had not guessed existed?

"Don't be a widgeon," she said.

"I believe it is too late to tell me that now."

Tess did not want to own she had been talking to herself. If he took umbrage at her comments, so be it. Anything to get him out of her room . . . and out of her thoughts.

"Can you walk to the door?" she asked.

"I shall know once I have tried." Lord Hawksmoor pushed himself to his feet. Swaying, he held out his arms like a rope dancer performing beside a gypsy wagon at a market day. He took one careful step, then another. He smiled triumphantly. "It seems I am steadier than I—"

She caught him as his knees folded. The legs of the chaise longue thumped against the floor as she collapsed beneath him, unable to keep him on his feet. When she moaned with the last bit of breath she had, for most of it had been squeezed out of her when he fell atop her, he shifted so his weight was not over her.

"Are you hurt, Miss Masterson?" Lord Hawksmoor asked.

Opening her eyes, she realized he was lying beside her on the chaise longue. Not just beside her, one arm was beneath her with his hand cupping her shoulder, while his other hand was pressed to the cushions on the opposite side of her. She raised her eyes to meet his right above hers. She started to edge away, then realized his leg was across hers, pinning her to the cushions.

"I did not mean to do you any injury," he continued when she did not reply, for she was too shocked to utter any of the thoughts racing through her head. "Tell me you are all right."

A satisfied laugh from the other side of the room swept

away any words she might have spoken. She heard Lord Hawksmoor curse, but she could only stare at her father who stood in the doorway. Tearing her eyes from his smile, she looked up at Lord Hawksmoor again. A desperate push against his chest persuaded him to sit up, then rise unsteadily to his feet. She grasped the blanket, which had fallen to the floor. Throwing it over her shoulders again, she stood.

"Papa," she whispered, "please let me tell you what has happened. It is not as it seems."

She wondered if he had heard her when he walked past her and offered his hand to Lord Hawksmoor. The marquess stared at it in an amazement she understood far too well. Why was Papa smiling when he should be furious to find a man in her private rooms?

"Welcome, Cameron, my boy," Papa said. "Welcome to the Masterson family."

"What?" gasped Tess at the same time as Lord Hawksmoor.

"I know the welcome is a bit late." Papa laughed loudly. " 'Twas something I forgot to say last night when you married my daughter."

Two

Tess stared at her father, then dragged her eyes toward Lord Hawksmoor, who was doing the same, his mouth agape before he closed it in a scowl. Married? Married to this marquess she had met only yesterday? What flummery was this?

Papa came to where she was sitting. There was a lilt in his step she had not seen in several months. That devil-may-care saunter had drawn the eyes of many women, even when Tess was old enough to notice. His sandy hair, still full, matched a neatly trimmed mustache. Although he wore the wrinkles of time on his face, they seemed to vanish when he smiled.

He kissed her cheek. "Many congratulations, my dear. This marriage is everything I would have wished for you."

"Marriage?" She wanted to accuse Papa of being as muzzed as Lord Hawksmoor, but no odor of brandy billowed from him. "How can I be married to Lord Hawksmoor?"

"I understand your confusion, Tess." He patted her cheek as he had when she was a child and had pelted him with dozens of questions, one after the other. "When Dr. Tucker arrived so late last evening to preside at the ceremony, we did not wish to wake you."

"You did not wish to wake me last night *for my own wedding?*" Her voice had a hysterical tinge to it, but she could not help herself. "Papa, you are making no sense. What is going on?"

"Yes, Masterson," added Lord Hawksmoor, coming around the chaise longue to where they stood. He kept one hand on the back of a chair by her bed, but his steps were steadier than they had been just moments ago. "Do tell us what is going on. This jest is not amusing, neither for me nor your daughter, who has the most to lose from your hoax."

" 'Tis no hoax." Papa's smile did not waver as he faced Lord Hawksmoor, whose face was now blank of any emotion. "You should know that, Hawksmoor, because *you* were present during the wedding."

"I recall nothing about a wedding ceremony. There was conversation among us as I recall—quite convivial conversation, but a wedding ceremony? You are mistaken, Masterson."

"I feared you might be questioning what had happened when I realized this morning how many times you had refilled your glass with my best brandy. That is why I have intruded upon your honeymoon even before the start of the wedding breakfast." Papa withdrew a sheaf of papers from beneath his coat. "I thought you might want to see these to help you remember. You signed these in front of me, the vicar, and Knox." He held up two fingers. "Me and Knox. The required number of witnesses to make this wedding legal."

"Very conveniently," Lord Hawksmoor said.

"Yes."

"But no wedding is legal without a license."

"There was one. You will see a special license amid the papers."

When Papa added nothing else, Tess wanted to reach out to grab the pages he held. What had Lord Hawksmoor signed in the presence of her father, Dr. Tucker, and the marquess's traveling companion, Eustace Knox? The special license? But why would he come here with a marriage license when he had not known her before they were introduced last night? This was making less sense all the time.

Lord Hawksmoor took the pages and scanned them. His fingers curling into a fist crushed the papers in his hand. He tossed them onto a table, every motion taut with anger. Still his face remained blank and his words calm. "This is madness, Masterson. I was completely foxed last night, if my aching head is any indication. If I was so foolish as to agree to a marriage to your daughter, it was because I had too much brandy."

"You insult my lovely daughter!"

The marquess bowed his head toward Tess. "Belittling you in any way was not my intention, Miss Masterson, for I am indebted to you for your kindness with my pounding head this day." Looking back at her father, he said with a hint of an emotion she had not heard before in his voice, "I do not comprehend why you believe I would be a willing party to any such match, Masterson. By the elevens, I never laid eyes upon your daughter before yesterday."

"But you have had the opportunity to see far more than her pretty face since then." Papa's smile began to fade.

"Regardless of that, this marriage is in error. It is time to put an end to this conversation and this unwanted marriage."

"Are you saying you wish to annul whatever ceremony took place last night?" Tess asked, unable to keep hope from her question.

Her father frowned, but the marquess smiled tightly at her as he replied, "It would seem, Masterson, your daugh-

ter wishes this marriage no more than I do. There is no
time to delay. If we get a quiet annulment . . ."

"No!" Papa's voice was thunderous.

Tess stared at her father in astonishment as Lord
Hawksmoor cursed and winced with pain as he held his
hand to his head. Papa often expressed himself with enthusiasm and candid fervor, but she had never heard him
speak with such cold vehemence.

"Papa—"

"Stay out of this, Tess."

She opened her mouth to protest, but closed it. Getting
into a brangle with her father would humiliate him in
front of Lord Hawksmoor. She sat on the very end of the
chaise longue as she watched the two men face each
other. They reminded her of two dogs sizing up each other
as they met for the first time.

But that made no sense. Papa had known Lord Hawksmoor's father for years, for they once had belonged to the
same club in London. Papa no longer belonged to that club,
because, she guessed, the money was not available for the
dues. He had traveled often to London in recent months,
but she had not heard him speak of the club again.

When the duke had died last year, Papa had delivered
his condolences to the duchess in person. He had been
at the family's estate of Peregrine Hall for nearly a week
for the funeral. Surely Papa must have spoken with Lord
Hawksmoor, the duke's younger son, while there.

So why were they acting as if they were strangers? It
was all too puzzling.

Lord Hawksmoor's eyes narrowed, but no other expression eased his taut face as he took another wobbly step
toward her father. "Masterson, why do you wish to bring
your daughter unhappiness in being wed to a man she
barely knows?"

"Because if you annul this marriage, she will never find
another man willing to marry her." Papa flung out his

hands, his voice still booming so loudly Tess suspected it would reach the kitchen. She wanted to urge him to lower it, especially when he added, "You spent the night with Tess, Hawksmoor. Who would have her now?"

"She is untouched."

"So you say."

"And so she says." Lord Hawksmoor put his hand on the blanket over her shoulders. Was his motion meant to comfort her? It did not, for his chaste caress brought to mind how his arms had enveloped her and held her to his firm body. "Speak the truth to your father, Miss Masterson."

"Nothing untoward happened, Papa," she hastened to say. "Lord Hawksmoor is being honest about that." She clenched her hands under the blanket as she gave her father a supplicating look. He must be able to find a way to put an end to this, and she longed to beg him to do so. Unable to speak the truth—that this man frightened her—for she did not want to heap insult on Lord Hawksmoor, she shivered. 'Twas not Lord Hawksmoor who scared her, but the power his kisses had had over her, stealing her good sense and teasing her to find a way to sample another one.

She could not keep her gaze from him. His wrinkled shirt clung close to his muscular chest, and its full sleeves could not hide his brawny arms. With his hair tousled and his eyes still heavy with sleep, he had a charm that teased her to trust him.

Was she as mad as she had accused him of being? This man had spent last night drinking so much that he had agreed to marry her.

Agreed? Why had Papa even allowed Dr. Tucker to begin the marriage ceremony? Had Papa *and* the vicar been so intoxicated as well? She wanted to ask her father that question, but did not have a chance.

"He is being honest that he did not touch you?" her father asked, now scowling. "Is that so?"

"Yes, I did not know he was here in my room until he woke me."

"Woke you?" Papa demanded. "How?"

Tess was sure her cheeks were aflame, because a potent heat surrounded her. In the glass in the hallway, she could see servants clustering near the door, eager to eavesdrop on what was happening within her rooms. The door beyond the bed was ajar, held open by a single finger, so Jenette must be listening there as well. Alone? There might be others with her abigail, each one agog with what was taking place. Even if Papa ordered the servants not to gossip, she knew at least one of them would be unable to keep this tale untold. Before day's end, everyone in the parish would know of how Miss Masterson had found herself surprisingly married to a marquess.

"Tess," Papa said sternly, "you may now be a marquess's wife, but you remain my daughter, and you will give me the courtesy of an answer to my question."

She raised her head and met her father's eyes evenly. Yet, in spite of herself, her gaze shifted . . . to Lord Hawksmoor's. Why was he not revealing any hint of what he was thinking? He should be furious, stamping about the room with a curse that would burn her ears.

Lord Hawksmoor might be stolid, but Papa was not, for his impatience heightened his voice. "Tess? How did this man wake you?"

"He woke me with a kiss," she answered, knowing that lying now would only worsen the situation.

Lord Hawksmoor's fingers bit into her shoulder before he snatched them away. "This whole discussion is ludicrous, Masterson. I was drunk last night. Your daughter was horrified to find me in her bed this morning."

"Her bed?" Papa's mouth twitched, and something sparked in his eyes. She had an odd sensation that *this* was what Papa had waited to have said.

"Where we slept as innocently as two pups."

"Without a watch-dog, however."

"True," Lord Hawksmoor said. He reached for his coat, which had been tossed, she noticed, on the foot of her bed. Seeing it there suggested a familiarity that did not exist. "And it is just as true your daughter remains a maiden—if she was one before last night."

Tess leaped to her feet and closed the door to the hallway. She heard the door to her dressing room click shut, and she guessed Jenette did not want to be caught eavesdropping. Picking up her dark blue wrapper, she pulled it on and buttoned it from her waist to her chin. Only then did she face her father and the marquess.

"I trust, my lord," she said coldly, "you can continue this conversation without resorting to demure hits. I have made every effort not to point a finger of blame at others involved in this bumble-bath. If you will recall, I am an innocent victim of this *contretemps*."

"Innocent being the critical consideration, I collect." Lord Hawksmoor shrugged on his coat.

"Yes." She would not be intimidated by his unrelenting calm. If he thought to betwattle her and her father with it, he was wasting his time . . . and theirs. She had seen the passion in his eyes when he stood by her bed and drew her into his arms.

Something flickered through his eyes now before he looked once more at her father. Was Lord Hawksmoor astonished she would not cower before his frigid serenity?

Smoothing wrinkles from his coat, the marquess said, "You have heard your daughter's comments, Masterson. Neither she nor I wish to be married to each other. If we handle this quietly, we all can return to our lives as they should be."

"You know that is impossible."

"I know there are ways of resolving any problem."

"Mayhap you do, but I believe there is nothing else to be said." Papa patted the front of his coat. "I have

Tess's copies of your marriage agreement here, and I will repeat what I told you when I entered the room. Welcome to the family, Hawksmoor." He glanced at Tess, then walked out of the room, closing the door behind him.

Tess was tempted to run after him and throw the door aside and shout that she would not be forced into this marriage with a man who did not want to be her husband. She did not move as she continued to stare at the flowery design on the rug.

"Weeping will gain you little favor in my mind," the marquess said.

"Weeping?" She raised her head and scowled at him. "I am giving in to neither tears nor vapors, my lord. I fear I am too enraged for either."

"I have no interest in your scolds."

"I have already seen what you have interest in." She crossed her arms in front of her. "First finding the bottom of a bottle of brandy and then seducing me when you believed I wished to welcome you into my bed as my husband."

He lowered himself carefully to the bed, and she flinched. She did not want him making himself so comfortable in her private chambers.

"You are my wife," Lord Hawksmoor said.

"You did not remember that when you tried to persuade me to surrender to you. You did not know then I had been buckled to you by proxy." She arched a brow. "I understand it is the way of a fine lord to have his wife and his mistresses, but—"

"Arguing will gain us nothing."

The very tranquillity of his words vexed her, but she had to acknowledge the wisdom of them. "That is true."

Pushing himself to his feet, he said, "I suspect you would like to dress, Miss Masterson."

"Yes." Again that unwanted heat soared up her face. "I own to wishing to wear something that has not been slept in." Reaching for the bellpull beside her bed, he added, "I assure you I will do all I can to straighten out this muddle."

"As I will."

"Talking some sense into your father's hard head might be a good place to begin."

"Why are you lambasting my father for being unthinking when you are more at fault than anyone in this?"

"I am aware of my complicity. My only excuse is that I, for some reason I cannot fathom now, drank too much, and I let myself act before realizing the consequences."

"Which you do not customarily do?"

He regarded her with eyes as cool as his frown. "It is not my habit to act so out of hand, Miss Masterson. You need only ask anyone who knows me well, and they will reassure you there must be more to this whole thing than drunken revels."

"Papa is the only person I know who also knows you."

"He seems an untrustworthy witness to my character at this time."

"Or a very accurate one."

He stepped toward her. Hearing the dressing room open behind her, she could not look to Jenette for help, because he took her chin in his hand and tilted her face up. "Ask yourself, Miss Masterson, why your father would think so poorly of me at the same time he rejoices in the fact we are wed."

Jenette's gasp was loud in the room. Tess was held by the cold anger in Lord Hawksmoor's eyes. There were so many answers she was ready to give him, but each one disintegrated into illogic before she could speak it.

"I do not understand any of this," Tess murmured.

"On that, we agree wholeheartedly." He released her and bowed his head toward her. "May I ask that we have an opportunity to discuss this before I leave for London?"

"Leave?"

He nodded. "I had intended to be on my way at first light, but . . ." He walked to the door with slow but even steps.

Tess put her hand over her mouth to keep from shouting at his back. How could he be considering taking his leave when they were in the midst of this insanity? Slowly she lowered her left hand, staring at it. No ring announced that she was now a stranger's wife.

"Oh, la," murmured Jenette as she inched closer. "What a fine looking man you have taken as your husband, Miss Masterson!"

"He is *not* my husband!"

"But Mr. Masterson said—I mean, I heard the marquess say that—"

Tess waved her abigail to silence. With two fingers, she rubbed her forehead, which now was aching, too. What a mess! There must be some way to find a way out of it with her reputation—and Papa's—intact.

Sending Jenette to order bath water and to bring the blue gown she wished to wear today, Tess went to the table where Heddy's cage was covered with its cloth. She started to lift the cloth, but the little hedgehog would be asleep now that the sun was up. Although she longed to talk to her beloved pet, she would not disturb Heddy, who could be ill-mannered when she was bothered.

She walked away from the table and threw open the draperies at the closest window. Sunshine flooded into the room, chasing away her gloomiest thoughts.

Those thoughts returned, doubly strong, when she turned to face the bed and saw the indentations on *two* pillows. Two questions remained that she must have an answer to before this marriage lasted a day longer. Whose idea had it been for Lord Hawksmoor to marry her? And why had nobody halted it?

Three

The breakfast-parlor was filled with enticing scents when Cameron entered it. On a sideboard, steaming trenchers offered eggs, kippers, bacon, potatoes, and other foods that would add to the nausea in his gut. Two maids stood by a door he suspected led to the kitchen, and a footman was as still as the dour man in a portrait by the arched window. A delicate wallcovering of some sort of flower entwined with vines added an inviting touch to the walls, but Cameron would have gladly been anywhere else but here.

At the table, Eustace Knox sat gustily enjoying a heaping plate of food from the sideboard as well as a stack of toast and at least one muffin from the basket close to his left hand, if the crumbs on the white damask tablecloth were any indication. He was a man who obviously savored life, for his belly was round and his smile broad. Dressed as always in the finest fashion, he also was a man who had the misfortune to be born into a family whose fortune came from trade rather than title. Eustace's father had followed in his own father's footsteps as an ironmonger. A fortune filled Eustace's pockets as if his family's forges were minting coin rather than iron and steel.

But it was Eustace's zest for life and all the pleasures

it offered that had gained him welcome among the *ton*. There were whispers a title might come his way when the Prince Regent assumed the throne. No one spoke too loudly of that, however, for it would be paramount to wishing mad old King George dead.

"Ah, Cameron," called Eustace, holding up a forkful of egg in a bizarre salute. He laughed. "I had not thought to see you here alone this morning . . . or so early, if the truth be told."

"Is that so?" He suppressed his vexation. Why was his friend smiling? Didn't *his* head pound?

Dozens of times, Cameron had nursed his friend through a hangover, so he knew Eustace was not immune to the headache Cameron was enduring now. Eustace enjoyed his brandy, seldom passing up any chance to share a fine bottle, whether at the club or dining with a friend.

Cameron massaged his throbbing brow. Everything about the past day was a puzzle: why Eustace had suggested they stop here at this out-of-the-way house to visit Masterson; why Masterson had kept them talking for long hours last night with every bit of gossip he could wring from them; and, most importantly, why Cameron had imbibed so much last night. That was not his way, for although Cameron appreciated savoring a good glass of an excellent vintage, he refused to drink until his good sense was drowned in wine, brandy, or ale. Eustace had no such compunctions. Mayhap his regular experience with a bottle was the reason he seemed unaffected by all he had swallowed, and Cameron was suffering from far more than a headache.

"You are not a very attentive bridegroom," Eustace added. Craning his neck to look out the door, he asked, "Where is your charming bride?"

"I should not be any sort of bridegroom, and Miss Masterson is in her rooms doing whatever she deems necessary before we meet to discuss this whole shocking mull." By exerting all his will, he kept his feet from plodding along the rug as he walked to the closest chair. He dropped heavily into it. Too heavily, for the motion resonated all through him, and he groaned.

His friend regarded him over a full fork. "You look horrible."

"Thank you."

"And I see your temper is as odious." Eustace continued eating as if he had not seen food in a year.

"Wouldn't *your* temper be odious if you discovered yourself with a bride you barely know?"

He shrugged and shoveled another forkful of fish into his mouth. "If she looked like Masterson's daughter, I might think I had gotten a bargain out of the deal."

"Why are you acting bacon-brained?" Cameron leaned one elbow on the table, then moved the newspaper that crackled under his sleeve. Shoving it away, he barely noticed it was from last week. "Forget that question, and answer this one: Why didn't you say something to stop that travesty of a wedding last night?"

Eustace dug his fork into the food on his plate again, then leaned back in his chair with the fork balanced between his plate and his mouth. "You would not be stopped."

"What?" He frowned, sure he must have heard his friend wrong.

"You were fairly shouting that you wanted to wed— and I quote—that luscious red-haired angel. No one could talk you out of it, and you had Masterson send posthaste for the vicar so you would not have to leave—and I quote again—that luscious red-haired angel here where someone else might find her and win her heart before you could."

"And you believed that?" He shook his head. "It must have been the brandy talking."

"Mayhap, but I have not seen you so forceful about

anything since your return to England. I could not help seeing how you took such eager notice of Masterson's daughter."

"I do not argue she is lovely."

"No, *you* would not waste your time on such a futile undertaking." Reaching for some jam to put on a piece of toast, Eustace shrugged again. "I have to own, my friend, I was pleased to see you so enthused over something. You have not once lost your blastedly boring equilibrium since you returned from the Continent."

Cameron took a deep breath and released it slowly. Why was Eustace babbling on about this now? His friend knew how hard Cameron fought to keep from losing his temper and giving in to emotional upheavals. Eustace knew why as well, for even Eustace, as outrageous as he could sometimes be, was placid compared to Cameron's older brother Russell, the present Duke of Hawkington.

Russell's seeming inability to keep his desires in check had created problems that, if they continued, even a duke would not be able to extract himself from without damaging his name and place in the Polite World. There had been a duel that fortunately ended with both men so inept with their pistols the only wound was to a tree. There had been carriage races where only luck had prevented someone from being killed, as had happened last summer in St. James's Park to two young ladies who must have wanted to prove they had driving skills to match a man's. As well, the rumors of Russell's prowling the dusky corners of Covent Garden and Drury Lane had not closed any doors to him.

A duke could do as he pleased. How many times had Russell bragged about that to Cameron when they were younger? Whether or not it was true, Cameron had been well aware that the younger son of a duke, in spite of the possession of a courtesy title, must not be so foolhardy. He must have spoken that last thought aloud, because

Eustace asked, "Do I assume from your questions you are having second thoughts this morning?"

Cameron muttered a curse under his breath before saying, "Neither I nor Miss Masterson wish to be wed to each other."

"You called her that before. You, of all people, should not forget she is now Lady Hawksmoor, my friend."

Rolling the newspaper into a tube, he slapped it against his hand. "No matter what you call her, she wishes to be addressed rightly as Miss Masterson, for there is something not right about a wedding ceremony where the bride is asleep in another room and the groom is lost in his cups."

Eustace chuckled heartily. "Is calling her by her maiden name a demand she made to you? Did she fly up to the boughs and dress you down?"

"Quite to the contrary. She has been the pattern-card of calm and rational thought. Her mien has been gracious, and she is willing—"

"You are a lucky man."

"—to help me put an end to this marriage as quickly and quietly as possible," Cameron finished, scowling at his friend. "I find her behavior exemplary."

"Do you?" Eustace chuckled.

"What is so amusing?"

"She must be as wise as she is lovely. A very dangerous combination in a woman."

"Why do you say that?"

"That she is wise? Because she is playing your own game with you."

"Game?"

"That cool serenity you assume when you want to unsettle everyone around you." Eustace picked up another muffin from the basket on the table. Slathering it with a generous portion of butter, he took a hearty bite and washed it down with the fragrant coffee. "You have succeeded with that pose very well, but you may have met your match in your wife."

" 'Tis no pose."

"For you or for Masterson's daughter?"

Cameron folded his arms on the table. The very idea of eating sickened him. His head still seemed too light and the pain in his stomach too heavy. If he could keep his eyes from drifting out of focus, he might be able to think more clearly.

"I have no reason to believe she is pretending, Eustace."

"And you?"

"What reason would there be for me to pretend?"

Eustace chuckled again, sounding a bit too self-satisfied to Cameron. "I do not know many men who would pretend to be displeased to find such a lovely lass waiting upon waking."

"And finding themselves wed?"

"There is that small matter." He stirred more sugar into his coffee. "It is a complication."

"An understatement."

"A habit I may be assuming from you."

"One thing I fail to understand is where that accursed special license came from. I certainly did not carry one in my pocket on the off chance I might decide to be married during this trip to Town."

Eustace took a deep drink of his coffee and yelped. "Hot! Blasted hot." Wiping his mouth with the back of his hand, he set the cup on the table. "I would be curious about that myself, but the license must be legitimate, or the vicar would not have married you." He glanced at the servants gathered by the kitchen door, then lowered his voice and leaned toward Cameron. "Your scowl suggests you intend to be done with this marriage posthaste."

"You are right. It is what I want."

"Despite what such a hullabaloo will do to Masterson's daughter?"

"I don't give a rap about Masterson's daughter," he growled. Drawing himself up short before his anger could gain the upper hand, he said, "I, of course, do not wish to see her reputation destroyed."

Eustace laughed. "So you have changed your mind about her?"

"I had no time to make up my mind before I found myself wed to her."

"Nonsense." He chuckled again and took another bite. "I saw how you admired her when we were introduced yesterday afternoon. You even smiled, something you have not done frequently since you returned to England."

"Do not confuse being polite to a woman with being intrigued with her."

"I don't. Do you?"

Cameron pushed back his chair, but a maid came forward to inquire what he wished to eat. "Coffee." When it was set in front of him, he lifted the cup and let the steam wash over his face. Blast! Even its feathery fingers hurt against his skin. Only Tess's touch had eased this pain.

What an irony! The cause of his anguish was the only solace for it. He gulped from his cup, ignoring how it burned his mouth. Blaming Tess for the ridiculous actions Eustace had gleefully outlined for him was contemptible. *He* was the one who had demanded to marry her in a drunken madness.

Luscious red-haired angel. They did not sound like words he would speak. Eustace was the one who spouted nothing-sayings to woo a woman. But those words were the perfect description for Tess. She was unquestionably a rare woman, in his estimation, for she had seen the impossibility of their situation and had offered her help to rectify it. If Masterson had not come in as he had . . . blast! This was becoming more and more complicated.

"All right," Cameron said as he set the cup back on the table. "I made a horrible mistake. Now I must do what I can to rectify that mistake."

"It will be costly."

"Costly?" He had not given that part of the matter any thought. Staying wed to Tess Masterson would be even more costly. Not to his accounts, but to his state of mind. He had come back from the war with Napoleon determined to pick up his life where he had left it. That meant long days at his club, where he could discuss matters of political concern with his friends or enjoy cards.

However, he had planned his first call to be at Pamela's house. He did not try to bamboozle himself into believing she would set aside her current protector, Lord Stedley, for Cameron knew she would not wait for him faithfully. That was not her way, although she had been his alone before he had bought his commission and set off to save England from Napoleon's dream of a vast empire. Pamela was a practical woman.

As Tess Masterson seemed to be.

"I am aware of the costs," Cameron said, pulling his mind back to the conversation.

"Good. And I assume Masterson's daughter is, as well."

"Yes, she is well aware of them. In fact, she mentioned several of them to me before I had thought of them."

Eustace arched a brow. "Egad, she sounds as logical as your mistress. Mayhap logical thought is what you seek in a woman, rather than passion."

"Quite the contrary. In many ways, it would have been simpler if she had screeched and threatened to do harm to herself and everyone else involved in this muddle."

"As volatile as Masterson is . . ."

Cameron sighed and took another sip of his coffee. Its

strong flavor bolstered him. "That is true. I would not have guessed his daughter would show so much restraint."

"Especially when she responded so ardently to your seduction?"

He put his cup back on the table and leaned toward his friend. "Watch what you say, for I suspect there are, already flying through this house, enough rumors of things that never took place."

"You did not—" He flushed as he looked past Cameron. "Ah, here is the pretty bride now."

Hearing Mr. Knox's words, which might be announcing her arrival or warning Lord Hawksmoor to take care what he said, Tess paused in the doorway to the room that once had been her favorite in the house because sunlight welcomed her each morning. Noticing how the maids and footman exchanged clandestine smiles, she affixed one of her own in place. She could not be vexed with them. For her to marry the son of a duke would be deemed an excellent match. But not this way! She had dreamed of being courted and learning to love the man she would marry. Instead she had been denied that.

She knew her smile was brittle as Eustace Knox came to his feet and bowed over her hand. If Papa had arranged for her to marry Mr. Knox, who gushed with congratulations she doubted were any more sincere than her smile, Tess wondered if she could have kept from fleeing into the woods and going to another town and changing her name and . . . a shudder raced along her. She *had* changed her name. She now was Tess Hawksmoor. *Lady* Hawksmoor.

When Mr. Knox clapped Lord Hawksmoor on the shoulder as the marquess stepped forward, she saw the marquess's smile was feigned, too. He held out his hand, and she placed hers on it. His gaze slipped along her. Did he find her gown too outmoded for his Town taste?

It was her very best one, but it could not compare with the perfect cut of his navy blue coat and his waistcoat, which had been skillfully embroidered in a paisley pattern.

A titter came from the other side of the room, and Lord Hawksmoor's fingers tightened painfully over hers. She did not remonstrate with him or with the maid, who now had her fingers pressed to her lips as she stared at the floor. How could Tess chide Sally for laughing when the situation was unquestionably silly?

"If you are agreeable," Cameron said in a near whisper, "I would ask you take your breakfast with me somewhere where we may talk without being overhead."

"I find I am not hungry this morning." She motioned toward the hall behind her. "May I suggest we go to the parlor? With the doors closed, it is impossible to hear inside." She hesitated, then added, "I know because I tried to listen at the doors when I was much younger."

Was that a smile she saw slip across his lips so swiftly? She could not be certain.

He offered his arm as he said, "Eustace, old chap, I trust you will excuse us."

"Go on, go on," his friend urged, waving the fork he had brought with him from the table. "I shall finish up my breakfast here. My lady, your father has an excellent cook. Please offer him my thanks."

Tess nodded as she put her hand on Lord Hawksmoor's arm. The strong muscles hinted at beneath his shirt were no illusion. She wondered what he had been doing that had created this unyielding strength. It was only one of a thousand thousand questions she longed to ask him. Or mayhap even a thousand thousand thousand, because every beat of her heart brought another she wanted to ask.

Knowing she was prattling like a gabble-grinder, but unable to let silence reign between them because then she would have to think of all that had not yet been said, Tess pointed out the portraits of her ancestors lining the hallway from the breakfast-parlor to the more formal room near the front of the house. She was not sure if Lord Hawksmoor was heeding her commentary until he paused in front of one picture.

"Your mother?" he asked in that controlled way that gave her no idea what he was thinking.

"Yes."

"I thought so. There is a definite resemblance beyond her hair, which is the same shade as yours." He peered at the portrait. "Are those chrysanthemums in the background?"

She had to look, because she had not paid much attention to what was behind her mother. Whenever she looked at this portrait, she tried to re-create her mother's living face, but nearly a decade had passed since her mother's death. Now it was impossible to remember the different expressions Mama had worn. "Yes, I believe they are. I have few memories of my mother, but I have heard she was greatly interested in her garden."

"I would like to see her plantings, if you would show them to me."

"The garden has suffered much neglect in recent years, although Papa told me just last week he intends to hire a gardener again."

"The other one was let go?"

She nodded. "With a good character recommendation, because there was not enough . . . that is . . ."

His mouth quirked. "You need not think you are betraying your father by divulging he has been purse-pinched for several years."

Realizing how close she stood to Lord Hawksmoor, she backed away a step. His mouth hardened again, but he drew her hand within his arm and let her lead the way to the parlor. He said nothing as she opened one of the double doors and walked in. His gaze swept the room, and she wondered what he sought.

The room had the best furniture in the house, although many of the pieces of art that once had graced the rosewood tables and walls covered with red silk had been sold quietly to pay for the upkeep of the house. The red and silver striped curtains were too gaudy, in her estimation, but there had been no money to buy new ones. Now it would not matter, because this would no longer be her home. Her home would be with her husband.

"Are you chilled?" asked Lord Hawksmoor.

Realizing she had shivered in response to her own thoughts, Tess closed the door and said, "No, I am fine."

"Then may I be forthright?"

"Please."

He walked away from her, pausing to look at a stack of books on a nearby table. "I have been giving our situation and possible remedies much thought since I last spoke with you."

"As I have."

Glancing at her, he turned and walked back toward her. "Because of our circumstances this morning, no one will believe our marriage is unconsummated."

"So you will ruin my life to protect your reputation as a rake?"

He clasped his hands behind his back, even though the fury in his eyes suggested he was giving thought to clasping them around her throat and putting an end to this with all due speed. "If you would take a moment to think, madam," he said coolly, "you will realize yours is not the only life which has taken an unexpected turn. And 'tis not my reputation that concerns me, but yours."

"Mine? I was asleep in my own bed, aimlessly dreaming of who knows what, when this scheme was set into motion."

"Which led to you being in your own bed with your

own husband." His smile was as icy as his words. "For that reason, an annulment would be most unlikely. The alternatives are to accept this situation or to seek a divorce."

"A divorce?" She shook her head. "But that would mean you must accuse me of adultery."

"Ironic, is it not? I would need to label you a wanton when you may remain a maiden, for all I know."

Her hand rose to strike his cheek. She gripped her own wrist, pulling her hand back, and stared at her fingers in horror. When his fingers covered hers, she lifted her eyes to his face, fearing she had angered him beyond all good sense. She could not keep from cowering when his hand rose toward her. Something flickered through his eyes, but they grew cold again when he touched her cheek as gently as if she were a child.

"I fear," he said quietly, "my frustration has been directed toward you, when you are not at fault. I owe you an apology."

"I never have . . . I mean, I should not have slapped you before or tried to now. 'Tis not a habit I wish to gain."

"You have never slapped a man's face before this morning?" His chuckle surprised her. "I trust you have never been given such cause before this."

"No."

"Honest, I see."

She jutted her chin toward him. "You have no reason not to trust me, my lord. 'Twas not at my instigation that we became husband and wife. Nor was I present, as you may now recall, although unquestionably you were too deeply lost in your cups to take note of the solemnity of the vows you spoke." Tugging her hand out of his, she went to sit on the bench beside the window. "How could you have been so foolish?"

"A question I have asked myself repeatedly." He

leaned on the wall beside the window and gazed down at her. "Miss Mas—madam . . . blast it! Calling you Tess would be easiest just now."

"I would not wish to inconvenience you further."

His mouth tightened, and she regretted her sarcasm. Yet he had appreciated her honesty. She could not pretend she was joyous at the tidings that she had become his wife.

"I do not think of being inconvenienced, but of finding a way to put an end to this with all due speed." He looked out the window, and she guessed he was wishing he was far from here. He sighed before adding, "If you are willing to allow such a slight intimacy, it will not suggest we have shared further intimacies."

"You are right. There is no reason to be silly."

"Save that everything around us is skimble-skamble."

Tess smiled, surprising herself. Under other circumstances, she believed she might have enjoyed exchanging words with Cameron. Her smile faltered. Friendship would be denied to them because they were in this absurd situation.

"As soon as I can, I shall seek legal advice," he continued. "There must be a choice other than divorce, which would destroy your good name, or an annulment, which I fear will be impossible to obtain now."

"I hope you are right."

"You sound dubious."

"I am dubious."

He nodded. "As I am, but I promise you I will contact our solicitor as soon as I reach London. There must be a way out of this, and I swear to you I shall find it."

"And if that is not possible?"

He did not give her answer as he looked again out the window. She understood why. There was none.

Four

Wind battered the eaves and slammed against the windows. The glass rattled while the fire cowered and cringed before the air being forced back down the chimney. Something struck the house before clattering to the ground.

A branch, Tess suspected, as she fought to calm herself. Every nerve was on edge, even though she had tried to hide that fact. When rain washed down the windows, she slumped against the bright blue settee and laughed uneasily as the clock on the landing chimed ten times. She was unsure if she should be grateful the storm had prevented Cameron and his friend from taking their leave today or furious they remained here, reminding her of how her life was no longer her own.

From where she sat alone in the library, she could hear male voices. Papa had invited his guests to join him in the parlor farther along the hallway for after-dinner wine and cigars. Glad for the reprieve, Tess had come here. Her hopes of losing herself in a book had been for naught. The book sat on her lap, and she had not turned a page since the clock had last chimed.

Closing her eyes, she leaned back against the settee's well-worn cushions. This was her haven, the place she came when she yearned to think. She loved the odor of sunlight on the oak shelves as well as the dusty warmth from the books. The leather bindings added a thick scent to the room. Beneath her feet, the carpet was dilapidated, for it had once been in the front parlor before it had been moved back here. Now the rug in the parlor was nearly as worn.

The rug should have been replaced last year. Tess had looked at one in a London shop, but her father had given her excuse after excuse until she no longer asked when they might order it to replace the one there now.

Often she brought Heddy here and read aloud to the hedgehog as the moon rose. She had no illusions that the little creature gave her words any mind, for Heddy's thoughts were purely on the grubs and insects trapped in the garden so Tess could put them in the hedgehog's cage. Sometimes, Tess took Heddy out of the cage and held her, but never when anyone else was about. The hedgehog, which was no more than six inches long, was skittish and would curl up into a snorting ball if anyone else approached.

But tonight, Tess had wanted to be alone to try to sort out her thoughts. It had been useless, because her thoughts had gone around and around until *she* wanted to curl up as Heddy did and wait for this to pass.

A shadow appeared in the doorway, and she smiled when she recognized the silhouette as her father's. Coming to her feet, she started to walk toward him. He motioned for her to stay where she was as he drew the door closed.

Tess gnawed on her lower lip. Papa's steps were furtive, almost as if he were an interloper in his own home. She lowered herself back onto the settee and, closing the book, set it on the shelf beside her. He stopped in front of her and sighed.

"This has all become even more complicated than I thought it would," he said without preamble.

"This? I assume you mean my abrupt marriage." Tears weighed in her eyes as she whispered, "Papa, how could you agree to let me be married like this to a man I do not know and who does not want me?"

"Tess, I had no choice."

"What do you mean? Of course, you had a choice. You could have refused to go along with that drunken sport." She closed her eyes before the tears filling them burst forth in a springtide.

When her father put his hand beneath her chin and tipped it up, he said, "Tess, look at me."

She opened her eyes. She had thought she was familiar with every expression her father might wear, but she had never seen this taut one before. The muscles at the back of his jaw worked, adding the illusion of a tic to his cheeks. His eyes burned with strong emotions, and his mouth shifted from a consoling smile to a straight line before she could draw a single breath.

"There is something you must know," her father said. "Something that is very painful for me to tell you, but it is clear I cannot be false with you any longer. You have a right to know the truth, because it has now had a terrible impact on your life. 'Tis ironic that the very thing aimed at protecting you has turned your life topsy-turvy."

"What is it, Papa?"

He gazed at her steadily as he said, "I did not choose to have you marry Hawksmoor. Knox insisted I must do nothing to halt the ceremony."

"Mr. Knox? Why should he have had anything to do with this?"

"Because of blackmail."

She sucked her breath in with a horrified gasp. "Blackmail? You are being blackmailed by Mr. Knox?"

"Hush!" He put his finger to his lips before going to the sideboard to pour himself some wine. He filled a second glass and brought it back to her. "Hawksmoor's older brother apparently is so desperate to have Hawksmoor wed and therefore keep him out of trouble—"

"Marriage does not keep all men out of trouble, Papa."

He took a deep drink, and his tight smile returned. "It appears you are more worldly than I had guessed."

"Even here, one hears the gossip of the *ton* and their antics."

"You are now part of the *ton,* Tess."

Coming to her feet, she put her untouched glass on the table beside the settee. "Papa, I do not want to be part of the Polite World, nor do I wish to be Lord Hawksmoor's bride. But I do wish to understand why you let Mr. Knox force your hand in arranging a marriage guaranteed to make neither me nor Cameron happy."

"Cameron?"

"That is his name." She arched her brows. "And I *am* his wife. It is not inappropriate for me to speak of him thusly."

"You are accepting this bumble-bath with equanimity."

"What good would a tantrum do?"

Her father chuckled. "If I had had your equanimity, I might have found myself in less difficult situations throughout my life. I should have known I did not have to prepare for vapors or hysterics with you."

"You should have known I would be unhappy with this match."

Dropping onto the chair beside the settee, he waited until she was sitting again before he said, "Tess, I explained my predicament. To be honest, I doubt I could have arranged a marriage that would offer you such a secure future. Hawksmoor is not the heir, but he has a fortune of his own, and even before he went off to the war, it was said he was not the rakehell his brother is. I have heard of only one mistress he had, and if *on dits* are to be believed, he was quite faithful to her."

"Papa, this is not the time for prattle. I do not understand why Mr. Knox played a part in this."

"I told you already he was acting on behalf of the duke." Impatience sifted into her father's voice. "There are few women willing to marry a second son, especially one who is scarred."

"Scarred?" Her forehead wrinkled as she frowned. "Do you mean that tiny mark over his right brow? It is barely visible."

"It is enough, compounded with his position as a second son, to compel many women and their matchmaking parents to look elsewhere. However, the Duke of Hawkington, your husband's brother, deemed it important for Hawksmoor to be wed. The duke and Knox are also in each other's pockets, so Knox must have seen this as a chance to gain the duke's favor."

"Are you saying Mr. Knox arranged all this?"

"I believe it was his idea to stop here on their way to London."

She came to her feet, unable to sit still while she swallowed the whole of this incredible scheme. "And Mr. Knox arranged for the special license that allowed Dr. Tucker to marry us?"

"That I know for a fact." Papa picked up his pipe from the table beside his chair and began filling it with tobacco. "He let me know within minutes of his arrival he had obtained the license."

Tess searched back in her mind and remembered now how Mr. Knox had been talking intently with Papa while she was greeting Lord Hawksmoor. At the time, she had given their conversation no thought, for she had guessed it to be of no more importance than any other when her father's friends called. They spoke of fast horses and luck at the card table and their comrades who were not present.

And she had been mesmerized by Lord Hawksmoor's smile. Only now did she question whether it had been an unusual expression for him or if he had barely smiled since because the situation was so bizarre. Mayhap it was just as well he did not, for his smile seemed to have a way of making her forget everything else—even herself—as she delighted in the charming twinkle in his eyes. If someone had asked her opinion of him then, she would have spoken of his polite demeanor and of his smile that had stirred something within her to a boil.

Now . . . now she wanted only to be done with Cameron Hawksmoor and everything to do with him.

Her thoughts must have been clear on her face, because her father put down his pipe, unlit, and hid his face in his hands. Shaking his head, he moaned, "What have I done? I thought to save both of us, and I fear I have sacrificed you and your happiness, Tess."

She knelt beside him. Putting her hand on his arm, she whispered, "Papa, I know you did only what you believed you must."

"Yes." His words were muffled behind his hands. "Please promise you will speak to no one about what I have told you."

"Cameron—"

"Most especially not him, Tess. There is already much anger between him and the duke, and it is sure to escalate if Hawksmoor discovers how his brother has arranged this marriage for him." He shuddered. "And we would be ruined. Utterly ruined. Promise me this, Tess."

"Yes, Papa."

"Yes, what?"

"Yes, I promise I will speak to no one about your being blackmailed into agreeing to this wedding."

"And you will say nothing to your husband?"

"I told you I would not. I would do nothing to cause you more harm, Papa."

His shoulders drooped even lower. "I wish I could ask

you to forgive me, but how is that possible when I have done what I have done?"

"Papa, of course I forgive you. That is what one does for those one loves."

When her father lowered his hands and looked past her, whatever he had intended to say went unsaid as his mouth hardened. She turned to see Cameron opening the door. His face was, for once, not expressionless. Instead it was tight with a frown.

Tess came to her feet. Her father stood, positioning himself between her and Cameron. Even though she was tempted to allow Papa to shield her from Cameron's fearsome scowl, she was sure he had suffered enough already in being forced to agree to her marriage. This was her battle to fight.

Forcing a smile onto her face, she stepped around her father and walked toward Cameron. She saw, for the first time, his friend Mr. Knox was standing behind him.

"Do come in and join us," she said. "We are having a conversation before retiring for the night. If the wind does not lessen, I fear we all shall be kept awake while it howls around the roof. Thank heavens you arrived last night, rather than tonight, because you would have been soaked. If—"

"Yes, we were lucky to arrive last evening," Cameron said, striding across the room.

Papa poured two more glasses of wine and held one out to Cameron. When he offered the other to Mr. Knox, Tess was astonished to note her father's smile had returned. Was Papa trying to hide his despair? Although Mr. Knox may not have been in a position to take note, Cameron surely had seen Papa hunched over, his face in his hands.

Cameron set his glass on the table next to Tess's and aimed his frown first at Mr. Knox, who was drinking his wine with obvious gusto, then at her father. "It is my duty as your guest, Masterson, to thank you for your hospitality. I wish to let you know Knox and I will be taking our leave at dawn on the morrow."

"You and Knox?" Papa asked, his voice becoming a low growl.

"Yes."

"Does that mean you are planning to leave Tess here?"

Tess looked from her father to Cameron, as she had so often in the past day. "Papa, I believe—"

"Hush, Tess! I am discussing this with your father."

In astonishment, she realized Cameron had interrupted her. How dare he treat her as if she were too witless to have a say in her own future!

"There is nothing to discuss," her father said, glancing at Mr. Knox.

Tess clenched her hands at her side. Did Papa fear Mr. Knox would spout out whatever he was using to blackmail her father?

"You are quite correct," Cameron replied. "There is nothing to discuss on this matter. Tess would be best off here."

"Do not lather me with such nonsense. She will not stay here. She is your wife. Her place is with you, Hawksmoor. Don't you agree, Knox?"

Mr. Knox looked up from where he was refilling his glass with Papa's best wine. "What?" Even on that single word, his voice was slurred, and she wondered if he was on his way to becoming intoxicated again tonight.

"Don't you agree a wife's place is with her husband? I believe," Papa continued, "you mentioned that very thing to me earlier today."

Mr. Knox set the bottle back on the table with a thump. His chuckle sounded forced, but he said, "I do believe you are right, Masterson." He tried to slap Cameron's shoulder companionably, but his fingers missed, warning he was more fuzzy than Tess had guessed. "Sorry, old chap, but I believe I did say those very words."

"If you will not heed my counsel," her father said, "then you should heed your friend's." He kissed Tess's cheek. "I bid you both good night. Tess, I trust you will give instructions for an early breakfast."

"Masterson," Cameron said in the quiet tone Tess was beginning to believe he assumed when he did not want to reveal his thoughts, "it would be better for Tess to remain here until I am able to work everything out."

"What do you need to work out? You and Tess are legally wed, and that is that. The sooner you face that fact, the sooner you can build a life together." He tweaked Tess's cheek. "And the sooner I will be able to bounce my grandson on my knee."

Tess opened her mouth to protest, but her father walked out of the room as assuredly as Cameron had entered. Mr. Knox picked up the bottle and followed. Looking at Cameron, she said, "I fear Papa is much more accepting than we are of the inevitability of our future together."

"Then he shall be disappointed." He took her hand and drew her down to sit on the settee. "Tess, I suggest you remain here simply because the Polite World can be most unforgiving of any mistake."

" 'Twas not my error that ended up with us married."

"True." Leaning back against the settee, he set his arm along its back. Anyone walking past the library door would assume he was relaxed, but Tess was not betwattled.

Although he did not touch her, she was aware of every inch of his arm's length behind her. Some sort of energy billowed outward from him that she could not ignore. No one else had ever affected her like this, and she was unsure if she liked it or not, for it seemed to leave her too vulnerable in his company.

"Do you want to go to London?" he asked.

"I have always heard a wife's place is at her husband's side." Her attempt at levity failed miserably.

"You agreed to go to London because your father requested it. Do *you* want to go to London?"

"There is nothing I can do here bring an end to this debacle." She folded her hands in her lap. "Mayhap I can do something worthwhile in London."

"What do you think you can do?"

"I have no idea."

"Then—"

She came to her feet. "What do *you* think you can do? I suspect you, too, have no idea." Grabbing her glass from the table, she raised it to her lips.

He seized her wrist. "Tess, do not make the same mistake of drinking too much as I did." He lifted the glass from her fingers and placed it back on the table. His fingers loosened on her slightly. Then one slid in a slow, sensual caress along the inside of her arm.

"A single glass of wine will not leave me foxed," she whispered, watching the sinuous motion of his finger.

Releasing her arm, he argued, "But you were not about to drink this wine for enjoyment. You were looking for escape from all of this that troubles you so deeply."

She stared at him, but he refused to meet her eyes. "Escape? Is that why you drank so much with Papa and Mr. Knox?" Not giving him time to answer, she asked, "From what were you trying to escape?"

"I don't know."

"This makes no sense."

He arched a brow. "I fear nothing will until we work out a solution to this."

"Do you believe we can?"

"I believe we must."

Five

This is nonsense. She will not stay here. She is your wife. Her place is with you, Hawksmoor.

The words, in Papa's most authoritative tone, echoed through Tess's head as she listened to the steady sound of the horses' hoofs on the road. Every pace took her farther from home and Papa. She tried not to think how long it might be before she returned.

Cameron was looking out the window beside him as if he hoped to find an answer to all that troubled him. She was still amazed Cameron had not insisted, at the last minute, that she remain behind at her father's house. Mayhap he had realized he needed her help in rectifying this bumble-bath, even though she had no idea what to do to find a way out of this problem.

No one would guess anything was amiss with him, for his face suggested he did not have a concern beyond which cravat to wear at dinner this evening. Only his fingers, tapping in an endless rhythm against the bottom of the window, hinted at the turmoil within him. She wished he would share his thoughts with her, because they might then be able to devise an answer.

She glanced to the other side of the carriage, where Mr. Knox was dozing. His light snores could barely be heard beneath the rattle of the wheels. She wanted to grab him by the shoulders and demand he answer her questions. Why was he blackmailing her father? Every chance Tess had given her father to explain to her this morning during the hurried breakfast and the even more rushed farewells had come to naught. Papa changed the subject, avoiding telling her the truth. She tried not to think what might have happened that was so appalling he could not speak to her of it.

"I trust you have been to Town previously." Cameron's voice was hushed, so as not to wake his friend.

Startled, for this was the first time he had spoken since they left Papa's house nearly two hours ago, Tess replied, "Yes, I have been there three times. The last time was to pay a call on my grandmother before her death."

"When was that?"

"About five years ago."

"Three times, but no trip more recent than five years ago?" He shook his head. "You might as well say you never have been at all, for I doubt you have ever attended any sort of assembly."

"No."

"Do you know how to handle yourself in such company?"

"Of course." She raised her chin, but did not lean toward him to make her point. She did not want to chance bumping into Heddy's cage, which was next to her feet. If Cameron had been curious why she had brought it here instead of leaving it with the other bags in the cart that followed the carriage, he had not asked. "Do not write me off as a hopeless bumpkin."

"Knowing the rules is not the same as knowing how to comport oneself when one is faced with a challenge among the Polite World."

She clenched her hands together, glad her gloves hid how her knuckles must be bleaching with her fury. "I promise you I shall do nothing to embarrass you, Cameron, such as flirting with the Prince Regent."

"Are you always so outspoken?"

"I am always this *honest.*"

"A perilous trait in London."

She laughed. "Then I must risk that peril, because honesty is a habit I do not wish to lose."

Cameron shifted on the seat, sliding his arm behind her. Again, as when they had spoken last night in the library, he did not touch her. She was glad, because she was unsettled even when he was this close. If he let his fingers drop to curve along her shoulder, she doubted she would be able to form a single logical thought.

"I hope you feel the same after you have spent a fortnight or two in London," he said with the inkling of a smile.

"A fortnight or two? You think that is all I will need to stay?"

"On that I have no idea." The smile was gone again. "Mayhap it would be for the best for you to refrain from involving yourself with the *ton* during your sojourn in Town. It would make it simpler for you to leave once our marriage has been brought to a satisfactory end."

She frowned at him. "Do you intend to keep me imprisoned in your house like a heroine held by some horrible villain in one of those outrageous novels?"

"What do you know of such books?"

"Only what I have read."

Cameron started to reply, then chuckled. She wished he would laugh more often, because the sound had a spontaneity missing in his other actions. Everything else about him, save for when he had awakened her in her bed, was so sternly controlled.

His hand rose from the back of the cushion to tap the top of her bonnet. "Most honestly, I have to tell you I may be doing society a great favor by shielding them from your sharp wit. I suspect there are wretchedly few among the Polite World who would be prepared to counter your sarcasm with any skill."

" 'Twas not sarcasm, Cameron. Simply the truth."

"Ah, that honesty again."

"You would prefer something other than honesty?" She was growing more certain with every passing moment he was the most contradictory man she had ever met.

"I would be foolish to say no, wouldn't I?"

"Would you?"

He leaned his cheek on his hand. With his elbow propped on the back of the cushion, he slanted toward her. She had to tilt her head back to meet his eyes, and her bonnet bumped on the seat. He hooked a single finger under its brim and tipped it aside.

"I would be foolish to let down my guard in any way with you, Tess," he said, his voice hushed, but penetrating. "You see everything very clearly and without compromise."

"It is the only way I know."

"Really?"

Tess edged away as far as she could. "I do not like that question."

"Why?"

"Because it sounds as if you are accusing me of some misdeed."

"Not you."

"Papa?"

Cameron's brows rose, but all suggestion of a smile vanished. "You leaped to that conclusion very quickly, Tess. Do you have a reason for that?"

"You could be speaking only of Papa or me, because I doubt you are discussing Jenette."

"Who?"

"My abigail." She glanced over her shoulder, although

she could not see the wagon that followed this carriage and carried the servants and luggage. "You do not know her, Cameron, so you must have been speaking of Papa or me."

"Yes."

She waited for him to add more. When he continued to look at her as if he expected *her* to reply, she turned to look out the window beside her. She would not sit here and listen to him criticize her father.

A sigh edged through her tight lips. She could not fault Cameron for being furious at Papa, because Cameron must wonder why her father had allowed the wedding ceremony to take place. If she could explain . . .

But she must not. She had promised Papa she would not reveal the truth to anyone.

She had not guessed how difficult that promise would be to keep.

Tess stretched her arms, holding Heddy's cage with care, as she waited for Cameron to wake Mr. Knox. She had not guessed the man would sleep all day during their journey, save for when they had stopped for their midday meal. If Mr. Knox had been awake, he might have offered some conversation to fill the long miles of silence. Or mayhap it was just as well that he had slept, because she had heard the sharp words exchanged by the two men this morning as she was walking toward the carriage. How she had longed to tell Cameron he should be more than vexed at his friend. Mr. Knox's crime had not been agreeing with her father last night that Tess should come to London. It had been blackmailing her father into arranging the wedding.

Jenette rushed over from where she had been speaking gaily with a tall, skinny man who had been pointed out to Tess as Park, Cameron's valet, when they set out this morning. "Are we staying here, Miss . . . my lady?" Her gulp was so loud Tess was surprised no one else seemed to hear.

"Yes." She gave her abigail a tentative smile. How could she blame Jenette for having a hard time adjusting to this sudden change? Again she was taunted by how readily she could set her abigail's mind at ease with the truth, but she had promised Papa to say nothing. Handing the cage to Jenette, she pretended not to notice how her maid grimaced. The hedgehog and Jenette shared an intense dislike for each other, for Jenette was squeamish about the bugs and worms Heddy ate.

"Please make sure our bags are brought promptly to where we are sleeping tonight," Tess continued. "I am not certain if I shall need to dress for dinner."

"Will you be eating here?"

"Yes." She showed no sign of her doubt. Did Cameron intend for them to eat in the public room here? Mayhap he planned on having their evening meal brought on trays.

She had no chance to ask him as he took her arm and guided her toward the inn. Mr. Knox trailed behind, rubbing his eyes and grumbling under his breath. The inn's whitewash had fallen from its timbered front, revealing its age, but the windows were clean and unbroken. Both sounds and odors from the left revealed where the stables were. The wind was coming from the right, so those scents should not fill the inn.

The inside of the inn was not as simple as Tess had suspected. A flowered rug ran along the stone floor, and the wooden floors in the taproom gleamed with care. A vase filled with white and pink blossoms sat on a table covered with an embroidered cloth. A painting of the front of the inn with a coach unloading passengers dressed in the style of a half century before hung on the opposite wall. Other frames were shadowed by the dim light, so she could not discern what was within them.

To the right, a dining room was visible through a partially open door. A stone floor and low rafters offered a welcoming touch. The fire on the hearth eased the chill coming with the end of the day. So many times, she and Papa . . . and Mama . . . had lingered at the table in the dining room in the oldest section of the house and watched the fire burn down to embers as they spoke of whatever filled their minds. She was amazed—and saddened—to realize she and Papa had not done that since Mama's death.

"Are you hungry?" Cameron asked.

Tess looked back at him. She should not be unsettled that he seemed to be watching her closely and questioning what she did, because he barely knew her. "Why do you ask?"

"You are staring at the dining room like a child looking at a beloved toy."

"I am recalling some beloved memories." She debated whether to share them, for she hoped Cameron would share some insight about his past as well. She halted when a raw-boned woman emerged from the shadows.

The woman smiled broadly, creasing her cheeks, which were unlined despite her gray hair. "Welcome to the Primrose and the Crown. I am Mrs. Hunt. Are you seeking something to eat or a place to rest or both?"

"Supper is what we want first, then two rooms as well as lodging for those accompanying us."

The woman looked from him to Tess and then on to Mr. Knox. "Two rooms?"

"One for Lady Hawksmoor, and one for the two of us," Cameron replied smoothly, acting as if he had not seen Mrs. Hunt's curious look.

"Very well." Mrs. Hunt smiled at Tess. "This way, if you please, my lady."

"Tess?"

She turned to look at Cameron. "Yes?"

"Do not linger to change for dinner. I think it would

be best, if Mrs. Hunt's kitchen can manage it, if we dined as soon as possible."

Mrs. Hunt replied, "Your dinner can be served at any time."

"I would like to wash up," Tess said, not adding she had looked forward to ridding herself of this dusty dress. "Then I shall be back down to join you for dinner."

"Excellent." He went to where Mr. Knox was entering the taproom.

Going with Mrs. Hunt up the stairs, Tess was pleased to find the room comfortable, albeit utilitarian. The bed with its high headboard was simple, and a chair, a dressing screen, and a table were the only other pieces of furniture set before the wide hearth. The floor was as clean as those below, and some sort of pattern had been placed upon the wall, although she could not discern it, for the room was shadowed, with only a single candle burning.

Jenette rushed in with word that the bags were on their way up. While Tess cleaned her face and hands with the tepid water in the bowl on the table, a fire was laid on the hearth. She guessed by the time she returned, the damp odor of a room that had not been used in a while would be banished.

She paused only long enough to peek under the cloth of the cage. Heddy was lying on her side, her soft brown underbody contrasting with the spines that grew along her back. Her eyes on either side of her narrow snout were closed, and she was making some sort of snuffling sound, even though she was still asleep. Wanting to reach into the cage and scratch Heddy's belly, Tess did not. She simply smiled and drew the cloth back before going out of the room, glad she had Jenette and the hedgehog as connections with what had been.

Cameron and Mr. Knox were waiting by the door to the dining room when she came back down the stairs. She understood why Cameron had not wanted to delay.

The room was already filling with other guests. He must have seen other carriages by the stables.

"Go ahead," said Mr. Knox. "I will be right with you." He turned to where a lad was standing by the front door. A flash of coins exchanged hands.

Cameron asked, as if to himself, "What is he doing now? Any polish he has placed on his boots will be ruined before he arrives in Town."

Tess had no answer as they went into the dining room, with Mr. Knox hurrying after them. A small square table was set aside for them not far from the hearth. Tess was aware of the curious eyes aimed at her as she walked through the room. When Cameron's hand settled over hers on his arm and then tightened, she knew he had seen the stares as well. That they bothered him astonished her, because he was not her true husband to be distressed by the admiration of other men.

Mr. Knox chuckled as Cameron sat Tess so her back was to the room. "You are the envy of every man in the room," Mr. Knox said as he pulled out a chair on the other side of the table. "You should be grateful to Masterson for saving his pretty daughter for you."

Cameron drew out the chair across from Tess's. "That is not a topic for dinner, Eustace."

"Why not?" Mr. Knox leaned both elbows on the table and propped his chin on one hand. "I can think of no better topic for this meal than to speak of your pretty bride."

"You are going to embarrass Tess."

She started to smile at Cameron in gratitude, but before she could reply, Mr. Knox laughed and said, "I cannot believe any woman would be embarrassed by a compliment, especially Masterson's daughter. She has been shut away in that country house while Masterson waited for the perfect match for her. Then along you came, my friend, and the marriage was made."

"I would rather not speak of that." Cameron's face was calm, but she noted how his hand had closed into a fist on the table.

"Then shall we speak of how glad I am to have Masterson's house behind us?" Mr. Knox smiled up at a maid who set a loaf of bread and some sliced beef on the table. With a wink at her, he added, "The scenery is much more pleasurable here now that we do not have Masterson glowering at us every minute."

"Papa might not have glowered if . . ." Tess lowered her eyes from the abrupt shock in Mr. Knox's. How could she so quickly forget the promise made to her father to say nothing about why he had agreed to the wedding?

"If what?" prompted Mr. Knox.

"I have said too much already." She reached for a slice of bread.

"Too much?" He laughed. "You keep your tongue so firmly behind your teeth that one would think you did not have one. Like a little mouse in a shadowed corner. Your good fortune, old chap." He snatched several pieces of meat and put them on the plate in front of him. "You do not need a prattling shrew who babbles endlessly and says nothing of value like her father."

"Eustace, that—"

Tess interrupted Cameron as she scowled at his friend. "Mr. Knox, I would ask you not to speak so of my father when he is not here to defend himself from your scurrilous comments."

"I am saying nothing here I would not say to his face."

"Then I shall be as forthright. I find your manners intolerable, Mr. Knox. If it is the way of the *ton* and their hangers-on to so cruelly ridicule decent folks, then I am glad I shall not claim a place among you."

"Not claim?" Mr. Knox's eyes widened. "As Lady Hawksmoor, you are a part of the very thing you despise."

"I shall be part of it only as long as—"

"That is enough, Tess," Cameron said quietly.

She looked at her husband, despising his composed expression. If she had not seen the powerful passions in his eyes when he had pulled her into his arms, she would be able to forgive him now for acting as if he had divested himself of all emotions. Did he hide them because he did not trust them or because he was as disgusted with them as he appeared to be with her at the moment?

"I shall not sit here and listen to this son of a sow speak so of my father, who is a well-respected man."

Mr. Knox snorted in disagreement.

Tess started to reply, but Cameron's hand over hers was a silent admonition not to give voice to her anger. She looked down at her plate. The idea of eating sickened her. She did not want to stay here with her father's blackmailer, who took every opportunity to belittle him. Nor did she wish to eat with Cameron, who seemed not to care what Mr. Knox said but censored every word she tried to speak.

"Excuse me," she said, coming to her feet. Even though she felt a momentary pulse of malicious delight that Mr. Knox had to stand as well as Cameron, she turned and walked out of the dining room.

Her ears strained for the sound of Cameron calling after her to come back and accept his friend's apology. She heard nothing but the rumble of the voices from the dining room. Climbing the stairs, she slammed the door as she entered her room. The sound did not give her the satisfaction she had hoped for, but it was, she knew, the only satisfaction she would get out of this unwanted marriage.

Six

Stomping across the room, Tess glared at the fire crackling on the hearth while rain ran down the uneven glass in the windows. The cheerful wallcovering was bright in the glow of the extra candles she suspected Jenette had badgered from the innkeeper.

As if a bit of extra light could lighten my dark spirits tonight! Walking past the small bag that contained the clothes brought into the inn for her, her hands fisted on the footboard of the bed. A mocking laugh filled her head. How self-assured she had been when she told Cameron she could deal with anything that might happen on their journey to London.

She wanted nothing but to go to bed and put the whole of this evening behind her. Ringing for Jenette, who should have been here instead of flirting with Cameron's valet Park, she began to undo the buttons down the back of her dress. Two flew off, clattering like small hailstones as they rolled under the bed.

"Oh, my!" gasped Jenette as she rushed in and bent to retrieve them. "My lady, you should have waited for me."

"I know." Tess did not want to argue with her abigail, so she let Jenette undo the rest of her dress. Going to the glass by the dressing screen, she knelt in the overstuffed chair beneath it. Her fingertips touched her straight lips. They would soften beneath one of Cameron's kisses. Too easily she let her desires for them persuade her to toss aside her good sense when Cameron was near. His touch was the most wonderful thing she had ever experienced. The very thought terrified her, because she would be a widgeon to become more involved with a man who wanted only to put her out of his life.

A knock was set on the door. Realizing she wore nothing more than her chemise and stockings, she sprinted behind the dressing screen while Jenette answered the door. "Thank you," Tess heard her abigail say, before the latch closed again with a soft click.

Peering around the edge of the cotton-covered screen, Tess asked, "Who was it?"

"The innkeeper . . . Mr. Hunt."

"What did he want?"

"He delivered this bowl of soup, a pot of hot chocolate, and a bottle of brandy for you." Smiling, she held out the tray. "The note is from Lord Hawksmoor."

Gingerly, unsure what this gift meant, Tess took the pewter salver. She placed it on the table by the bed and stared at it. Brandy? Why would Cameron send her brandy? She did not need to recall he had been drinking Papa's brandy when he became so intoxicated that he was a willing participant in the wedding ceremony, for every waking second was a reminder of that. Or had been it sent for some other reason? With quaking fingers, she lifted the unopened bottle.

Mayhap in London Cameron was accustomed to women who drank such a quantity of spirits. She shivered as she wondered what sort of women he usually consorted with when he was in Town. In spite of Papa's words about Cameron's position as a second son and how women were disgusted by the barely discernible scar, she suspected there were many women in London who would appreciate the attentions of such a handsome man who was the brother of a duke and clearly plump in the pockets.

Putting the bottle on the tray, she was ready to send it back untouched. Then she remembered Jenette had said there was a note. Tess unfolded it. The short message was written in a bold hand, which matched Cameron's demeanor.

> *My dear Tess,*
>   *Please accept this to eat and drink in hopes it will bring you a pleasant night's rest. Our journey on the morrow will be shorter, and tomorrow evening we shall dine more comfortably in the privacy of my house. That will allow us time to work out a way to deal with the uneasiness of our lives together until I can find a way to end this.*
>
> *Cameron*

She blinked back unexpected tears. What had she expected? An apology that he had given her a scold in front of the inn's other guests when she had wanted only to defend her father? Or had she dreamed—foolishly—of a profession of adoration he had been unwilling to say aloud?

She resisted the temptation to crumple the note and throw it back onto the tray before she sent for the innkeeper to take away this unwelcome gift. Looking down at it again, she bristled as if she were a hedgehog like Heddy when she reread, *until I can find a way to end this*. She needed to show Cameron she was not entirely witless, even though he obviously believed that in the wake of this evening's conversation.

Her fingers refused to close over the paper to wrinkle it into a ball. As much as she wanted to dismiss his note as coldhearted and unfeeling, she could not keep from recalling how gentle his touch had been when he led her to the carriage and away from her home to begin a new life which neither of them had anticipated when they first met two days earlier. In the rarely unguarded depths of his eyes, she had seen the powerful emotions he tried to conceal.

Hearing a chuckle, she looked up to see Jenette smiling.

"What is so amusing to you?" Tess placed the letter on the table.

Folding Tess's gown and placing it on the foot of the bed, Jenette said, "Forgive me, my lady. 'Tis nothing. Nothing at all." She went to the tray. "Do you wish me to pour for you?"

"Some of the chocolate, please."

"With a dash of brandy?"

Tess bit her lip as she stared at the full bottle. It must have cost Cameron dear. If she left it behind untouched, the innkeeper would sell it again. It should be enjoyed, although she doubted Cameron would drink very much brandy again so soon after letting it betray him.

Picking up the bottle, she said, "Jenette, I need you to do me a favor."

"Of course, my lady."

"Pour me a cup of chocolate while I dress. Then I want you to do an errand for me."

Behind the screen, Tess drew on her simple white nightgown. She closed her wrapper over it before going to her bag. She was about to open it when she heard scratching sounds from the hedgehog's cage. She lifted the cloth from it and opened her bag, then took out the small box that contained the food she had brought for Heddy's journey to London. Opening it, she gave the hedgehog a serving and set the cage in a shadowed corner by the bed where the moonlight would please Heddy. She ignored Jenette's grumbles about bringing insects into a perfectly clean room.

Leaving Heddy to enjoy her dinner, Tess found the writing box she had not intended to use until she reached London. She lifted out a single slip of paper and thanked Jenette, who put a cup of the fragrant hot chocolate beside her along with the cup of soup. Tess began to write. Words which usually came to her with ease faltered, and she stumbled her way through a few sentences. Reading it, she was unsatisfied. She considered throwing it away and starting over, but she doubted if she could do better. Folding it, she held it out to her abigail.

"Jenette, would you take this and the bottle of brandy to the innkeeper and ask him to deliver it to where Mr. Knox and Lord Hawksmoor are staying?"

"No need to bother Mr. Hunt. His lordship and Mr. Knox are just across the hall." Her eyes twinkled, and Tess suspected Jenette was hoping for the chance to see Park again. "I shall deliver it myself." Before Tess could chastise Jenette for such unsuitable behavior, her maid had slipped out the door. It remained slightly ajar behind her.

Curiosity teased Tess to sneak closer and listen to what was said. She wrapped her arms around herself, shivering at the thought. But at the thought of what? Of being discovered lurking there like a naughty child or of having Cameron catch sight of her when she was dressed so inappropriately?

She laughed aloud, but there was no humor in the sound. Cameron had seen her in *déshabillé* already. To play the shy lass flirting with a dashing rogue was something she could not do.

Jenette's laugh floated into the room. It possessed the coquettish tone Tess had dreamed would be in her own laugh when she met the man who touched her heart so much she was willing to spend the rest of her life with him.

Footsteps faded in the distance. Where was Jenette bound now? The door swung wide.

Tess took one step toward it to close it, then gasped,

"Cameron! What are *you* doing here?" She clutched the neck of her wrapper to her chin as his gaze swept over her as if he had never seen her before.

He had removed his coat and cravat and loosened the top two buttons on his shirt, just as he had when he had been lying beside her in her bed. Then he had gathered her into his arms and against the hard breadth of his chest. Her breath grew uneven with the memory of those splendid sensations.

When a smile drifted across his lips, she realized how intently she was staring at him. She looked away from his knowing eyes to see he carried the brandy, a glass, and her note.

"That was not the pleasant greeting a wife should offer her husband, Tess."

"I did not invite you here."

"I am quite aware of that." He closed the door, ignoring her frown. "Jenette and Park have gone to sit by the fire-place in the dining room, and Eustace is sharing tales in the taproom. Your gift of this brandy raises questions—"

"Gift? You sent it to me!"

"You are mistaken. Why would I send you *brandy* of all things?" He pointed with the bottle toward the steaming pot of hot chocolate. "I asked the innkeeper to send that to you."

"The brandy was with it."

He set the bottle on the table. "Now I understand the cool tone of your note." Opening it, he began with, "Cameron." He looked up. "Not even a 'Dear Cameron,' which you seem to believe would suggest some obligation on your part."

"I was distressed."

"Clearly." He looked down at the note and read, *"I would be an ungrateful wretch not to say thank you for your thought in sending a tray to my room. So please accept my thanks. You need not worry that I shall delay you on your journey to London on the morrow."* Tossing it onto the table, he said, "It is signed *Tess Masterson.* Your signature now, even though neither of us may like that fact, is Lady Cameron Hawksmoor. Mistakes like that could create even more problems for us in Town."

"Oh." She closed her eyes and sighed. "Forgive me for falling back on habit when I was upset. It was thoughtless of me."

"As you believed it was thoughtless of me to send this brandy to you." He set the bottle on the tray and picked up a cup. "May I?"

Tess nodded, breathing with silent relief when he poured some of the hot chocolate into the other cup. He handed it to her and then took the one that had been cooling beside the soup.

"Thank you," she whispered. "It seems I am developing an intolerable habit of jumping to baseless conclusions."

"To the contrary. Your conclusions, especially in this case, have a very strong basis. Why wouldn't you believe I was parading before you that you could be as want-witted as I if you emptied that bottle of brandy?"

"I do not have such cruel thoughts."

"Nor do I." He motioned toward the chair by the foot of the bed. "May I keep you company while we quaff this delicious chocolate?"

"You are bold, Cameron."

"Bold?" He sat in the chair and leaned toward her, his elbows on his knees.

"You think I will forgive you for the way you scolded me at dinner simply because you are not the one who sent the brandy."

"I do not suffer scenes well."

She bristled and crossed her arms in front of her. How dare he speak to her as if she were a child! She could not keep her anger out of her voice as she said, "I must ask you to leave. It is time for me to finish readying myself for bed, and I am not dressed to receive company."

"I noticed that."

Trying to ignore his smile, which spread slowly from his lips to his glittering eyes, she stated tersely, "I am sure you did. Now will you please leave?" Her fingers shook as she gestured toward the door.

Standing, he placed his cup on the tray and walked toward her. She stepped back in rhythm with his steps to keep the space between them unchanged. When she bumped into the turned-down bed, she raised her hands.

"Cameron, this is silly. We are trying to convince people we are *not* married. Your being here contradicts that assertion."

"I know." He put his hands on her shoulders. "You are trembling."

"Yes." She knew she should not look into his dark blue eyes, but she could not halt herself.

"Why? I collect you are not frightened of me."

"No, of course not." She had repeated the lie so many times to herself it did not taste bitter when she said it to him.

"Then why are you trembling?"

"I believe I am overmastered by everything that has happened in the past two days." There. That was the truth.

He nodded. "I share that feeling, but I came here for one reason, Tess."

"And what is that?" she asked, trying to ignore how his fingers stroked the curve of her arm.

"I must learn to trust you."

"I told you that myself."

"And I have realized you are correct. Now I ask you invest the same trust in me." One corner of his mouth tilted. "After all, I have not thrown you on that bed and kissed you until you surrendered to the ecstasy I am quite certain we could share."

"Cameron!" She edged away, startled he would speak so.

He stepped in front of her again to keep her from slipping past him. "I am more of a gentleman than you seem to think I am. Can't you trust me for just a few minutes?"

Staring up into his face, which still revealed too little of his emotions, she could not disregard the familiar delight billowing up from deep within her. She wanted him to stay. Talking with him might be the best antidote to the unhappiness that had burst out of their mutual frustration this evening.

"Can you be trustworthy for a few minutes?" she asked as she lowered her crossed arms to her sides.

"You wish honesty from me, I assume."

"Yes."

"Then I can honestly tell you that, with you, being trustworthy will be a struggle. That I must own. You inspire in me two very different desires: One to kiss you again because you are such a lovely woman." His lips tilted in a smile as his eyes twinkled with sapphire fire. He abruptly scowled as he added with a threatening growl, "The other is to send you to sit in the corner, because you insist too often on acting like a child."

"Mayhap I would not act so if you stopped trying to control everything I said and did."

He drew back his hands and regarded her with astonishment. "I do not—"

"To the contrary, you do!" She put her hands on her waist and regarded him with a cold smile. "I am not a child, nor am I a possession—a most unwanted possession, I should add. I shall not be ordered about like a dog who waits to do your bidding. Mayhap I do not know as much as I should before embarking upon a Season in London, but may I remind you I do not intend to stay any longer than it will take to dissolve this marriage?

Then, *my dear* Lord Hawksmoor, I shall not be a problem for you, nor shall I be subservient to your commands."

Cameron was surprised he was not burned by the sparks in Tess's eyes, which glittered like dew-kissed grass at sunrise. This woman was too unpredictable. With other women, he always had been able to conjecture when they would erupt into anger or become fawning. Tess baffled him completely, for her anger, though volatile, could be icy cold. There was a gentleness within her that bewildered him even more, because, for some reason he could not fathom, she had forgiven her father and *him* for this marriage she so clearly hated.

"Mayhap," he said, "I have been overly long involved with the army, because it seems I have become accustomed to giving orders and expecting them to be obeyed without question."

"I am not one of your men."

"Most definitely you are not."

He was treated to that beguiling color that flooded up her cheeks, turning them the same deep rose as the curtains around her bed. His finger brushed one cheek's downy warmth before he could halt himself. When she turned her face away, he wanted to curse. She was right. They must make the best of these uncomfortable circumstances until they could put an end to them. Or the worst of them, he added with a sigh. The best would be to have her in his arms. The worst was this wanting to hold her and knowing, if he did, how completely he could be destroying any chance for them to end this marriage.

"Tess?"

At his hushed question, she looked at him again. "Cameron, I am fatigued. If you wish to continue to harangue me, can't it wait until we are in the carriage in the morning? We still have many miles to travel before we reach Town, and you can use them to list all my shortcomings."

"That is not what I intended to say."

"Then what did you intend to say?"

"Will you sit?" He motioned toward the chair.

He thought she might throw his polite words back into his face, but she nodded. As she crossed the small room, he could not keep his gaze from following the graceful sway of her hips. What was it about this woman? He had met her only days ago, but she continued to fascinate him. If he had half the wit of a goose, he would leave. She was a temperamental woman, no matter how she tried to pretend otherwise. She might look at him with an expression as dispassionate as any he wore, but she could not hide the passion he had tasted on her lips.

Handing her one of the cups again, he sat on the bed. Tess's eyes widened, but she said only, "This chocolate tastes very good on such a damp night."

"I thought you might enjoy it."

She drew her feet up beneath her and smiled, startling him. "A pot of chocolate seems to be the best prescription for any number of woes."

"Something you learned from the stillroom at your father's house?"

"No. Something I learned through practice." She chuckled again. "Tell me, Cameron, how do you deal with your tie-mates when they engage you in a battle of wits?"

"Do not mistake an honest attempt to learn more about you with a lack of wit on my part."

She started to answer, then began to laugh. When he asked what she found so funny, she said through gasps of laughter, "You equate a lack of wit with becoming better acquainted with me. How flattering, Cameron!"

"You must own I would be jobbernowl to chance exploring the oddities of a woman's mind."

"My mind is not odd."

"From your point of view."

" 'Tis the only one I know." She took another sip and smiled. In spite of himself, he could not keep from noticing how her eyes sparkled as she nestled into the chair. His arms suddenly felt empty, and he knew just now she would be the only one who would satisfactorily fill them.

He set his cup on the tray and reached out to take her hand. Running one finger along her willowy ones, he watched her lips part with a soft sigh. He needed only to cup her chin and tilt her face beneath his. Her mouth would be sweeter than the chocolate.

"Cameron," she whispered.

Yanking his gaze away from her lips, he released her fingers before he could pull her closer.

"I think it would be for the best if we put an end to this conversation." She set her cup next to his and came to her feet. "We must be leaving very early in the morning if we plan to reach London before nightfall."

"Yes." He stood and discovered she was so close not even a half step separated them. Her head tipped back as she looked up at him. When his hand cupped her cheek, her eyes closed and she leaned her face against his palm. In a whisper, he said, "It appears you were honest when you told me earlier today you are always honest."

"Yes, even at unfortunate times like this evening."

"Even fortunate times like now?"

"Fortunate?" she whispered.

"Yes, when we are alone like this when we can talk plainly and . . ."

She opened her eyes, and he knew his warning to her in the carriage was one he should remember now. Honesty was a dangerous trait when one stood this close to a beautiful redhead who just happened to be one's wife. An unrestrained need rushed through him, hot and demanding.

His mouth was on hers before he could take his next breath. Slowly, as if he had never kissed her before, he explored each delicious morsel of her mouth. Unhurried, but with an impatience that refused to be denied, he lured her lips to soften and offer up all their pleasure to him. He stroked her back, drawing her even closer to him. The softness of her against him threatened to undo every bit of his self-control.

He released her, stepping back before his traitorous arms could enfold her again. He was seven times a widgeon, for Eustace had conceded Cameron might be right that there was more to this marriage than Masterson wanting a well-placed husband for his beloved daughter. But who would have been Masterson's ally in this and why? Eustace had owned to having his hand forced so he could not halt the ceremony, but refused to say by whom or why. That, his friend had warned, might endanger all of them.

He did not want to think of that now as he gazed at his wife, whose breathing was as frayed as his. He forced his voice to be even as he said, "You are not, by any stretch of the definition, a little mouse, despite what Eustace said. I am not sure what you are, but I suspect, before we can gratefully bid each other *adieu,* I shall have learned."

She smiled, and he wondered how long any man with a heart beating within him could resist such a lovely sight. "Will you?"

"Without a doubt." His arm was around her waist again and her lips beneath his, branding him with the sweet fire that he craved and which, as her arms slid around his shoulders, he feared ultimately would betray him to whichever enemy had been behind this scheme to see him wed.

Seven

This was so strange.

Not strange in that Tess had never seen anything like the houses that edged Grosvenor Square, but because she could not imagine calling a town house on this elegant square home. Along the walkway, a man followed a small black dog stretching to the full extent of its leash to test every scent. Two children chased each other in the center of the square, sending the pigeons flitting up in front of them. As soon as the birds settled, the boy and girl raced through them again.

The carriage slowed on the north side of the square. Before it came to a stop, the tiger had jumped down from the boot and was preparing to open the door. He stepped back and bowed with a flourish that would have befit the Prince Regent himself.

"Thank you," Cameron said as he stepped out. Turning, he offered his hand to her. "Tess, what are you waiting for?"

Tempted to tell him she would prefer to sit here until she could understand how she was to maneuver through the maze of the life that had become hers, she sighed. She would be silly to remain in the carriage, because the only way she could decipher this puzzle was to spend more time with this so very puzzling man. When he had pulled her into his arms last night, she had been astounded and thrilled. The latter reaction frightened her.

Her hand settled on his broad palm, and she recalled again, most unwillingly, how he had held her last night. His kiss had been devastating to her determination to keep him distant, for it had coaxed her to abandon caution. Nothing should have changed, but everything had when his lips caressed hers. She might have been able to toss aside the memory of his kisses in her bedroom when he woke her, but not the ones in the inn. Then she could have pushed him away, could have ordered him to leave, could have reminded him of the jeopardy of any hint of affection between them. Instead she had melted against him like a sweet left out in the sunshine.

When he did not meet her eyes as he handed her out, Tess withdrew her hand quickly from his. He walked to where the cart was almost unloaded. It had reached the house before them, because the carriage had paused on another street Tess had not been able to identify to let Mr. Knox take his leave.

Jenette came over to where Tess waited and held out her hand for Heddy's cage, which a footman had taken from the carriage and was regarding with obvious curiosity. The maid was wide-eyed as she turned slowly around to stare at all sides of the square. "Oh, my, isn't this grand?" she murmured over and over.

Wishing she could do the same, Tess put her hand on Cameron's arm when he returned to her side and motioned toward the door of the house directly in front of them. She must not gawk like a bumpkin, for she had no idea who might be peering out of one of the dozens of windows facing the square. A single mistake now could put an end to all her hopes of getting back the life she had dreamed would be hers.

Yet . . . she looked up at Cameron's face, which could have been carved from the same pale stone as pillars on the front of the houses. Even a day ago, she could not have imagined how such a kiss would alter all her assumptions. She had been certain she wanted nothing more than to put an end to this debacle and get this man out of her life.

She should be grateful he had taken his leave right after that mind-sapping kiss. He had said something as he left, but she could not recall what it was. She had been so overwhelmed by the longing his kiss evoked that all thoughts had been tossed, willy-nilly, from her head. This morning, he had been the epitome of gracious and distant politeness. Nothing more. If he thought to act as if he had not kissed her again, she wished she could comply. That would be the sensible thing to do, and she always had been a most sensible lass, her father had told her. But she could not be reasonable about her most unreasonable longing to be in her husband's arms again.

The door opened as they neared. Hearing Jenette repeat, "Oh, my!" Tess was tempted to echo it as she entered the foyer. She had thought her grandmother's house was elegant, but even that fancy London house seemed simple compared to the grandeur of this one. Red striped wallpaper accented the height of the ceiling on this floor. Although the doors opening onto it were closed, the mahogany floor glistened with obvious care. The wood was topped by rugs she knew must come from the East. Matching carpet climbed stairs edged with metal newel posts engraved with what appeared to be some sort of a herald pattern.

Arches opened in the gallery above, although a pair were closed, as if someone had decided there were too many views from the upper floors. Lamps of bronze and crystal hung from the two of the arches where their soft light would wash down over the foyer. But the most magnificent part of the entry was directly above. A stained glass window was set in the roof four stories above them.

It splashed light in a rainbow of colors onto the floor and onto them.

Cameron greeted the man who had opened the door, then added, "This is Harbour, the butler. You need only ask, Tess, and he will see you have what you need."

"Thank you," she said, although she wanted to remind Cameron what she needed was a way to sort out the confusion in her brain.

"Please have someone get Lady Hawksmoor's bags from the boot," Cameron said.

"Lady—" The gray-haired butler regained his composure more quickly than a footman who stared agog at her from one of the doorways. "Of course, my lord."

"She will be using the front room to the left of the staircase." Cameron drew off his gloves and dropped them onto the table. Picking up a card from a silver tray there, he smiled as he read it. He slipped it beneath his coat, then frowned when he looked again at his butler. "Is there a problem, Harbour?"

"I wish only to be sure you wish her things taken to the left-hand room."

"The left-hand room."

Tess noted how the butler avoided looking at her. Was there a reason other than his obvious astonishment? Mayhap the man, in pristine livery the same shade as his hair, did not want to reveal his thoughts. In that, he might be very much like Cameron.

"Yes, my lord." Harbour went to give the orders to the footman and the rest of the staff.

"I will take you upstairs, Tess." Cameron offered his arm. "I suspect you will be glad to rest after our journey."

"I will." She did not add anything else, and she suspected he was pleased she was remaining as quiet as she had during the long hours of the day's journey to London.

Climbing the stairs by his side, she saw, when she reached a landing where the stairs turned to the next level, that the same herald design was placed over the front door. A lion and a dragon faced each other behind a bare sword in the talons of a great bird. It was a crest that suggested a warning to any outsider, because neither the dragon nor the lion could pass by the hawk and its sword.

"The crest is left from a time when the Hawksmoors were involved in more than the proper business of this century," Cameron said. "It seems out of place in this time, but the family deems it a reminder of past heroic deeds."

"I was thinking how perfect it seemed to be for you."

"For me?" He shook his head. "Do not paint me with the glories of great heroes, Tess. I am not your knight in shining armor, nor your prince who has come to rescue you from that dragon."

"But you are much like that hawk." She raised her hand. "Flying high above and considering the world, alone with your thoughts as you keep yourself apart from everyone and everything else."

"I doubt that is what my ancestors had in mind when this crest was designed."

"Mayhap, but mayhap not."

His mouth twisted into the caricature of a smile. "If you had the misfortune to meet my brother, you would know at least one Hawksmoor wishes to sample every bit of the world and its pleasures."

"Is your brother in London?"

"He seldom leaves Town. Here, he has his club and his tie-mates and his mistresses."

"Mistresses? More than one?"

His smile became more sincere. "You derided me for thinking of you as a bumpkin, but I suspect from that question you are more naïve than you wish to own to being. A man can have as many mistresses as he can afford."

"And what about you, Cameron?"

She had thought he might not answer, but he said, "I never found it prudent to be involved with more than one woman at a time."

Tess was unsure if she should be comforted or uneasy at that comment. Cameron did not intend to become involved with her now. Did that mean he had a mistress or . . . she closed her eyes in despair. What if he had been coming to London to call upon his fiancée? She had not given thought to the idea that more lives than their own might be ruined by this marriage.

As they climbed another set of stairs and stepped out into the upper hallway, which was filled with plants in pots of all shapes and sizes, Tess wondered if she was somehow dreaming the whole of this. Imagining she was married to a stranger made more sense than the jungle before her eyes. She could name only a few of the plants. The rest were ones she had never seen before.

"This is incredible!" she exclaimed as she tried to take it all in at once.

Behind her, Jenette was once again whispering, "Oh, my!"

"I did not know," Tess added, quickening her pace so she could walk beside Cameron, "that you enjoyed having flowers about."

"Why should you know that?" He did not slow his steps, but did lower his voice when a maid edged past them in the hall made narrow by the broad leaves of some flower Tess did not recognize. "What do you know of me other than I made a mistake that has upset our lives?"

She grasped his sleeve, halting the procession. When she motioned for Jenette to go with Cameron's valet along the hall to wherever they were bound, she did not let Cameron draw his sleeve out of her hand. "Would you please stop it?"

"Me?" Genuine surprise widened his eyes. "Stop what?"

"This constant grousing."

"I know you sing oh be easy, but I cannot."

"I what?"

"You do not complain when you have every reason to. I forget that you are not familiar with Town cant."

She shrugged, but continued to hold on to his coat. "I do have many reasons to complain, and I would if I thought it would do any good. However, nothing can be done until you seek the advice of your solicitor. I believe that it would be easier on both of us to accept what has happened for now—"

"*I* cannot accept it!"

"I said for now." She released his sleeve. "You might find, Cameron, that you can endure this with more equanimity if you would stop assuming I am delighted to be your wife. You may be the son and the brother of a duke, but you apparently find that fact far more impressive than I do."

He halted her from walking past him by putting out his arm. "Are you always this disagreeable?"

"Are you?"

"No."

"Then why are you trying to be at daggers drawn with me on the few occasions when you deign to talk with me?" she asked.

"Because it is simpler."

"Than what?"

His arm swept around her, tugging her toward him and giving her the answer she should have guessed. A hushed huskiness added fervor to his words as he murmured, "Do not think to use these airs of innocence to betwattle me."

"It is no pretense. Simply an unthinking question."

"Unthinking?" He laughed quietly. "Too often, I find myself thinking of holding you like this and even closer, Tess."

Although she longed to remain in his embrace, she put her hands on his arm and pushed it away. He did not release her gaze as willingly. Knowing she should look away, she did not. Her nails bit into her palms as she fought to keep her hands from reaching up to caress his cheek, darkened with the shadow of more than a day's growth of beard. Her fingertips tingled as she imagined letting them sweep across his rough skin.

"Ah, Lord Hawksmoor, I . . ." The butler gulped nearly as loudly as Jenette had yesterday in front of the inn. "Pardon me, my lord."

Tess dragged her gaze from Cameron's to see the butler's face fall with consternation. When she heard what most remarkably sounded like a chuckle from Cameron, she was amazed to see him smiling. She wanted to ask why, but was constrained by the butler's announcement that the baggage was on its way upstairs.

Cameron nodded, then walked toward the front of the house. Tess, her curiosity unsatisfied, for she suspected the butler had planned to speak to Cameron of other matters than the luggage, followed. When she reached the end of the hall, she was surprised that no window offered a view of the Square. Instead, a simple table almost invisible beneath the wild profusion of leaves sat between two doors facing each other across the hall.

Opening the door to the left, Cameron motioned for her to enter. The light from the hallway was swallowed by the golden shadows of the walnut furniture arranged elegantly in front of an unlit hearth. Around the furniture and in front of the tall window and edging each wall between the two closed doors were more pots with plants. A few were blooming, but the dim light consumed the color. When he drew her through the door, her slippers nearly disappeared into the royal blue carpet. She paid no attention as she stared up at the painting hanging above the mantel. It was of an orchard with a grand manor house in the distance. Beneath one tree, a lad sat, reading a book that appeared to have pictures of apples, although it might have been meant to show he had picked the fruit from that tree. The lad had hair as dark as Cameron's, and she wondered if it was a portrait of him as a child.

He allowed her no time to admire the grand frescoes and the art parading along the walls of what she realized was a sitting room. He drew her through one of the other doors. She faltered, for, set in a shadowed alcove, was a magnificent bed. Curtains that gleamed like cloth-of-gold were draped around it, but could not hide the carving that climbed all the way up the testers and even along the façade of the wooden canopy. Stag, foxes, and rabbits ran before hunters who were giving chase on foot and on horseback. Over their heads swooped a trio of birds. Hawks, she realized.

The bed was more than twice as wide as hers at home—at her father's house. Trying to act nonchalant, instead of revealing how she could far too easily imagine sleeping in such a grand bed with the man who was now her husband, she looked out into the other room and saw Jenette had the third door, the one closest to the front of the house, open. From what she could see, it led to a dressing room. Odd that it would be on the far side of the sitting room, but it was built against the front wall of the house, so that might explain its location. There were so many puzzles in this room, but the greatest one was Cameron Hawksmoor.

Untying her bonnet, she took it off. Setting it on the table beside the window that was as tall as the one in the sitting room gave her something to do with her hands instead of kneading them together as she had been doing since they entered the room.

"I trust you will be quite comfortable here, Tess." Cameron pointed to a bellpull next to the bed. "That will ring in the kitchen, so you may let Mrs. Sheridan, the cook, know when you want a breakfast tray brought to you."

"There is no breakfast-parlor in the house?" Oh, how grateful she was to speak of everyday matters, even though they were standing in this splendid chamber.

"There was one, but what use have I had for one when I have been living here by myself? It has been simpler for me to enjoy my coffee and the daily newspaper in the privacy of my rooms."

"I will make every effort not to intrude upon your habits, Cameron."

"You may do as you wish." He walked back out into the sitting room, pausing to cup the leaf of one plant. He glanced at her and hastily dropped it. "It matters little, for I expect I shall soon be able to obtain legal assistance to end our marriage. Until then, you are to stay here and make yourself quite at home."

"Staying *here* with you might not be wise."

"Why not? Do you have someplace else to go?"

"A guest's chamber would be more appropriate."

He smiled tautly. "Ah, now I see your concern. You need not worry about your husband demanding his espousal rights in yon bed, Tess. This is *your* room while you are here. I will have my own chambers on the far side of the hall. That will satisfy your fear about my encroaching upon your virtue, I assume."

"Yes." She was about to add more, then saw the intensity in his eyes. He wanted to pretend now that the kisses they had enjoyed last night had never happened, although she had been certain he would kiss her again if they had remained much longer in the hallway. That did not unnerve her as much as the discovery of how much she longed for him to kiss her again . . . and again.

"Then you must stay here. Although it may not be to

your liking, you *are* my wife, and it behooves me to take proper care of you until the proceedings are completed."

Tess nodded in resignation, but she wondered if a divorce would be as easy as he expected. If not, her life would be enmeshed with Cameron Hawksmoor's for longer than either of them wanted.

Eight

"My lord, your—"

A lanky form pushed Harbour aside from the doorway of the small parlor as if the servant had no more feelings than one of the velvet ottomans. Tess glanced at Cameron, who had been working on a letter to the solicitor while she had been writing a note of her own. She hoped Brenda Rappaport was in London. The woman who lived in the neighboring house of Tess's late grandmother had always made Tess feel welcome. Would Mrs. Rappaport have some advice for her now?

She folded the half-finished note and set it on the table beside her as she watched a man stride into the room as if it belonged to him. He smiled broadly and with obvious anticipation. His tousled, rabbit-brown hair had thinned to near extinction on his high forehead. His eyes were almost lost in the deep hollows of his face, and his expression pulled his thin lips into a parody of a grin.

Tess did not flinch as his gaze settled on her. She met it evenly, but in silence. The elegant cut of the man's dark coat and breeches bespoke a ready acquaintance with wealth and authority, yet they could not hide his spindly limbs. Bony hands emerged from the lace at the wrists of his sleeves. It was not a natural state for him, because his skin hung loosely on him. Mayhap he had been ill.

"Russell, what are *you* doing here?" Cameron asked as he came to his feet, closing the letter he had been penning.

Tess stared. This gaunt man was Cameron's brother the duke? She looked again and saw only a passing resemblance. If Cameron had not spoken his brother's name, she would not have guessed them to be related. Only their height and blue eyes were similar.

The balding man smiled and held out his hand toward the door. A woman appeared by his side. Tess forced herself not to stare at a carrot-topped woman, whose full curves suggested too many chocolates and too little activity. The heavy paint on her face concealed her age but hardened every feature.

"Are you going to forget your customary gentlemanly manners, Cameron? Come here and greet Isabel." The duke's scratchy voice resembled an unoiled shutter hinge being played with by the wind. "She is a very dear friend."

"Very dear," seconded the garish woman. Her outrageous accent exposed her low class beginnings in one of London's decrepit streets. Holding out her pudgy hand, she pushed it directly in Cameron's face.

Tess clenched her hands in her lap as she waited for the explosion of fury she could see tensing the muscles across Cameron's jaw. She had not seen his anger explode, and she feared it would be fearsome. She could imagine no other reason why he struggled to keep all his emotions in check.

"Miss—" Cameron glanced at his brother.

"Miss van der Falloon."

Cameron almost smiled at the absurdly fancy name for this bit of fluff. He forced himself not to look at Tess. If she could not overcome her country manners and giggled at this ludicrous name, he feared he would lose any control over his own mirth. The temptation to grin vanished when his brother's mistress waved her hand impatiently in his face, triumph oozing from every licentious angle of her sharp features. He had thought his brother, now that he held the ducal title, would have better taste in women than the she-cats that crawled through the alleys around Covent Garden.

Miss van der Falloon—How had she devised *that* name?—smiled more broadly as he bent over her hand. Her expression, which revealed a pair of broken teeth, dimmed when he did not raise her hand to his lips. She might have his brother wrapped around her fingers, but not him. He released her hand and folded his own behind him as he regarded her without expression.

Not willing to be defeated by a show of good manners, she put her hand on Russell's arm and cooed, "My dear, dear Russell 'as been so anxious fer ye and me to meet. When 'e 'eard ye'd returned to Town, 'e positively leaped outta our bed to rush to call 'pon 'is little brother."

Cameron's jaw tightened with the curses he wanted to let fly. How could Russell parade this tawdry woman through Cameron's house and through Town? Did Russell believe Cameron would accept this strumpet when both of them knew Russell would soon tire of her and seek another bed? If Russell thought—

"Please sit," came a melodic voice from beside him, "and I shall ring for some hot chocolate. The morning air still has a chill in the wake of last night's rain, doesn't it?"

He turned to see Tess coming to her feet. She was smiling, every inch the gracious hostess who would not be unsettled even if the Russian army marched through the parlor. As her hand swept out toward the settee, he caught it in his. Too tightly, he realized when she winced, her smile faltering.

He let his gaze linger on her, pleased by how charming she looked in her simple gown of a soft ivory that added more fire to her glorious hair. Her pretty face had no need for cosmetics, and the scent that came from her was sweet, not thick with perfume like the woman beside his brother.

Cameron's pleasure vanished when his brother asked, "Wherever did you find this lovely creature? I had heard that you had returned to Town, but the *on dits* did not suggest you had brought such endearing company with you."

"I found her at her father's house."

His brother chortled. "A bold move, Cameron, but one worthy of a great war hero, I must say."

Blast and double blast! He did not have to look at Tess to know she was regarding him with astonishment and that gentle aura of disappointment she showed each time she discovered he had withheld yet another fact from her. She had been reticent about the flowers and bushes in the hallway and in her private chambers, but he had seen the questions in her eyes. Could she guess he balked at explaining because to invite her into his private life even that small bit suggested she might remain there? That this whole debacle was real?

The great war hero . . . Balderdash! He was a coward who had let brandy gain the better of him and steal his wits and his future plans from him in one drunken jest.

"Will you introduce me to your delightful companion?" Russell asked with more than a touch of impatience.

"This is Tess." Cameron knew he should not hesitate, but he did before adding, "Tess Hawksmoor, my wife."

"Wife?" repeated his brother. With a chuckle, he walked across the room, steering his garish convenient ahead of him. "This is, indeed, a surprise, Cameron."

"Yes, I suppose it is."

"I did not expect to be meeting *your wife* today. I had not even heard you were betrothed. Father would have been very pleased to see you settled. He always said you would be wise and set up housekeeping with the proper woman, and I must say you chose a properly pretty one." He seemed unaware of Isabel's jealous scowl, and Cameron knew his brother would soon be giving the woman her *congé* if she insisted on being in a muff.

"Not as pleased as he would have been to see you wed with an heir on its way."

"Ah, that is true." Russell reached past him and grasped Tess's hand. "Tess Hawksmoor, is it? I welcome you to the family, my dear."

His quick tug nearly pulled Tess off her feet. As he kissed her stoutly, Isabel fumed. That did not surprise Cameron. What startled him was his own reaction. Before he could halt himself, he jerked Tess away from his brother. Her whispered thanks would not reach any ears but his.

"Do not be a jealous bridegroom." Russell laughed as if he had made a great joke. "Then she will have the right to be jealous as well, and *you* would not want that, I know."

Cameron's curse was silent, but he said only, "Tess, please ring for chocolate and coffee now."

She slipped around him, as ethereal as a wraith. When she reached the bellpull and gave it a tug, he could not miss the dismay in her eyes. He knew it was not because of his brother's overly passionate kiss, but because Russell had suggested Cameron would soon give any wife cause to be jealous that his affections were not offered solely to her. Dash it! Did she expect him to be faithful to this mockery of a marriage?

He could not ask that now. Not when his brother, who could not keep from repeating every bit of poker-talk he had ever heard, was within earshot. Instead he said, "I trust there is some reason for your call at this early hour,

Russell. You seldom are up before noon. I collect you are in need of funds."

"Money? Do not be crude, Cameron, and speak of such things when ladies are present."

Cameron smiled tightly. Russell had never been averse to asking him for a loan in the past. Twice his brother had even sent a note to Pamela Livingstone's house to request money to cover his gambling debts because Russell had been anxious not to leave the table when no one else would take his IOU.

"I agree it is not a subject fit for female company," Cameron said as he watched Tess give her request to a footman before returning to stand beside him. "I am simply inquisitive."

"What reason do we need now that we have your nuptials to celebrate?" Russell laughed again as Isabel plucked a bottle of wine from a sideboard as she passed. When Russell snagged two pairs of glasses, she gleefully uncorked the bottle and emptied it into the goblets. Wine splashed on the dark rose rug, but she ignored it as Russell shoved a glass into Tess's hand. He held out another to Cameron, who did not take it.

Raising the glass high, Russell crowed, "To your future happiness, brother dear."

Cameron did not move, save to look at Tess. Her cheeks remained gray with distress that she was coming face-to-face with his brother's mistress. She must learn the ways of the *ton* were different from what she had known in daisyville. No, he knew Isabel was not the reason for her ashen appearance, because she had been fine until Russell spoke of Cameron giving her cause to be jealous.

"Aren't you going to drink to your future?" Russell asked, his smile fading.

"At this hour of the morning?" Cameron returned.

"The idea of a cup of coffee appeals to me far more than wine."

"Ever the puritan, aren't you?" He dropped the bottle back onto the sideboard with a crash. He disregarded the sound and the puddle on the polished mahogany. As he raised the goblet to his lips, he locked eyes with Tess. "How about you, Lady Hawksmoor? Why aren't you drinking to my toast? Aren't you pleased with your good fortune in marrying into this family?"

"I prefer to wait for the hot chocolate." Relief filled her voice. "Here it is."

Tess motioned to the maid carrying the tray to set it on a table between a trio of chairs. A footman had followed the maid into the room, and he moved a fourth chair closer to the low table. Smiling her thanks to them, she wished she could go with them out of the room.

"Please sit," she said. "You must forgive Cameron and me, for we are still tired from our long journey from my father's house."

The duke poked Cameron with an elbow. "A good excuse for guests, isn't it?" Leering at her, he added, "You need not speak gently for me, dear sister Tess. Lustiness is a Hawksmoor family trait." He put his arm around the waist of the woman by his side. "Right, Isabel, my love?"

"Wotever ye say, dearie."

"I was being honest, Your Grace," Tess replied, trying to keep her frustration in check. She poured out two cups of coffee and two of hot chocolate. It did not surprise her that the duke and his mistress did not set down their glasses to take one. "I meant only what I said."

Beneath the duke's laugh, Cameron said, "Pay him no mind. He is so seldom in a real lady's company I fear he has forgotten how to act graciously."

"I heard that," growled the duke. "Do not become all fancy on me, little brother. If your new wife is fatigued because of her journey here from . . . where did you say you met this charming flower of femininity?"

Tess's fingers clenched her cup so hard she feared that she would crush it. She kept her face blank as she waited for Cameron to give the ignoble explanation guaranteed to add to her shame as an unwanted and unwilling bride. When she looked at Cameron, her outward composure almost crumbled, for she had not expected to see an apology in his eyes. He was, she realized with a start, ashamed of his brother and the earthy woman by his side.

When he took her hand, no sign of his indignity could be heard in his serene voice. "If you recall, I told you that I met her at her father's house. We were introduced and wed there."

"And Mother approved of this?"

"Mother does not know."

Mother? Tess stiffened. Cameron had mentioned his father was dead, but had not said anything about his mother. The duchess was certain to be in a snit over her son's marrying without her approval.

Cameron put his arm around Tess's shoulders. Did he think she was about to flee? Mayhap he understood how much she wished to—to flee back to Papa's house and the life she had known there. She wanted nothing to do with the fast life of a duke and his mistress and his brother and their friends who spoke of people she had never met. He tightened his fingers into her arm, and she glanced at him. His taut smile warned he wanted to prevent his brother from suspecting anything was peculiar about their marriage.

Quietly he said, "No doubt Mother shall be infuriated with me. That should deflect her vexation from you for failing to wed."

The duke laughed again. "This is so unlike you, little brother. You have always been the good and obedient son, the one who makes the family proud with your devotion to duty. Now you have gone and done something completely out of hand. Could it be you have a reason to have been in such a hurry to make this lovely lass your wife?" He stretched across the tray and patted Tess's stomach. When she gasped and pulled away, horrified at his outrageous action, he winked at her. "Could it be you want to make your child legitimate? Mayhap you have learned something from your wayward brother." He stood and lifted his glass. "To the next generation of the Hawksmoor family!"

"That is quite enough." Cameron put out a hand to block his brother from reaching behind him for the wine bottle again. "If you want to drink yourselves into oblivion, I suggest you return to your own house, Russell."

Isabel pouted, the expression out of place on her thickly powdered face. The duke started to argue, then stammered as he met Cameron's cool eyes. Mumbling an excuse that Tess suspected was aimed at maintaining his dignity, he stood and put his glass on the sideboard, then led Isabel from the room without another word.

Cameron turned to her. Motioning for her to stay where she was sitting, he went and tugged on the bellpull. When a maid answered the ring, he ordered a full tray of breakfast. Belatedly, he added, "I assume you are hungry, Tess. Harbour mentioned earlier to me you had not called for a tray to be brought to your chambers."

"Yes." She wanted to say something else, but was not sure what would be appropriate, so she added only, "Thank you."

"I suppose I should apologize."

"Apologize?"

"For Russell's behavior." He cocked one brow toward her. "Do not say what I fear is in your mind."

"Do you profess to read my thoughts now?"

"No, I think only what I would be thinking if our situations were reversed. I would be sure nothing your brother did could outweigh what you had done in a drunken moment."

"By marrying without obtaining your mother's approval on the match?" She came to her feet and wrinkled her nose as she looked at the wine splattered on the rug. "I may not know the ways of the *ton* well, but I cannot see how your behavior compares to your brother's."

"You are right. You do not know the ways of the *ton*. A mistress is a passing fancy; a wife is a way for a man to advance himself in the eyes of his family and friends."

"I am sorry I do not meet your expectations or theirs."

"I did not say that. I said only I am sorry my brother has been inflicted upon you."

"What good would an apology do now?" She met his eyes steadily. "What good would any sort of apology do now?"

Sitting beside her, he smiled, but the warmth failed to reach his eyes. "You have been prettily spoken until now, quiet as a mouse, according to Eustace, who has not taken notice of how you can be very much the opposite."

"I warned you I prefer honesty. You must own this is hardly a normal situation."

"True." He sandwiched her hands between his. "I feel compelled to apologize for my brother and his latest high-flyer calling when you have just arrived in Town." His lips tightened, but he took a calming breath. "I fear you will be unable to avoid them, but I must speak with Eustace about spreading the news of our arrival about London with such alacrity."

"Mr. Knox? But he was traveling with us."

"I should have been suspicious when he gave that lad a tuppence at the inn." A wry smile settled uncomfortably on his lips. "It seems he owes me an explanation of why he believed he should do that." He looked again at the door. "As Russell owes me an explanation of where he found that low creature."

"Miss van der—?"

"You may as well call her Isabel," he interrupted with a terse laugh. "I doubt if even that is her real name. I never met her before this morning."

"Never?"

"She has never been received at Peregrine Hall. After meeting her, you can understand why. Mother would fly up to the boughs at the very idea of Russell bringing his latest mistress to our ancestral home."

She drew her hands away and stood. "As she will be in a pelter to hear you have wed, Cameron."

"Quite possibly."

"The duke—"

"He is your brother-in-law. You should accustom yourself to calling him Russell."

Color flashed along her cheeks. "I have never met a duke before."

"Is that why you acted so overmastered by him?"

"No. I was not impressed by him, but I am by his title."

"I can assure you Russell is not the only duke who takes advantage of his position to seek his pleasure as he wishes."

When he stood, her gaze moved along the white shirt covering his broad chest to his linen stock, which was wrapped perfectly beneath his chin. As she met his eyes, curiosity taunted her. Unlike his brother's glazed eyes, Cameron's revealed his quick wit and his tightly controlled passions.

Before she could speak, although she was unsure what she would have said, a maid brought in a tray topped by silver serving dishes. When she had spread them out on a low table and curtsied before hurrying away, he urged, "Eat, Tess. Mayhap this coffee will finally loosen my frozen brain, and I can recall what happened the night we wed."

"You remember none of it?" Once she would have found such an assertion preposterous, but she could not disbelieve what was before her eyes. Cameron Hawksmoor was not a man who surrendered his will readily. She could not imagine him drinking until he was so foxed he was made a party to wedding a woman he had spoken to only in passing upon his arrival.

"Bits and pieces, but what I recall is like some half-remembered dream." He scowled into the cup he was pouring for himself. Sitting on the settee, he met her gaze without apology. "Mayhap some fresh air will help me remember more. I have some calls to make today."

"To whom?"

"The first shall be to a solicitor who may be able to help us. If all goes as I hope, I shall be hurrying back to tell you the good tidings. Then you can be done with the Hawksmoor family once and for all."

Nine

There was more comfort than Cameron had guessed in seeing how little had changed on the street. So many times he had driven along it, and the brick fronts of the houses had been the backdrop to the anticipation of pleasure. He had thought of this pleasant street many times when the bitterness of the battlefield had threatened to drag him down into melancholy.

He swung off his horse and handed the reins to the lad who ran forward to take them. Noting the new livery the lad wore, he smiled. His erstwhile mistress, Pamela Livingstone, had made good use of Stedley's generosity. That was no surprise. Before he had left England, her intelligence had drawn him to her almost as surely as her sensuality.

As Tess does to you now.

Where had that thought come from? He did not want to tangle his life up with the woman who was now his wife. Mayhap if they were not prisoners in this marriage, he would have determined if she might be interested in an *affaire de coeur.* A worthless pursuit, for she might allow him to sample a few kisses, but she had thrown him out of her bed.

Cameron forced his frustration aside as he walked into the parlor where he once had felt more at home than at his own house on Grosvenor Square. His vexation bubbled forth again when he noted how the room had been redecorated in shades of green and gold. It was far more pretentious than it had been when he last called here, for the furniture was gilded, and the rug was clearly new. He had hoped something would remain the same as before.

"Cameron, how kind of you to call."

He looked toward a tall bay window. As a slender figure rose, silhouetted against the day's feeble sunlight, he smiled. Pamela was the same. She walked toward him, and he saw she was as graceful as he had recalled during those long months when he had been far from England. Her golden hair was lying perfectly about the shoulders of her cream wrapper, which was edged with intricate lace.

Taking her hand, he bowed over it, then kissed her cheek and smiled. "You know I would not be long in London without giving you a look-in."

"Do come and sit down. You can tell me about all your experiences since you left."

"If I not am intruding when you are expecting another caller—"

She smiled. "Dear Cameron, you know John would be as pleased to see you as I am. He has said so often he is grateful for your introducing us."

"So you still are with Stedley?"

"Yes." She sat in the green tufted chair, where she had been obviously enjoying a cup of tea when he arrived, for a tray was set in front of her. When he brought a painted chair to face hers, her smile broadened. "He is a kind man, and he is devoted to me. I am grateful, too, Cameron, that you took the time before you left England to arrange for us to meet. However, I wish to know about how you have been. I have heard congratulations are due you."

"On my marriage?"

"Yes." She laughed lightly. "I am so pleased for you, Cameron, although I should chide you for not telling me about this before I heard the *on dits.*"

He took a deep breath and released it slowly. "By the elevens, Eustace is losing no time in spreading the word of my nuptials."

"And why not? It is joyous news. So tell me, however did you get your mother to agree to let you wed Tess Masterson?"

"Your spies are very efficient."

"Because I know her name?" She laughed again, the sound like sunlit bubbles bursting in midair. "You must know such a quick wedding in daisyville without anyone being aware of your plans is sure to create a great deal of talk. No one had a chance to debate the planned wedding before it took place, so now everyone feels the need to prattle about it."

"It is not a wedding I had planned."

"What?" She lost her nonchalance and frowned. "You plan everything, Cameron, to the tiniest detail. How could you fail to plan your own wedding?"

It did not take long for him to tell her the ignoble tale of how he had come to find himself with a wife. As he spoke, Pamela came to her feet, motioning for him to remain seated. She paced from the window to the table where she kept a bottle of wine for guests.

"Outrageous," Pamela said. "It sounds as if Masterson's hand is deep in this."

"She is his daughter."

"That is true." Sitting again, she added, "I have heard nothing of her, for Masterson has kept her secluded and away from his cronies."

"Those cronies are not the type of men one would wish to know one's daughter."

She nodded. "I have heard he cares little who sits across the table when he holds the flats in his hands. He is known to be strident when he is in his cups and refuses to listen to any opinion save his own."

"In that, he is much the same when sober." He poured himself a cup of tea from the pot on the tray.

"And his daughter? Is she like him?"

Cameron shook his head. "She is very different. She listens when someone speaks, even though she may not agree." He chuckled as he recalled her heated words at the inn. "She is not afraid to let one know her opinions, but she has a gentleness about her that is completely contradictory to her father's character. I suspect she is well read."

"A bluestocking?"

"Mayhap, but her country ways are because she has seldom been to Town."

"So Masterson has never spent any of his winnings on launching his daughter into the Polite World?"

"Winnings? From what I saw at their house, I would have guessed Masterson was at point non plus. The garden—" He threw up his hands. "The garden was a disaster."

She laughed. "I should have guessed you would notice the state of the garden. What of your wife's wardrobe?"

"It seems to me it is not as fashionable as among the dandy-set here in Town."

"Which means you took little notice of what she was wearing." She wagged a finger at him. "Either I should chide you for paying more attention to Masterson's gardens than his daughter, or I should wonder if she has so beguiled you that you have taken no note of what she wears."

"Feel free to chide me."

"Really?" She smiled and relaxed again in her chair. "I think you are wanting to avoid the truth, Cameron— she intrigues you."

"Whether she intrigues me or not is immaterial. Nor

does it matter that Masterson is so bothersome he would not hear of Tess's remaining in the country while I made an attempt to unravel this mess."

"Unravel?"

"I am looking for a way to put an end to this marriage."

Pamela's dark eyes widened. "Oh, no, Cameron! If you divorce her, she will be forever ostracized." Reaching across the table, she put her hand on his arm. "She is your wife, Cameron. Your very new wife. Please go to her and make certain you are aware of what you are doing."

"What I am doing? I know quite well what I am doing." He scowled. "I know now, even though I clearly did not then."

"Mayhap it is not all for the worse. *On dits* suggest she is lovely."

"She is."

Pamela laughed. "Cameron, there is no need to act as if you have done something out of hand by owning to the fact your wife is a lovely woman."

" 'Twould be easier if she were a shrew and a nag and threw tantrums each time I walked into the room."

"Mayhap you should be grateful she is kindhearted and willing to do what she must to make your marriage work, for there may be nothing you can do to change it now."

He shoved himself to his feet. "Pamela, I have heard disparaging talk from everyone else. From you, I had hoped to hear more optimistic thoughts."

"I could be dishonest with you and tell you whatever you wish to hear."

"As you have in the past."

She smiled as she lifted her teacup to her lips.

Cameron chuckled. It was a wise mistress who filled her lover's ear with nothing-sayings. "I came here hoping you might know of someone who is more interested than the family's solicitor in looking for a way to bring this marriage to a quiet end."

"There may be someone."

"I suspected you would know someone."

She set her cup on the tray. "Cameron, I do not *know* this man, but I have heard of him. He helped a friend of mine with a difficult parting between her and her gentleman friend." She hesitated, then added, "He is not for the clutch-fisted, for his services do not come cheaply."

"I am not miserly." Looking about, he gave her a reluctant smile. "Or mayhap in comparison to Stedley, I would seem so to you."

Rising, she kissed his cheek. "My dear Cameron, I never had any complaints when we were dear friends." She went to a writing table and opened a drawer. Opening a small book, she copied some information onto a slip of paper. She handed it to him. "If Mr. Paige cannot help you, I do not know where else you might turn."

"Nor do I."

The few windows of the solicitor's dusky office were shut tightly against the rain. Tess doubted they had ever been opened. An underlying stench of mustiness surrounded her as she sat on an uncomfortable chair in the antechamber, which was painted a dreary gray. A heavy door to the inner room was guarded by a young man she guessed was a clerk. He was scanning a heavy volume, his nose almost against the pages, his finger following each line in slow succession.

She fought not to tap her fingers on her lap. There was something about this place which disquieted her; something more than the dank odor and the dim light filtering through the windows draped by navy brocade. She glanced at Cameron. His shoulder rested against the win-

dow's frame, and he appeared to be watching the traffic
on the street below, but she knew his mood was closer
to outrage than complacency.

Not that she blamed him. They had been kept waiting
for almost an hour. She had seen him pull out his pocket
watch more than a half dozen times. The clerk had looked
up the first time when the small sound of its gold chain
broke the heavy silence, but had disregarded Cameron's
impatience.

She wondered if Cameron shared her misgivings at
coming here to seek advice. He had been vehement about
not going to his family's solicitor. Was it because he did
not want a suggestion of anything being amiss to reach
the rest of his family, especially his brother? Or had the
family solicitor told him what she suspected every honest
attorney would? Dissolving this marriage quietly was impossible. Cameron had told her only that a friend's suggestion had brought them to Eldred Paige's office near
the Inns of the Court.

Cameron turned and caught her staring at him. She did
not lower her eyes from his sapphire ones, but she could
not prevent her breath from catching. This man, who was
now her husband, would have drawn her eyes amid any
crowd. When the sun shone on his jet hair, the strands
glistened with blue-black fire. Yet it was the determined
set of his lips which held her attention. No one could
doubt he intended to have his way. A shiver sifted along
her spine, and she was grateful she was not his nemesis.

As his gaze swept past her as if she were no more
important than the chair beneath her, Cameron turned to
the clerk. "How much longer must we wait?" he demanded in a voice guaranteed to carry past the closed
door.

The clerk squinted and mumbled, "Mr. Paige is a busy
man. You were told he would try to squeeze you in this

morning, Lord Hawksmoor. As soon as he has time to meet you and your *wife,* he will send for you."

Tess recoiled from the emphasis the weasel-faced clerk used. Telling herself Lady Hawksmoor should be above letting the words of a common law clerk disturb her, she could not help noting how Cameron's back stiffened at the verbal jab. Not for the first time, she was curious about what had been said in the messages exchanged between Cameron and this solicitor during the past four days.

Cameron crossed the room and sat next to her. "How can you be so patient?"

"I am not patient. I hate waiting."

"You do not show it."

Tess kept her voice low, but did not hold back her fury. "Would you prefer I throw myself on yonder lad in a fit of temper?"

"He might not mind if you did so in a fit of a different sort of passion."

"Cameron!"

For the first time since they had entered the stuffy office, a suggestion of a smile pulled at his lips. "I thought you wished honesty from me."

"Yes, but I can assure you I honestly have no desire to throw myself at that man—in a temper or in any other way."

"I am glad to hear that."

"I never guessed you would be a jealous husband, Cameron."

"Jealous?" He regarded her with bewilderment.

"You may rest assured I have no interest in throwing myself at any man. In spite of what Isabel whatever-her-fancy-name-is said, such a thought would never come into my head." She lowered her eyes, so he could not see her distaste with her lies. She would gladly fling herself in Cameron's arms again if he would welcome her there.

Being false with him—and herself—was becoming increasingly difficult.

Save for when she had believed he was about to kiss her in the upper hallway after their arrival in London, Cameron had been the pattern-card of a polite stranger. He greeted her politely each morning if he chanced to see her after she took breakfast in the cheery orange breakfast-parlor, but he never joined her there. When he discovered she enjoyed reading the news, he offered her the newspaper for her perusal; yet he avoided discussing anything in it with her. He had secured a seamstress to make her clothes to replace her unfashionable gowns, even though he had said nothing about calls or going out among the Polite World. Without fail, he treated her with gracious indifference.

But he was no more indifferent to her than she was to him. She had too often caught sight of the same heat in his eyes as when she had awakened to find him lying beside her in her bed. He had not tried to hide it, and that added to her discomfort.

The door to the inner office opened, freeing her from her uneasy thoughts. Cameron set himself on his feet and held out his hand to her. When she rose, he drew her fingers within his arm as he led her toward the open door.

Her steps faltered when she followed Cameron through the doorway. By a large cluttered desk, stood a man. His chins compounded upon each other as they struggled to stay above his collar which had vanished in a cascade of flesh. His waistcoat contained enough material to make her a gown. Bright eyes peered from behind his full cheeks, which were edged by pale brown hair.

"Lord Hawksmoor?" he asked, and her eyes widened in shock. The high pitch of his voice did not match his girth.

Cameron either was not astonished or hid it, as he concealed so many of his thoughts. "Yes, and I trust you are Mr. Paige."

"Of course." He bowed his head slightly toward them. "I am Eldred Paige, Esquire."

"I trust as well this conference will be private."

Mr. Paige smiled, his wide cheeks broadening. "All my clients can be assured of complete confidentiality."

"Really?" Cameron glanced at the clerk on the other side of the open door.

The young man remained over the heavy tome, but had not moved his finger since the door opened. Mr. Paige motioned for his clerk to rise. That the clerk had been watching became obvious when he bounced to his feet, slammed the book shut, and strode out of the office with the air of an affronted grand dame.

"Forgive him," Mr. Paige said. "Delany does not like hearing his reputation disparaged."

Cameron said nothing as he ushered Tess across the solicitor's office. If she had thought it would be elegant, she was sorely disappointed. A scratched desk showed every dent its chair had made in it. Books were stacked against walls bare of any decoration.

Mr. Paige lifted a mountain of papers from a chair and smiled. "If you please, my lady . . ."

Tess sat gingerly. Dust met her gloved fingers as she put her hand on the chair's arm. Wiping them surreptitiously, she watched as Cameron selected another chair, set closer to the desk.

"You understand why we are here?" Cameron asked without preamble. "This situation is uneasy at best and must be handled with the utmost decorum and secrecy."

The obese man smiled. "I am aware of that, my lord. Your correspondence has informed me of your, shall we say, unusual circumstances."

"Then what is your opinion?"

Tess could not help admiring how Cameron ignored

the attorney's fawning tone. Tightening her hands on the ribbons of her bag, she leaned toward the desk, anxious to learn if Mr. Paige knew of a solution they had not considered.

"You have presented me with a unique and not easily solved dilemma." The solicitor sighed. "I have already told you an annulment may be impossible unless you are ready to offer proof you did not consummate your marriage."

Tess choked, and said, "I—"

"Lady Hawksmoor shall not answer your coarse statements, Paige," Cameron said quietly.

Mr. Paige relaxed back in his chair, which creaked an ominous threat from somewhere beneath his bulk. Disregarding the sound, he pyramided his fingers before his nose and nodded. "The facts you presented in your letter to me suggest any resolution will be, as I have already stated, far more complicated than a simple annulment. Not impossible, but complicated."

"Complicated?" Cameron pounced on the single word.

"A divorce—"

Rising, Cameron clenched his hands. His gaze fled past Tess as he fought to control himself. "I told you. A divorce is out of the question. I shall not have Lady Hawksmoor's name sullied with deeds she has not done."

Mr. Paige raised his hands. "My lord, I am not a magician. What do you expect me to do? It may have taken you only a few minutes to marry Lady Hawksmoor, but even if you were to choose to petition for a divorce, it shall take many months to undo the bonds of matrimony. If you do not decide to divorce her, then you are her husband, and she is your wife until death do you part. So name a correspondent in a charge of adultery against your wife."

"No!" Tess's voice squeaked on the single word. Heat flowed along her face, and she guessed her cheeks had reddened with mortification. Cameron must not consider this course. It would shame her father even more than whatever Mr. Knox was blackmailing him with.

When Cameron put his hand on her shoulder, she looked up at him. He was staring at Mr. Paige, his jaw fixed with his scowl. "Neither Tess nor I shall resort to perjury."

"Then neither you nor your wife shall be divorced."

She sensed Cameron's fury, even though she could not see him. The stiffness of his fingers along her shoulder warned her he was seething with his inability to end this problem swiftly.

"I see no reason to continue this conversation," Cameron said, holding out his hand to her. As he brought her to her feet, he added, "Good day."

Tess was no longer startled by the sharp sound in Cameron's voice. It was the coldness she had heard the morning she woke to discover him in her bed.

"Lord Hawksmoor?" called Mr. Paige. Turning, she saw him holding out a sheaf of papers. "If you change your mind, you need only fill out these with the appropriate names and return them to me."

Cameron took the pages and dropped them on the desk. "We will not be returning." Taking Tess's arm, he steered her to the door.

Tess wished she could think of something to say to ease the silence between them as they went back to where the carriage waited on the street. She knew so well the pain of having hopes dashed. But to say that was to chance refocusing his anger on her, because *he* was the reason her dreams were now disintegrating into despair.

"Damn my eyes," Cameron muttered as he sat next to her in the closed carriage on the way back to Grosvenor Square. Crossing one foot over the other knee, he clasped his hands around his ivory breeches. "Paige is an ass."

Although she silently agreed, Tess asked, "Why would you expect anything else from him? The law is the law."

"A friend told me Paige is very competent at handling difficult situations. I figured such competence might enable him to find an answer for us that would avoid the messiness of a divorce."

Shaking her head in disbelief, she watched his brows dip in a low scowl. "Why would you believe anything that *he* said or did?"

"He?"

"Mr. Knox? Wasn't he the one who told you about Mr. Paige?" Her face grew cold. "How many others have you told about this?"

"There is no reason for me to tell anyone anything. My friends have been sharing the glad tidings, apparently."

"Why are you surprised? After all, Mr. Knox is the one who—"

"The one what?"

She had said too much. Papa had pleaded with her not to speak to anyone, especially to Cameron, about the blackmail. Searching her mind, she asked, "Cameron, how can you trust him after what he did?"

"What he did?"

"He was a witness to the wedding vows you took. He should have halted you then."

"He was drunk." He grimaced as the carriage bounced into a chuck-hole. "Now he is eager to help undo what has been done."

"So he suggested you contact Mr. Paige." She folded her arms in front of her. "Does Mr. Knox have any other dead ends to suggest?"

He did not answer. Leaning his elbow on the window, he stared out it.

The carriage rolled to a stop in front of the town house on the north side of Grosvenor Square. When the door opened, Cameron glared at the footman who set the step by the coach door. The young man backed away, and Cameron stepped out. Turning, he held out his hand in a silent command to Tess. She wished she could ignore it, pull the door closed, and order the coachee to take her home. That was impossible.

Harbour opened the door. "Good morning, my lord, my lady."

"Thank you, Harbour," Tess replied.

Cameron said nothing as he thrust his hat and gloves toward a footman.

She looked at Harbour, but the butler did not seem surprised by Cameron's taciturn behavior. He took Tess's bonnet before she hurried to catch up with Cameron, who was going up the stairs.

When Tess entered the small parlor where they had talked to his brother, Cameron was pacing with the same impatience he had shown in the solicitor's office. He whirled as she entered and asked, "Are you following me?"

"I thought you might wish to discuss with me what we should do next."

"Do next?" He laughed tightly. "There appears to be nothing we can do next. We are husband and wife quite legally and quite irrevocably. We are lucky I am a second son."

She dampened her arid lips. "So you do not have to produce an heir to be the duke after you?"

"Now you understand."

Wanting to tell him she understood less and less with each passing hour, for she had seen the desire in his eyes, she said, "I do want you to know I appreciate that you did not consider Mr. Paige's suggestion of a divorce."

"It would be a waste of time."

"A waste of time?" She was puzzled by his answer. Facing her, he walked toward her as he said, "For a bill of divorce to succeed, there must be no doubt of the charges within it. Who would believe *you* were guilty of adultery?"

"I am not so loathsome that no one has looked upon me with interest."

"No, you are not." He lifted a single strand of hair that had fallen onto her shoulder.

A sudden heat seared her. Slowly she raised her eyes to meet the blue-hot fire in his. Knowing she should turn away or simply ignore it, she waited a second too long. She was caught by his eyes. The weakening within her center was no longer unfamiliar as his gaze slid along her arm, across her bodice, and up to her face. He took another step toward her, then stopped abruptly as if he had run into an invisible wall.

Not one she had built. Nor was it one she dared to break through, even if Cameron would allow anyone to penetrate that barrier. He kept it in place, especially with his unwanted wife. If she suggested they could be friends during the time they had to endure each other's company, she feared he would turn his back on her. She was unhappy and wanted nothing more than someone who would listen to her despair.

That was a lie. She wanted his fingers touching more than her hair, and she longed to have his arms around her as he held her with unrestrained ardor, as he had when she woke to discover herself in his embrace.

No emotion lightened his voice when he spoke, reminding her anew that her husband intended to have no obligation of friendship between them. "Ring for nuncheon when you are hungry, Tess. I will be in my study. Have a pleasant afternoon."

He was gone before she could answer. Looking at the doorway, where even his shadow vanished as his footfalls faded into the back of the house, Tess blinked back tears. She wished she could hate Cameron, but that was impossible. He was being kind within the limited parameters he set. If she remained quiet and did not disturb him, he was a genial host to a resented guest.

Nothing more. She would be wise to act the same, but she wanted so much more with this man whose touch thrilled her.

Ten

"This was delivered for Lord Hawksmoor." The footman gripped a pair of folded pages sealed with red wax as if he feared they would fly out of his fingers. "I thought he might be here."

Tess stood and held out her hand. "I shall take them to him."

The young footman faltered. Then color rose up his cheeks to swallow his freckles. " 'Twould be my pleasure to find him."

Had Cameron given orders she was not to receive anything here? No, that was absurd, because she had had a letter delivered from Mrs. Rappaport only an hour ago. Her late grandmother's neighbor was not in Town, but would be delighted to have Tess call when Mrs. Rappaport arrived back in Town after her own granddaughter gave birth by summer's end.

"Thank you," she said to the footman, "but I will see they are delivered to Lord Hawksmoor."

The footman placed the pages in her hand, an uneasy expression lengthening his face. If Tess had had any doubts that the servants were unaware of the strange marriage between her and Cameron, those doubts were now banished.

"Please convey to Harbour," she added, "that I will be taking tea in the book-room."

"Yes, my lady." He rushed away toward the kitchen, where Harbour would be gossiping with the kitchen staff while tea was prepared.

Tess walked toward the back of the house, where Cameron had his study. Although she had taken a tour of the house with Mrs. Astin, the housekeeper, she had not gone down this corridor. Mrs. Astin had pointed to it and explained the marquess preferred his privacy there.

The house was silent, as always, while Tess went down the steps to the room that must share a wall with the kitchen. Her ears ached for the sound of loving laughter and gentle words. In her father's house, she had always heard the servants chattering among themselves and listened to the cook's whistling as she worked. As a child, Tess had spent hours trying to copy how Cook could imitate several different birds. Cook could copy their songs so well that, when after dinner Tess held the hedgehog in the kitchen, Heddy would look about as if trying to find the bird.

"No," she whispered. She must forget her other life now that she was Lady Hawksmoor.

In the shadows beyond the staircase, she paused by the door that led into Cameron's office. She knocked gently, and the door swung open. Realizing it had been left ajar, she hesitated. She did not want to burst in on him if he was intent upon . . . she had no idea what he would be intent upon during the hours he spent here each after-noon.

Tess waited for an endless minute, then pushed the door wider. The scrape of a chair on the wooden floor resonated, but she did not look to see where it was. She stared at the room, which was nothing as she had expected. Unlike the rest of the tidy house, every surface was covered with opened books, papers, and strange instruments. A door opened into a small garden between the house and the stables. A wide window swept the disorder with sunshine as she turned to face Cameron, who was standing in front of a long table.

Behind him, a large map of the world covered the wall. Aware of his gaze on her, but saying nothing, she walked to where she could read the map more easily. The vast distances overwhelmed her when she realized how small England was. She saw the notes written on it. Some of the words were in Latin, and she guessed they were scientific names. She was not sure if they were of animals or of plants.

"These were delivered for you," she said as she held out the folded pages.

He set them on the table beside a pile of withered plants. "Thank you."

His terse answer warned her she was traipsing on unsteady ground, but she yearned to know more about this man who was her husband. Looking from the plants to the map, she asked, "Are these the names of various plants on here?"

"Yes."

"Do some of those cuttings come from these distant places?"

"These?" He picked up one from the pile. "No, these are quite common English weeds. I keep my more exotic cuttings in the files there."

She looked at the wall opposite the window. It was lined from the floor to higher than her head with long, narrow drawers. Each one was labeled, but she could not read the neat white squares from where she stood. Quietly she said, "I had no idea you enjoyed studying botany."

"It has been an interest for as long as I can remember," he said in the same emotionless voice. "I hope through my studies to identify a plant that is like no other ever classified."

She swallowed her laughter at his presumption, for surely every plant ever grown on Earth had already been discovered. The fire in his eyes warned her to silence, and she hastily looked again at the specimens.

"An admirable avocation for the son of a duke, don't you think?" he asked when she did not reply.

Was he trying to incite her to a heated answer with his icy cold question? Images of quiet hours in a sunlit garden filled her mind. She had loved to spend time with Jasper, the gardener, learning about all the plantings in the garden. He had taught her about each plant, and he had been the one who found Heddy as an abandoned baby and brought her to Tess to care for. That had been almost three years before. Jasper had been helping her learn more about rhododendrons when Papa had to release him with a good character reference after money became so dear. Because Papa was having to pay Mr. Knox for his silence? So much had become clear with Papa's admission of the darkness that haunted him.

She touched a dried blossom. A simple field daisy, its color faded and each petal as fragile as a dream. Raising her eyes, she met the vexation in Cameron's. Was he irked she had found out about his interest or simply that she had intruded on his private haven?

Deciding honesty was the best recourse, as always, because there were too many half-truths about, she retorted, "Sarcasm serves you well, Cameron, doesn't it? It keeps everyone from getting too close to you."

"I did not guess you had become an expert on my feelings."

"There is hardly any need to be an expert when you always resort to derision if someone probes too close."

He picked up the dried plants and set them on a cluttered shelf. "You are proving surprisingly insightful. If this was more than a marriage of inconvenience, I would think you look upon me with the clear eyes of love. But then, love is reputed to betray the senses. I offer my brother as an example."

"Love? Do you think he loves Isabel?"

"I believe he thinks he does . . . until he tires of her and finds a new love, whom he will swear is the very woman he has sought his whole life."

"Bitterness over something you cannot change will not heal the damage, Cameron."

"Do you have a trite phrase for every occasion?"

"Do you have cruel ones?"

"Cruel?" He came back to where she stood. "I did not think the truth could be deemed cruel. Simply the truth, and I believed that was what you wanted from me."

You have no idea what I want from you. She was tempted to give voice to that thought, but bit back the words. "It is true we are making a complete muddle of this marriage."

"Or it has made a complete muddle of us."

Tess smiled, in spite of herself. "You may be right. I doubt either of us is at our best. I understand I am an embarrassment to you, Cameron."

"Embarrassment? I am not embarrassed by you."

"I thought you had not had any friends calling because you were embarrassed by the situation we find ourselves in."

"I have not had any friends calling because I have been calling on them to seek their advice." He cleared his throat and looked away, as if his own words had unsettled him. "I must own, Tess, you are behaving in a very civilized manner."

"Is there any reason to be spitting at each other like two cats?"

"None that I know of." He went to the door and opened

it in a clear invitation for her to take her leave. "If you will excuse me, I should read the letters you brought."

"Oh . . . of course." She came around the table.

As she reached the door, he did not step aside. Instead he brushed his fingers against her cheek, then jerked them back, staring at them as if he had no idea why they had touched her. She steeled herself for a sharp comment, but he said, "I would be pleased to dine with you this evening, if you are willing."

"Are you as tired as I am of taking a tray in private each evening?"

"Partly, and partly because I realize there is no need for each of us to make believe the other does not exist. We might as well make the best of the circumstances dealt to us until a suitable denouement can be found." He took her hand and raised it politely to his lips. His kiss lasted no longer than etiquette allowed for strangers. "I trust I may enjoy your company then."

She nodded and walked out of the room. As the door closed behind her, her fingers touched the warmth left by his lips. Such a reaction was more dangerous than his anger, but she knew she would chance the peril once again.

Soon.

Tess pushed aside her bonnet, letting it hang by its ribbons down her back. She kept hidden the jar of insects and worms she had picked up beneath the trees in the center of the square. Explaining to Harbour, who was always at the door whenever she came in or went out, would take too long when she had run out of food for Heddy last night. She would give the hedgehog a feast this morning that Heddy could enjoy before sleeping the day away.

"Lady Hawksmoor," said Harbour as she greeted him

and hurried toward the stairs, "there is a caller in the front parlor."

She looked down at her gown, which bore the stains of where she had knelt on the ground. "Please express my regret at needing to change before receiving a guest. I shall be quick. I promise."

"Do you want me to have that taken to the kitchen?"

Tess knew *that* must mean the jar she held. "No, thank you. I will tend to it."

"You might find more treats for your pet to eat in the kitchen garden," he said, smiling. "When I had a hedgehog as a boy, it liked the big slugs found under the leaves beneath the plants."

"Thank you." She should have guessed the servants would know quickly that she had brought Heddy with her and had the hedgehog in her bedchamber. No doubt they knew all about what did—and did not—happen in her private rooms. "You are welcome to look in on Heddy, Harbour, although she does not take well to strangers."

"No hedgehog does." His laugh echoed oddly along the high walls of the foyer. "Mine growled like a dog. The dog stayed far from it."

Wanting to stay and talk to him more about the little creatures, Tess knew she should not keep the guest waiting. She gave the butler a smile and hurried up the stairs to her room. Pausing only to give a very sleepy Heddy some of the harvest from the green area in the center of the square, Tess changed into a pale yellow tea gown.

She rushed back down the stairs to the first floor where the parlor was. Hearing the servants on the ground floor below, she grinned wryly when a leaf fell out of her hair. No wonder Harbour had smiled when he looked at her. She patted her hair back into place as she reached the door.

Her smile faltered when she saw who was waiting within. Mr. Knox may have called since he traveled with them from her father's house, but Tess had not spoken with him. As he faced her, he was rolling a walking stick with an ivory handle between his hands. He leaned it against a settee as she walked into the room.

"My lady," he said, bowing over her hand, "may I say marriage appears to agree with you for you look even lovelier than I recall on our last meeting."

"Thank you."

When she said nothing more, Mr. Knox's practiced smile grew taut. Did he think she would welcome him with enthusiasm when he was blackmailing her father and had had an obvious hand in her wedding?

"I had called," he said, "to speak to your husband."

"Cameron is not here." She would not let him guess how he was disconcerting her by reminding her with every comment of her marriage, for she guessed that was his goal.

Mr. Knox scowled. "Blast! I did not guess him to be such a lovelorn fool after two years. He must be calling on Pamela again."

"Pamela? Who is Pamela?"

His scowl became an expression of dismay. "I thought you knew."

"Knew? Knew what?" She regretted the words, because she could not miss how his eyes twinkled. With mischief? Or was there a darker cause for his mirth?

"If you do not know, it is not my place to say anything. Pretend I never mentioned her name." He tipped his hat as he picked up his walking stick. "I bid you good day, my lady."

Knowing she was overstepping the bounds of propriety, she grasped his sleeve. "Mr. Knox, how can I pretend I did not hear what you said?"

"You should speak to your husband about Mrs. Livingstone. It is not my place to say anything to you about his very private concerns."

She jerked her fingers back off his sleeve. She should have guessed right from the beginning what he meant. This Pamela Livingstone must be Cameron's mistress.

Mr. Knox was instantly contrite, and she knew her re-action had been too visible. She wished she could be more like Cameron and hide her feelings when his friend said, "I am sorry to have mentioned her name. It was thoughtless of me."

"If you had not, someone else was sure to." A tight smile stretched her lips uncomfortably. "With my luck of late, it would have been Mrs. Livingstone herself when I chanced to pass her on the street."

"That is possible."

"What?" She had not guessed Cameron's mistress might be found so close to his house.

He walked to a table set in a corner of the parlor. Picking up a miniature, he said, "Just so you will know, this is Pamela Livingstone."

"He keeps a portrait of her in the parlor?"

"Where everyone can see it?" Mr. Knox chuckled coldly. "You must set aside your country ways, Lady Hawksmoor. An unmarried man flaunts his mistress, es-pecially when she is as comely and refined as Pamela Livingstone." He handed her the portrait.

Tess looked down at the woman's face as Mr. Knox bid her a good day and took his leave. He was right. This woman was extraordinarily beautiful, with an ebullience that burst forth even from the portrait that had not been done by a very skilled artist.

We are lucky I am a second son.

Cameron's words resounded through her mind. For the first time, she realized he might have been speaking more about his good fortune than hers. He had a wife, so he did not have to worry about friends matchmaking for him, and he had his stunning mistress to warm his bed. Yes, he was a very lucky man.

And so was Tess lucky. 'Twas her misfortune all her luck now was bad.

Eleven

"Lady Hawksmoor?"

From beyond her closed bedroom door, Tess heard her name called in the apologetic tone which suggested Harbour would have preferred not to deliver this message. In her short time in this strange household, she had learned the butler served as a gauge for what was happening elsewhere in the house. If Harbour was distressed, something was about to change in the house. She hoped it would be for the better.

How could it be for the worse? She had not spoken with Cameron for the past two days, and she was not sure even if he was here in the house. Heavy, cold rain had kept her imprisoned here, going out only into the kitchen garden to find food for Heddy. She had spent time trying to read one of the books from the library and making little progress in writing a letter to Papa. Complaining that she felt abandoned would gain her nothing, and she had nothing else to write. What good would it do to tell him she was appalled to learn her husband was continuing to call on the mistress he had kept before he married her?

She was tempted to laugh at her own silly reaction. She should not care that Cameron kept a convenient somewhere near Grosvenor Square. It was not as if he had married her because he had professed to love her. This marriage was a bother to him, and he clearly did not intend to allow it to intrude on the life he had made for himself in Town.

As for her . . . Tess sighed as she shifted in the comfortable chair by the window. Watching the traffic rushing through the rain was silly. She had spent the past hour looking through the arched window to the street below.

Before her abigail could answer the door, it opened. She came to her feet, too shocked to remain sitting. Harbour always treated her with as much respect as if she had been a long-awaited bride coming to this house, so she had not guessed he would enter her private rooms without permission.

Tension was ironing the wrinkles from his face as he bowed his head. "My lady, excuse me, but 'tis Lord Hawksmoor. He requests you speak with him immediately."

She nodded, not asking the dozens of questions racing within her mind. Cameron must answer them, not his butler. Her husband might consider her guileless in the ways of the *ton,* but she knew well how to deal with servants.

As she brushed invisible dust from her light green sprigged lawn gown, her stomach twisted. She knew how to live with the servants. What she did not know was how to live with the man who was her husband.

"Lady Hawksmoor, are you ill?" asked Harbour from the doorway.

"No, I am well. Why do you ask?"

"You appear a bit gray."

Tess hastily rearranged her face into a smile that was as false as her fib. Her cheeks were icy, and she doubted if she could do anything to return the color to them. "I am quite well, Harbour."

"My lord is very anxious to speak with you."

She stepped past him, but paused in the hallway. "Harbour, could you bring tea to the parlor? 'Tis near enough the hour for tea."

"Parlor?" His face became ruddy as he pointed to the door on the other side of the hall past the plant-laden table. "My lady, my lord wishes to see you in his private chambers."

"What . . ." When her voice broke on the single word, she choked back the rest of her question. Even the dullest of the servants must know the truth—something was amiss with the marriage of Lord and Lady Hawksmoor. Forcing her smile back in place, she said, "Thank you, Harbour."

"Of course, my lady."

Tess edged past him and the planters to go to the door across the hallway. She realized her dressing room must be behind the wall that separated her rooms from Cameron's. When she knocked on Cameron's door, she received no answer. She glanced along the hall, but Harbour must have gone down the stairs. She could not have misunderstood his message. Not when it was so unexpected. Setting another knock on the mahogany door, she waited with as much patience as possible for an answer.

"Come in," came the call from within.

She turned the knob slowly. Her forehead threaded with bafflement as she pushed the door open. The room was lost to the thickening twilight, and rain splattered against the window that was the twin of the one in her sitting room. In one corner mirroring the fireplace in her chambers, the hearth's gentle glow challenged the dusk. Uncertain, she entered the room. Had she misheard what she thought was an offer to enter?

When she saw a shadow move, she asked, "Cameron?"

"Please come in and make yourself comfortable."

Tess walked toward where a chair was silhouetted against the light from the fire. This must be a sitting room, although it was far more austere than her room. That surprised her, for the master should have the best chambers in the house. Three chairs faced each other, and a pair of settees were set in front of the window that was the twin of the one in her private rooms. Several framed paintings were arranged on the wall between two doors.

In amazement, she realized Cameron must have given her his chambers. She recalled Harbour's astonishment upon their arrival when Cameron had requested her bags be brought to the rooms she now used. Why had Cameron hidden his kindness to her? She wished she could thank him for his attempt to make her welcome, but that might create more barriers between them. Any sign of emotion seemed to drive him further from those around him.

When she came around the chair, Tess was surprised to see Cameron dressed so informally, with his waistcoat undone and his shirt collarless. She had seen him dressed in something other than but prime twig only twice—the morning when he woke her in her bed and when he had kissed her with such desire at the coaching inn.

A quiver threatened to shatter her fragile composure. She must stop thinking of the moment when her life had been changed beyond anything she could have imagined. Even more important, she must stop thinking of the kisses they had shared then and since and dampen her longing for more.

Cameron closed the book he had had open, turning it so she could not see the title embossed on the cover. He tilted an irreverent eyebrow over the rim of his glasses. "Why do you look so surprised?"

"I never knew you wore glasses to read."

"I did not before . . ." He put his finger to the scar just above his right eyebrow.

"Oh, I am sorry."

"You have nothing to be sorry for. I doubt if you were anywhere near the field where I last encountered the French." He sighed and set his book on the table beside him.

It was not a novel, she realized, but an account book. She wondered why he was sitting in this darkened room reading such dry material. Her breath caught when she saw the slip of paper he was using as a bookmark. The engraved address was that of Mr. Paige, the solicitor. Had Cameron changed his mind and had the attorney send to the house the paperwork for a divorce?

"Tess, you need not stand there like a naughty child sneaking down the stairs to view a gathering of her elders." He sighed. "What has unsettled you?"

"When you did not have someone open the door, I thought I might be intruding when . . . when . . ."

"Did you, mayhap, think I would invite you here to wash my back while I bathed? Tess, one would almost believe there was a hint of espousal affection in your disquiet."

"Then one would be mistaken."

Instead of retorting as she had expected, he looked away, as if he were embarrassed, and sighed. "Sit down, Tess. I must speak with you posthaste, and I honestly have no interest in the requirements of etiquette at the moment."

"What is amiss?" Despite the room's faint light, she noted lines in his face which she was sure had not been there when she last saw him.

"Please sit down."

She did, adjusting the fire screen so she could see him and still keep the flames from searing her face.

With another sigh, he lifted his glasses off his nose

and rubbed the twin dents in its bridge. "I usually find exchanging words with you an invigorating pastime, but not today."

"What is wrong, Cameron? You look positively distraught."

He smiled without mirth. "Did you ever consider your intuition can be exasperating to a man who wishes to keep his thoughts private?" Without giving her a chance to respond to the unanswerable, he stood. "You should know before you hear of it from the servants that Russell and Isabel were involved in a carriage accident last night."

Pressing her hand over her heart, which thumped against her breastbone, she gasped, "Was it bad?"

"Yes."

"How are they?"

"Dead."

"Dead?" She stared at him in disbelief. His voice held no more emotion than if he was talking of the latest news from Whitehall. Mayhap less. Her single meeting with his brother and the duke's current mistress had been horrible, but the duke *was* Cameron's brother.

As if he could read her jumbled thoughts, he said, "Do not waste any sympathy on them."

"Cameron!"

"Please lower your voice."

"My voice?" When he scowled, she added more quietly, "How can you be so heartless? If . . ." She wanted to bite back her accusation when she saw the undeniable pain in his eyes.

Rising, she put her hand on his arm. She guided him back to his chair and seated him. Looking about, she went to a table near the door where a tray had been placed. She must have missed it before when her eyes needed to adjust to the dark room. She poured a glass of wine from the decanter on the tray and brought it back to him, then knelt by his chair and handed it to him.

"I am sorry," she whispered. "I should not have said that."

"Why not? After what you have witnessed, you have no reason to believe there was anything but disgust between my brother and me." He took a slow sip. "If my words just now suggested that was the true depth of my feeling for my brother, then I am the one who should apologize. I am not expressing myself well." Rubbing his forehead, he stared at the fire. "I have been told they died instantly, and I am sure that is the truth, for I have seen the carriage. Even the horses were killed by the impact against the trees. I was also informed that riders were seen in pursuit of them. Thieves, it is believed, because the bodies were stripped of anything of value before the watch arrived."

She put her head down on the arm of his chair. "Cameron, I am so very sorry. I have no siblings, but I can imagine how painful it must be for you, because I recall how it hurt when Mama died. I feared Papa would lose his mind."

"I am not looking for your sympathy," Cameron said, his voice again sharp. "I am requesting your help."

Tess regarded him with astonishment. Gone was the honesty that had sifted through his words so briefly. What had caused the change? Her hands fisted on her knees. Had it been the mention of Papa? She wished she could reveal the truth to her husband—that his friend and his brother had arranged for their marriage and forced her father to acquiesce to their blackmail, but her promise to Papa precluded that.

"Of course," she said softly, "you have my help. What can I do? If you wish me to have the house opened for the funeral service, I . . ."

" 'Tis not that which I need your help with, because

Harbour can handle any callers. It is something very different." He came to his feet again. Setting the glass on the table, he took her hand and brought her up to stand beside him. He did not speak as he led her toward one of the doors.

The room beyond was lit with a single lamp, but that seemed overly bright to her eyes, which had become accustomed to the dim light in the other room. She blinked, trying to see.

"Come here, Tess," he murmured.

She started to nod, but froze when she turned to look at him. Past him, she saw, set in an alcove smaller than the one in her chambers, a bed. This one was not carved with all the animals that graced hers, and its drapes were a simple cream. She had not guessed he would stay in rooms so barren in comparison with hers.

"Tess, do come along." Impatience tightened his voice as he took another step toward the bed. "I thought you were willing to help me."

"Yes, but . . ." She found her own voice. Jerking her hand out of his, she said, "I find it uncommonly coarse you would use *this* moment to . . . to . . ."

Cameron smiled coolly. Tess did not need to complete her thought, because it was revealed on her guileless face. She had asserted she wanted nothing to do with sharing a marriage bed with him, a wise choice he had agreed with until he could sort the whole of this out. However, her reaction proved she was not as oblivious to the sparks that leaped from her to him with even the most casual touch. A frown curved down along her lips, drawing his gaze to them again. So delicious they had been, a feast to tempt a man who had been fasting too long. Now . . . no, he must not let his thoughts go in that direction when there was another problem that required more immediate attention.

"Do you think I would use my brother's death as an

excuse to seduce you?" he asked. "That I would be so anxious to do the duty of my father's heir to begat an heir I would not let another hour pass before bedding you?"

She flinched. "I did not mean to suggest that."

"But you thought I would suggest you join me in my bed." He laughed without mirth. "It would have been very crowded, Tess."

"Crowded?" She looked past him, her face tightening. "Are you saying someone else is here? How dare you bring me here when you have another . . . guest?"

"Guests."

Her gaze came back to him, and he saw horror in her eyes. Guilt pinched him, but he ignored it. He had not asked for a wife. Nor had he wanted a brother who could not keep wandering from bed to bed, nor did he want any of the other obligations now foisted on him.

"Mayhap," he replied, "if you would not paint me with every evil you can imagine, you might be willing to give me the benefit of the doubt long enough to look at this." He walked to the bed and drew back the drapes that had concealed two small mounds. In a whisper, he said, "Russell, in his final act of insanity, named me the guardian of his children."

"Russell's children?" she asked as quietly. "You never mentioned your brother had children."

"I did not know until these two young boys were brought to the house not more than an hour ago."

Tess came closer to the bed, and he was treated again to the delicate fragrance of her perfume. He did not move aside as she leaned forward to look at the children. His fingers ached to sift through her hair, which had become an intriguing flame in the flicker from the hearth. His hand started to rise, but he forced it back to his side as she turned to face him.

Her eyes grew wide, and she tried to move away from him. She bumped into the bed. When she put her hand out to the mattress, he was surprised it was to steady it so they did not wake the little boys.

"Mayhap," she whispered, "it would be for the best if we spoke of this in the other room. The children must be exhausted to be sleeping so soundly."

She looked at the little boys again, and he tore his gaze from her enticing profile. On the green satin coverlet, the youngsters were rolled into balls beneath a single blanket. He saw her eyes narrow, and he guessed she had noticed how both boys had hair the same rusty gold as hers. That had surprised him, as well, until he had noticed the strong features of the Hawksmoor family in their childish faces. He wondered which one of Russell's mistresses had borne these two children.

The boys moved, and one mumbled something in his sleep. Cameron dropped the curtain to allow them to sleep undisturbed. Taking Tess's hand, he tugged her away from the bed, although every inch of him demanded he draw her into it and rediscover the pleasure of having her lying beside him.

"Your brother never spoke of these children before?" she asked.

"Never."

"Then how do you know . . . that is, upon hearing of the tragedy of your brother's death, someone might have brought these boys here to—"

Drawing her toward one of the paintings on the wall, he lit a lamp. She gasped, and he did not fault her. Save for the red hair, the portrait could have been of the two sleeping boys.

"Russell and I when we were of an age of those children," he said, still whispering. "That was painted at Peregrine Hall. The artist took some liberties with it because Russell had dared me to climb a tree and I ended up with a broken arm."

She went back to the doorway and looked within.

When she faced him, her eyes were bright with tears. They did not fall, and he would have been amazed if they had, for she had endured with dignity every setback and indignity since he had met her.

Cameron wished he could persuade her to show him how she was maintaining her serenity, because he was suffering from an overwhelming urge to ram his fist into the closest wall. *This* was not the way his life should have unfolded after he returned home from battle. " 'Twas insane for Russell to leave me with the responsibility for two children I never knew existed."

"Not insane, for you are his brother. I am sure he had no wish to have them raised by strangers."

"That is true, but now I find myself the guardian of two children." He rubbed his aching forehead. "I think the oldest is about six or seven years old. The other appears to be about a year younger."

"You think?"

"I told you already I was not aware of these children's existence. Since Russell left Peregrine Hall after a huge argument with our father and came to Town, I have never had much interest in my brother's private life."

"A huge argument?"

He allowed himself a smile. "Our father wished Russell to be more responsible. More like his younger brother, as Father was fond of saying."

"I am amazed your brother would even speak to you when your father compared him in anger to you."

"Russell spoke to me usually only when he wished to borrow money. He never told me why he needed it, only that he was short of funds." He did not pause to let her answer before he added, "Nor do I wish to know more now about his life. That is why I want you to take over the obligation for these children now."

"Me?" Tess's eyes widened, and he wondered if the depths would be as changeable as the green waves of sea that they resembled. A stormy sea, he corrected himself, when she added, "Why would you want me to take responsibility for those children? You were designated the *responsible* one."

He bit back the curse that would make the situation only worse. "You are my wife. It is your duty." He picked up his glass of wine and took another sip. "As you have no interest in your other wifely duties, the very least you can do is to assume this one."

"You are beastly!"

"Mayhap, but I know I am not the right one to oversee the raising of two youngsters."

"You are their uncle, and they have no one else. I will not let you foist your duty off on me so you can continue to live your life as you want."

"That is not why I am asking this."

Motioning for her to sit on a simple settee near a hearth, he dropped next to her. She started to rise. He reached for her hands, but she clasped them in her lap and met his fury without emotion.

"Listen to me," he began.

"No, Cameron, I shall not listen to you. I am sorry your brother is dead. I am sorry as well that you feel you have been burdened with his children, but it is your duty." She gave a laugh as cold as one of his. "After all, you have no respect for your brother because he did not do his duty as you and your family expected. Will you be like him and ignore your obligations?"

"I do not like having the by-blows of his love affairs handed over to me."

"So you will hand them over to me?"

"You have been bored having so little to do here."

"I did not realize you had noticed."

He put his hand over hers on her lap. "Even if I had not, Harbour was quick to let me know. It seems you have made a very favorable impression on him, which is not easy to do."

"You are changing the subject—or do you think flattery will bend me to your will?"

"I think taking this responsibility for Russell's sons will give you something to do while we work out the muddle of our marriage."

Tess sighed, owning to herself that he was correct. She had been lost in this house while she waited for an idea of what to do now that she could not go to Mrs. Rappaport for advice. "Mayhap, but Russell named *you* as their guardian. Not me. If—"

He gripped her shoulders, interrupting her in mid word. "Tess, do not make me beg."

"Beg?" She smiled in spite of herself. "I would wager you do not do that well."

"Then you would win." His hands gentled as they edged up to curve along her face.

It took every ounce of her strength to turn her face away before he could tip it toward his. His kisses could persuade her to succumb to his demands . . . and not simply to take care of his nephews. In his embrace, pressed to his hard chest, she would promise almost anything to sample another of his kisses.

He stood and strode to the bedroom door. He glanced into the room—to check on the children?—then faced her. She waited for him to speak, but he did not.

She met his stare without lowering her eyes. "What will happen if I refuse?"

He sat again and entwined his fingers around the knees of his breeches. "Father always said there was no need for us to bring our bastards to Peregrine Hall, because they would find no welcome. I suspect Mother will heartily agree with that sentiment."

"Are you suggesting she will cast out these children, who are part of her own blood?"

"Yes, it is possible."

She wrung her hands as she glanced at the doorway leading to his room. "You could keep them here in London."

"That is what I intend to do, but they must not be allowed to run about without some supervision. If I were to let them do that, I might as well turn them loose in whatever decrepit section of London spawned their mother."

Tess bit her lower lip, then nodded. He was correct. The children needed someone to care for them. She rose and walked to the tall window overlooking the formal gardens of the park across the street. Tears boiled into her eyes, turning the garden into a collage of wavy green. Before the past few weeks, she had dreamed of a husband and children. How could she have guessed her wish would come true like this?

When she remained silent, he said, "I know you have every reason to deny me this request. No one would fault you for throwing it back into my face when I have ruined your life."

"But now you intend to shift the circumstances so the blame will be mine if two other lives are ruined?" She turned to him. "How easy it is for you to twist things about so you get what you wish, Cameron."

"Not easy." He set himself on his feet. "Tess, I know it is a great imposition, but I need your help in hiring a governess. As a woman—"

"Just hire a governess? Is that all you are asking me to do?"

"Did you think I was asking you to adopt them yourself?"

She stared at him in disbelief. "I thought you wanted me to assume their care."

"No wonder you called me a beast."

"I will be glad to help hire a governess." She hesitated,

then said, "Until one is hired, I will work with Harbour to watch over the children."

He sighed. "No need. I have already obtained his agreement to have two of the footmen oversee the children until a governess can be hired."

"Footmen? Will you abandon them to servants again?" Pain sliced through her when she saw the grief in his eyes. "Forgive me, Cameron. I am not thinking clearly."

"I have had several hours to think about this. It kept me from having to think about devising a compassionate way to tell my mother that her wastrel son is dead."

"Cameron, I am sorry," she whispered. Looking at the bedroom door, she shook her head. "The poor children. How can we ease their grief?"

"They seem more frightened than sad. I doubt they knew Russell, and I have no idea if Isabel is their mother or if one of his other mistresses is."

"If we ask them—"

"I already have. They could not describe their mother, although they were able to describe quite accurately several servants in their household."

"That is ridiculous! How could they not know their own mother?"

"The woman who delivered them here said the children had been left with her as a housekeeper in a house not far from Covent Garden. She heard of Russell's death and brought them here because it was clear she would no longer be paid by my brother."

"The poor things!"

He nodded. Taking her hands again, he drew her back to sit beside him. "How delighted Father would have been with you! You have that sense of responsibility and obligation he despaired of ever inspiring in his carefree sons." Slipping his arm along the back of the bench, he let his fingers rest on the curve of her shoulder.

She plucked his hand off her shoulder. At the soft padding of stockinged feet, she turned, as Cameron did, to see a tangled-haired moppet in the doorway.

"Oh, my!" Tess looked at Cameron as she whispered, "What is the child's name?"

"One of them is Donald and the other is Philip."

"But which is which?"

"I am not sure."

She was about to retort when she heard his regret. Touching his arm in condolence, she looked up at him for the length of a single heartbeat. Then she went to the little boy. Kneeling in front of him, she forced a smile.

"Who are you?" the little boy asked before she could.

"I am Tess. Your Aunt Tess. What is your name?"

"Donald." He tugged at his wrinkled shirt and regarded her through squinting eyes. Rubbing them with his knuckles, he yawned, but lurched forward. He had eyes as blue as a summer sky . . . just like his uncle's.

"Good evening, Donald," she said softly. "Did you have a pleasant nap?"

The child nodded.

Putting her hands on her knees, she waited for the youngster to speak. She must avoid overwhelming him, but she wondered how much attention the children had gotten in a home without anyone to supervise the servants. He searched her face, clearly looking for anything familiar. She kept a smile in place.

Just when she was losing hope that he would answer, he murmured, "Tess is a pretty name."

"I like your name, too." She pointed toward the bench. "Do you know his name?"

The child bowed deeply. "My lord."

"No, no," she said. When the child regarded her in abrupt terror, she seethed inside. Being furious at the little boy's selfish father was useless now that Russell Hawksmoor was dead. Holding Donald's short fingers, she stood. "You need not call him 'my lord.' He is your Uncle Cameron. He and your father are brothers."

"Brothers?"

"Like you and Philip." She gave him another smile. "Please say 'good day,' to Uncle Cameron."

"Good day, Uncle Cam—Cam—"

"Cameron," she said, patting her head.

"Yes, Tess." Donald edged closer to her as Cameron stepped toward them.

Cameron paused as Tess knelt again and began to talk in a quiet, calming tone to the little boy. She looked directly into the child's eyes and waited with a patience for each answer he doubted he could copy. When Donald grinned, Cameron leaned one elbow on the marble mantel and listened to the child's chatter. He was impressed with how much information Tess was obtaining with a few questions, but he noticed how her hands clenched in unuttered outrage while Donald told a tale of abandonment and loneliness without shame.

Seeing her eyes spark as she stood, Cameron understood her anger. How could Russell have ignored his own sons? They were illegitimate, but they had Hawksmoor blood. Mayhap Cameron would have discovered that the children existed if he had become more involved in his brother's wasted life. The few attempts he had made to convince Russell to stop bringing shame on the Hawksmoor name had been futile, so he had given up.

"As there is no nursery in this house, which room will the children be using?"

Tess's question brought his attention back most gratefully to her. Astonished, he saw the smaller boy was now holding her right hand as Donald clutched onto her left one. When had Philip come out of the bedroom?

"You are welcome to choose any room for them you wish," he said.

"On the morrow." Smiling down at them, she said,

"Tonight, I think it would be best if they slept in my sitting room. Jenette and I can watch over them. On the morrow—"

"I must leave for Peregrine Hall in the morning to escort Russell's body home. If you are willing to remain here with the boys, it might be for the best."

Cameron frowned when her face bleached. Wondering why she found his brother's death so much more upsetting than he did, he nodded when she said, "I shall order supper for all of us brought up here."

"Tess, I should—"

"I know you have many preparations to make for the journey tomorrow, but I think it would be best if we became better acquainted during supper." She bent and said, "Donald, go across the hall and ask Jenette to ring for supper for us."

The little boys ran out, shouting with sudden excitement.

When Tess straightened, Cameron said, "Thank you."

"They need someone."

"Something that can be said for everyone."

He heard her breath catch, and he wondered why he could not draw in a breath of his own. He must be drowning in her deep green eyes. He could think of no place he would rather be. Cupping her chin, he bent toward her. As her compelling eyes closed, he wanted nothing more than to kiss her.

"My lord, I—" Harbour's embarrassed gulp was becoming too blasted familiar.

Tess swallowed her moan of frustration as the butler remained in the doorway. When Cameron motioned impatiently for Harbour to enter, she watched the butler hand him a folded page.

Cameron scowled as he read. "Forgive me, Tess, but I must go out. It seems his children are not the only things my brother ignored. The scavengers are gathering to collect the debts he never bothered to pay."

"Must you go *now?*" She glanced at her room. When she looked back at him, heat climbed her cheeks as she saw the hunger in his eyes. Had he thought she meant her question as an invitation instead of her plan for him to talk to his nephews? No, it was just that he must know she wanted to be in his arms as much as he wanted her there.

He smiled. "Sometimes I could almost believe you had affection for me, Tess."

"Why?" Her frustration flashed into aggravation. "Because I willingly assume your responsibilities?"

"No, not because of that. I might suspect you have some affection for me because of this." His hands encircled her face as he tilted her mouth toward his. The kiss was swift, but its fire seared her.

She stared after him as he left, Harbour following to arrange for a tray to be sent up to Tess's room. How many times would Cameron kiss her and walk away as if the fleeting touch meant nothing? Slowly she walked out of the room that belonged solely to him and back to her own. She halted in the middle of the hallway and stared toward the stairs, where she could hear him giving orders to bring a carriage to the door.

With Russell's death, Cameron now would become the duke. It would be his obligation to provide an heir. She grasped the molding on the door. Too late, she understood why Cameron had regarded her with such dismay when she had been furious with him beside his bed. He had told her only minutes ago he had had time to consider all the complications.

And one complication he had yet to deal with was obtaining an heir. A legal heir. Only one person could give him that.

His wife.

Tess Hawksmoor.

Twelve

The rain was heavy, and Tess drew the children closer to her beneath the umbrella as she stepped out into the humid day. The steady patter of the drops on the roof had drowned out the hushed voice of the bishop while he read the memorial service in the crowded church. Apparently Russell had gained many friends here in London, for even three months after his death, many had come to attend the service that marked the end of first mourning for his family.

Not friends, she realized, when she overheard two of the men talking. They had come here only to have the chance to speak with Cameron and remind him of the debts Russell had left as his legacy. A man pointed toward her, and she turned, not wanting him to come and dun her, too.

"Pay them no mind," Cameron said as he lifted Donald into the carriage. "They are ravens waiting to pick at the dead."

She watched him set Philip beside his brother. "Is that why you insisted on a quiet funeral at Peregrine Hall and this memorial service so much later in London?"

"My mother is still upset enough by Russell's death and the sudden realization she has not only a daughter-in-law, but two grandsons. She did not need to hear this gabblemongering as well." He took her hand to help her into the carriage. "That is why I urged her to remain in the country." He smiled sadly. "I know you have feared for weeks that she did not come to Town because she was furious I had married you."

"You knew I was fretting about that?"

"I suspected it." He handed her in, then sat beside her, facing the two little boys, who were giggling with each other. For a moment, she thought he would chide them, but he slapped the side of the carriage to give the order to return to his house on Grosvenor Square. Looking at her, he said, "You have much to learn about keeping your thoughts hidden, Tess."

"And will you teach me?" Even after nearly four months of marriage, she could not help bristling at the sarcasm Cameron used whenever anyone delved too close to his true feelings. "You seem to be a master at the skill."

"Hardly, for you seem to comprehend far too often exactly what I am thinking." He drew away from the window as rain blew in. Pulling down the curtains, he reached past her to do the same on the other side. He grasped the edge of the window, stretching in front of her, and faced her. "For example, I have no doubts you know what I am thinking of now."

He was right. She knew exactly what he was thinking as he slanted across her. In the past three months, she had not seen him frequently, for he had many obligations now that he was assuming the family's title. In addition, he had to work on clearing up the muddle his brother had made of his private life. Yet through all those long weeks of not seeing him, her desire to have him close had not ebbed.

He did not touch her, but he wanted to, she knew, and she wanted him to. Slowly her fingers rose to trace the stern line of his nose, then edge along the tilting line of his lips. His breath warmed her skin just before he laced his fingers through hers. Saying nothing, he turned their hands, which were woven together, so he could brush her cheek with the back of his fingers.

He yelped, and his fingers tightened around hers. When she gasped, he yanked his hand away and turned to look at the little boys. He reached down and caught Philip's swinging foot, halting it.

"By the elevens," Cameron said, "watch where you aim that boot!"

The little boy's eyes filled with frightened tears, and Tess put her hand over Cameron's. As his fingers slipped away, she patted Philip's knee, telling him to be careful.

"He did not mean to strike you with his foot," she added more quietly to Cameron. Even less than she had seen Cameron had the little boys had time with him. To them, their uncle remained a stranger. Their young faces disclosed their fear this unknown man would come between them and Tess, whom they had come to love and respect.

"I realize that," Cameron replied with a sigh.

"But you were so vexed."

"Because his kick reminded me that a boy can be foolish, but a man must not."

"Oh."

He frowned. "Just 'oh'?"

"You have made yourself very unclear on everything to do with me. I have found it simpler to say nothing until you decide if you wish this to be a marriage or not."

"Me? What of you? I cannot imagine Tess Masterson Hawksmoor accepting the dictates of her husband."

She looked away. Had he used her whole name as a reminder that he still harbored a hope, even after four months, that this marriage could be brought to an end? She thought of the page engraved with Mr. Paige's office address she had seen in his account book the day he told her of his brother's death.

"I wish only to know," she said in a near whisper, "what you are thinking on *this* subject."

"My mind has not changed." He hooked his finger beneath her chin and smiled. "My thoughts may have changed, but my mind must not."

"You are speaking in riddles, but I understand."

"I thought you might." As the carriage slowed in front of the house on Grosvenor Square, he added, "For I have few doubts your thoughts are as rebellious as mine."

Tess did not answer as the tiger opened the door. She was startled when Cameron motioned for the boys to scamper out and then for the tiger to assist her. When she stood on the walkway, safely beneath the umbrella held by a footman, she looked back at the carriage.

"Go inside," Cameron said. "I have business I must attend to."

"With Mr. Paige?"

That was the wrong question to ask where, even on the deserted street, others might overhear, she knew when his eyes narrowed. No emotion warmed his voice as he replied, "I should have said I have my brother's business to attend to this afternoon." He pulled the door closed.

She herded the boys into the house, knowing that by the time they were inside, the carriage would have driven out of sight from the square. Again so many questions waited to be asked, and too few had been.

"Mrs. Livingstone," Harbour said, his voice strained.

Tess came to her feet and stared as an elegant woman with golden hair came into the parlor, the very woman portrayed in the miniature Mr. Knox had told her was of Cameron's mistress. Pamela Livingstone drew off her lacy gloves as she paused on the other side of the chair where Tess had been sitting. Her deep blue gown was glorious, the perfect complement for her incredible beauty.

Tess struggled not to look down at her own dress that was not *à la mode* as Mrs. Livingstone's was. Her fingers wanted to reach up and make sure her hair had not escaped from beneath her cap yet again, but she must not reveal any nervousness until she discovered why *this* woman was calling.

"I am glad you are at home to me today," Mrs. Livingstone said in a voice like the song of a robin on a spring morning.

"I was not expecting company." This time she could not keep her fingers from patting her hair back. "Please sit while I ring for some lemonade." She faltered, then asked, "Do you like lemonade?"

"It will be lovely."

Tess turned to see that Harbour had lingered in the doorway. Asking him to have some lemonade brought, she gave him a smile to thank him for staying to make certain she would not turn Mrs. Livingstone away. Relieved that the boys were out playing in the square with two of the younger footmen, she took a steadying breath before she walked back to where Mrs. Livingstone still stood.

"I came to offer my condolences, for it would not have been my place to attend the memorial yesterday afternoon," Mrs. Livingstone said. "I was very sorry to hear of Russell's death."

"I will tell Cameron you have called." She sat facing Cameron's mistress, hoping that she could retain the remnants of her composure.

"I trust those were Russell's children I saw running about on the grass."

"Yes. I know there may be those who believe they should not be in such a public place just months after their father's death, but they need to run about in a space much bigger than the kitchen garden."

"Susan Baum's children, I assume."

Tess could not keep from blurting, "You know the identity of their mother?"

"Assuming only, because the children are ginger-hackled like Mrs. Baum was." Mrs. Livingstone held up a hand graced by a lovely emerald ring. "Before you ask, Lady Hawksmoor, Mrs. Baum died nearly five years ago. Mayhap even longer ago, for she may have not survived the birth of that younger boy. I no longer recall."

"So they truly are orphans."

"Yes. As Cameron takes his obligations seriously, I do not doubt he will continue to tend to those children as if they were his own." A twinkle abruptly brightened her brown eyes. "Or he will make arrangements for them to be properly cared for."

"He has."

"And you are the arrangement?"

Tess was tempted to tell Mrs. Livingstone the question was presumptuous, but arguing with Cameron's mistress would gain her nothing. "I offered to help him find a governess for the children, a process that is taking much longer than I had anticipated." She did not add that all the candidates she had interviewed seemed overly strict or more interested in flirting with one of the footmen.

"But until then, you have taken over the place of a surrogate mother for these children."

"I do not think they have ever had the company of a mother."

"On that, you are probably correct. You are showing a great deal of kindness in welcoming those children into your house."

"They are my husband's nephews."

"But not every new wife would open her door to her brother-in-law's side winds." Mrs. Livingstone smiled, and Tess knew her confusion must be on her face when Mrs. Livingstone said, "I mean by-blows, Your Grace."

Tess flinched at the form of address she could not accustom herself to, but did not reply as a maid set a tray with two glasses and pitcher of lemonade on the table beside her. Filling one glass, she handed it and a napkin to Mrs. Livingstone, then poured some lemonade for herself.

As soon as the maid had taken her leave, Mrs. Livingstone said, "I know you could have turned me away from your door, Your Grace, but I had a reason for calling other than expressing my sympathies now that you are out of first mourning. I have been away on a journey with a dear friend, but as soon as I returned to Town, I wanted to ease any concerns you might have about Cameron and me." She smiled gently. "The very first concern I wish to ease is that there is no longer a 'Cameron and me.' I am with Lord Stedley now."

"Thank you for telling me that."

"But you do not believe me?"

Tess wrung her napkin until she heard the fabric protest. Dropping it into her lap, she said, "I have no reason to believe or not to believe you, Mrs. Livingstone."

"Ah, 'tis Cameron you do not believe."

"That is not exactly the truth either. He has not said anything about you."

"But you recognized my name."

"Mr. Knox—"

Even Mrs. Livingstone's scowl could not ruin her perfect profile as she spat, "That man must have been fed with a shovel when he was a child, and he seems to find it impossible to keep that big mouth shut. You and Cameron had barely returned to Town before Mr. Knox was spreading the word of your wedding."

"I do not understand why Cameron considers him a

friend." She put her fingers to her lips. She should not be speaking so of Cameron to this woman.

"You are not saying anything I have not said myself." Mrs. Livingstone smiled again. "However, it is as simple as that, once Cameron selects a friend, he is loyal, no matter what."

Even when his friend used blackmail to arrange Cameron's marriage? She could not ask that. Falling back on the trite, she said, "That is an exemplary trait."

"He is an exemplary man in many ways. I do not need to tell you that."

Heat scored Tess's face. The intimacies that belonged to a husband and wife were what he had shared with this woman. Even a sip of the slightly sour lemonade could not ease the fire of embarrassment searing her.

"Your Grace, if I said something that has unsettled you, forgive me."

Tess looked up to see Mrs. Livingstone's honest chagrin. "Of course. I am not myself just now."

"Quite to the contrary, I would say. You seem very much as I have heard you described: pretty and pretty-mannered enough even to receive your husband's cast-off."

"I appreciate that you came here to express your condolences and to be so honest with me about your current relationship with Cameron." She had never guessed she would be speaking like this to her husband's former mistress. "It is pleasing for me to hear you state that what you shared is gratefully in the past."

"Gratefully? Do not mistake my words. I greatly enjoyed the times I spent with Cameron, and there are times when I miss his calls. He is a man, as you must know, who challenges anyone around him with his quick wit." She ran her finger along her glass. "Yet he has a gentle heart that is touched by the unhappiness of anyone around him."

Tess was unsure how to reply. Yes, she recognized the description of his quick wit, but a gentle heart? If Cameron had one, he had hidden it very well from her. Deciding to be honest, she said, "The unhappiness is his now."

"Yes." Mrs. Livingstone rose. "I have taken too much of your time, Your Grace, when I wished only to offer my sympathies."

"Thank you." Tess stood, too, glad Mrs. Livingstone had misunderstood her rash words.

"You are very kind." Mrs. Livingstone squeezed Tess's hand. "And you are, I believe, just what Cameron needs."

So shocked she could think of nothing to say, Tess just nodded. She heard a commotion just as Mrs. Livingstone was walking out of the parlor door.

Going out into the hall, she saw Donald and Philip running up the stairs with two of the youngest footmen close behind. Both boys were chattering and covered with dirt and grass stains. Donald's breeches had a torn knee. Philip had two torn knees. Their smiles were so broad Tess could not keep from smiling in response.

Mrs. Livingstone edged around the filthy boys, regarding them with wide eyes. She looked back at Tess, but did not ask the questions she clearly was thinking. Before Tess could decide how best to explain about the boys when they would be eagerly listening, Mrs. Livingstone had bid her a good day and vanished down the stairs.

"A squirrel," Philip was saying. "It ran right up the tree, but I almost caught it. Next time—"

"Who was that lady?" interrupted Donald as he peered over the railing to the foyer below.

"Mrs. Livingstone," Tess replied.

"She is pretty."

"Yes." She put her hand on his ruddy curls. "She is."

"I like her." Philip spoke with an authority that

brought his father to mind. "She smiled at us. Will she be coming back?"

Tess steered them toward the stairs to the upper floors. "Not today. You need to get cleaned up before supper."

The boys grumbled, and she heard the footmen chuckling. No doubt they recalled hearing similar words during their own childhoods. Turning, she asked the footmen to arrange for warm water to be brought to the room the boys shared. It overlooked the garden at the back of the house, so it was close to the stairs to the kitchen, where the boys enjoyed going to wheedle a treat out of the cook whenever they had the chance.

The little boys continued to complain until Tess offered to have them join her for tea in her rooms. When they were scrubbed and pink-cheeked and sitting on her settee holding a cake each, she listened to them laughing about their misadventures outside.

"So you like animals?" she asked when Donald barely paused in his story of chasing a squirrel to take another bite of his cake.

He nodded, frosting emphasizing his smile.

"Would you like to see my pet?" She had thought about this a great deal during the past week. Although hedgehogs were leery of strangers, she believed, after seeing how gentle the little boys were with the cat that loitered by the kitchen begging for scraps, she could trust them with Heddy.

Philip bounced to his feet. "See it! See it now!"

Standing, Tess held out her hands. Two smaller ones, sticky with frosting, grasped them. She took them into her bedchamber. Putting her finger to her lips, she watched their eyes grow big as she lifted off the cloth that allowed Heddy to sleep during the daylight.

"What is it?" Donald asked, standing on tiptoe to see into the cage.

She picked up Philip so he could see. "A hedgehog."

"But what is a hedgehog?"

She was shocked speechless. Several of the favorite stories she had read over and over when she was not much older than Donald had been filled with all sorts of animal characters. From the time when she was very young, she had seen hedgehogs in the garden and along the country roads.

"They live beneath bushes and in the hedgerows, and they eat insects and worms."

"Insects and worms?" Philip's face twisted in disgust.

"Do they eat caterpillars?" Donald shivered. "Those would tickle."

Tess smiled and covered the cage again. "I have never fed Heddy caterpillars. Mayhap we can offer her one if we find one in the garden."

"Take her out!" crowed Philip.

Herding them from her room, she put her finger to her lips again. "You must be quiet around Heddy. She is very afraid of strangers."

"Just like Philip," said Donald with a condescending glance at his brother. For the length of a heartbeat, Tess saw his father's expression on his face.

Before Philip could snarl back an answer, she replied, "Sometimes it is wise to be fearful. If Heddy lived in the garden and was not careful, a dog or a hawk could come and carry her off. She might step in front of a carriage or a rider. Even though she rolls into a ball when she is frightened, she could not fight off a dog."

Tess continued answering their questions about Heddy and promised them they could see the hedgehog again tomorrow. When she said the hedgehog would be wide awake with coming of dark, the boys pelted her with pleas to be able to stay up late enough to see that. She smiled as she agreed—if they would go to bed without complaint this evening.

The boys proved how much they wanted to see the

hedgehog awake when they were as good as they had promised. When she went in to kiss them good night, Donald asked as he climbed into bed, "Will Uncle Cam be coming to look at Heddy, too?"

She doubted they understood why she was trying not to laugh. The boys continued to call Cameron "Uncle Cam." Whether Cameron liked it or not, she was unsure.

She tucked the covers around him. "Mayhap. He will be pleased to know you are asking about him."

The two boys exchanged a glance she could easily read. They did not miss their uncle, whom they had seen seldom since they came here. She had been careful not to mention Cameron was busy trying to untangle the mess of debts and obligations his brother had left as a legacy.

As she closed the boys' door, she looked at the one across the hall. It had not been opened in the past week, because Cameron was too busy to enjoy his avocation. She sighed, hoping there were no more ways their lives could be turned upside down.

"Gone?" Tess stood, dropping her embroidery to the floor. "What do you mean?"

Large tears welled up in Philip's eyes, then fell along his face. "I did not mean to . . . I just wanted to . . ."

"He let Heddy out," Donald announced, crossing his arms over his narrow chest.

"You wanted to, too!"

"I did not. I knew Tess would be angry if—"

Tess had no interest in listening to them pulling caps. Most likely, both boys had been unable to resist the temptation of going in to see the hedgehog. "Did she bite you?"

"Only once." Philip held up his bleeding thumb.

Rushing to the bellpull, Tess tugged. Harbour and two

footmen arrived at the same time. The two footmen who were supposed to be watching over the children, she noted with a scowl. She gave quick orders. One footman took Philip to have his thumb cleaned and bandaged while the other and Harbour followed her up the stairs, Donald hurrying after them as quickly as he could. She slowed when she saw her door was closed.

"I shut it," Donald said, pushing to stand beside her. "I thought we could find Heddy more easily if she was still in your room."

"An excellent thought." She patted his head. "Take care when you open the door. I doubt if she will scurry out, because she is more apt to find a shadowy place to hide."

Harbour set the footman, Jenette, and Cameron's valet, Park, to work looking for the hedgehog in the sitting room. He went with Tess into the bedroom and got down on his hands and knees to peer under the furniture. When he chuckled, he said, "This reminds me of searching for my own pet before my mother was the wiser. Where does your hedgehog usually go to hide?"

"She never has escaped from her cage before."

"Then she may have not gone far." He bent to look under the bed.

Tess squatted to see under the dressing table. Her eyes widened when she saw something in the shadows. Although it was the wrong size for Heddy, she plucked the item out. It was a simple box that had been covered in leather. Opening it, she saw a military medal lying within. She was not certain which one it was, but it glinted silver in the lamplight. She slowly closed the box and put it on the dressing table.

"So that is where it went to," Harbour said, glancing over his shoulder.

"What is it?"

"Lord Hawk—His Grace's medal he received after his service at Boney's final defeat."

"I did not realize Cameron was at Waterloo," Tess said, pretending not to notice the butler's slip. It was difficult to get used to calling Cameron by his new title when he was rarely here.

"That was where he was wounded."

"Wounded?" she gasped, horrified.

"You never asked him about the scar above his eyebrow?" Harbour asked, still on his hands and knees as he peeked back under the bed.

"No."

"May I say, Your Grace, that you show an admirable lack of curiosity?" He sat back on his heels, then gathered his feet beneath him and stood. "When I was courting my wife, her father quizzed me about every facet of my life."

She hated lying, but she could not reveal the truth to the butler. Not only did she wish to spare Cameron the embarrassment of revealing the truth about their wedding, but Papa's request to conceal why he had been a party to it kept her from being honest.

"I have heard," she replied, "there is always more to discover about one's spouse."

Hearing shouts from the other room, Tess jumped to her feet and raced out there. Donald was hopping from one foot to the other as he pointed to one of the potted plants by the window.

"Right there, Aunt Tess. Right there!" he cried.

Tess gently elbowed past him and lifted a leaf to see Heddy curled up, her bristles pointing out in every direction. When the footman reached to pick up the hedgehog, Tess shook her head. She picked up the cloth that had covered the top of the cage. Draping it over her hands, she scooped the frightened hedgehog out of the planter and carried her back to the cage in her bedroom.

With a few soothing words to her pet, she set the cloth back over the cage. Then she turned to thank those who had helped in the search. She laughed along with the servants as they related how they thought they had found the hedgehog in a corner only to discover a shoe left by one of the little boys.

Cameron paused by his bedchamber door as he heard the laughter from Tess's room. He kneaded his brow, which ached from hours of poring over Russell's account books with the family's solicitor. They were nearly done, after three endless months of trying to make sense of them. The situation had been even worse than he had feared. Even after Russell's grand house on Berkeley Square was sold, the proceeds would be only a small percentage of what his brother owed. He could not guess why Russell had spent two hundred fifty pounds every month for the past year or more, but had not once accounted for where that money went. Every other debt, and there were many, were accounted for with signed IOUs or other slips of paper. The two hundred fifty pounds spent month after month were not.

Another peal of giggles came from the room, not from Tess or the youngsters. He watched, astonished, as several maids and a footman walked out of the room. Their amusement was masked when they saw him.

When his butler came out of Tess's room, Harbour asked, as if nothing unusual were taking place, "May I bring you something for tea?"

"Yes."

"Where?"

Cameron's brows lowered, and he was about to ask his butler why he was acting so oddly. Then Cameron realized he was still staring at the door opening into the rooms that once had been his. Going to the door, he said, "In my rooms, of course, Harbour."

"Which rooms do you mean?"

Pointing over his shoulder toward the chambers he was now using and resisting the angry words that would not help just now when he did not need his butler playing matchmaker, Cameron walked into Tess's sitting room. His gaze swept along her slender form. Even though he had been away from her for weeks at a time since Russell's death, he could not erase the image of her enticing beauty from his mind. Her hair was mussed, falling in auburn swirls about her shoulders. His fingers tingled to follow the curve of her lips and watch them draw up in a smile in the moments before he tasted their luscious warmth.

Her abigail glanced past Tess, then said something. Tess turned, her lustrous eyes widening. Her attempt to smooth back her hair was futile, and he was glad. With it loose like this, she urged him to think of nothing but her.

"Cameron," she said, walking toward him as she had so often in his dreams, "you missed all the excitement."

He gulped, wondering if she had any idea what images of excitement filled his thoughts just now. Her in his arms, soft and willing, bold and seductive. He tried to force those thoughts aside, the effort making his voice gruff as he asked, "What has been going on here?"

"Heddy got out." She looked down and smiled, and he realized Russell's sons were standing beside her. Until now, he had been so fascinated with the promise in her eyes he had not noted the children.

"Heddy?" he asked.

"My pet hedgehog."

He choked on his astonishment. "Hedgehog? How long have you had this pet hedgehog, Tess?"

"Since it was a baby. About three years ago."

"Three years?" He had expected her to say she had found it in the kitchen garden. "Did you bring this creature here from the country?"

"Yes."

"How?"

She walked into the bedchamber with the lads in tow. When she gestured for him to follow, every inch of him reacted, even though he knew she was not offering the invitation a wife should make to her husband. She walked to a table and drew aside the cloth on the cage where the hedgehog was asleep.

"You keep it here?" he asked.

"Surely you saw this cage in my room and in the carriage."

"I will own I had other matters on my mind the sole time I was in your chambers in your father's house. I did no more than give a passing thought to what sort of animal lived in the cage on your table. Nor did I take note of the cage on our way to London."

"I thought your lack of curiosity remarkable, I will say."

"And I will say I do not want vermin in my house."

"Heddy is not vermin."

"The hedgehog belongs outside in the garden. It is not right to keep a filthy creature in the house."

"She is well mannered, and I keep her cage clean." She arched a russet brow at him. "Why are you complaining about her being a filthy creature when you did not know she was here until I spoke of her?"

Before he could answer, Donald piped up, "I will help Aunt Tess keep the cage clean." The boy grinned broadly. "I was the one who found her in the pot over there."

"I will help! I looked, too!" Philip tugged on Tess's skirt. "Let me help, too."

"Yes," she said with a gentle smile, "you may help keep Heddy's cage clean. That way, she will become accustomed to you. Now Jenette will take you to have your supper."

Her abigail took each boy by the hand and led them out of the room.

When Cameron was about to follow, Tess said, "Please wait."

Could she hear his heart thudding at the soft warmth in her voice? When she went to the table which he once had used as a desk, but she had converted into a dressing table by hanging a glass over it, she picked up a small box and held it out to him.

He took it without speaking. Slipping it beneath his coat, he turned to go into the sitting room.

"Cameron?" She stepped in front of him. "You cannot pretend nothing of importance is in that box."

"What is in it had its hour of importance, but that hour is past."

"And that is that?"

"What else do you expect it to be?"

She folded her arms in front of her, clearly unwilling to put an end to this conversation. "I expect it to be something you are proud of."

"I have no wish to be lauded as a hero, so leave off with your mewling for the great hero you wished you had wed."

"Mewling?" Her hands clenched on her arms. "I can assure you, Cameron Hawksmoor, no one will ever use that word to describe me . . . if one sticks to the truth."

"So you are accusing me of lying?"

"I am accusing you of being shortsighted, short-tempered, and short a sheet."

He laughed dryly. "Another example of your wit, I see."

"Quite the contrary. Another example of how I tire of your tiresome tantrums. You act no older than Donald when you cannot have your way." She squared her shoulders. "Cameron, they are your nephews."

"So I was told."

"You think they are not? I know the boys were brought, unbidden, to the house, but didn't the paperwork found in Russell's house prove he had been paying someone to watch over his children?"

He waved aside her question. He did not want to think about what the paperwork at Russell's house had revealed. "That is neither here nor there. They are here now, as you are."

She took a deep breath, then released it as her shoulders sagged. "Cameron, I was a fool to listen to someone who told me there was more to you than you allowed anyone to see."

"Who told you that?"

"Pamela Livingstone."

He was certain he had misheard her. "Pamela? When did you speak with her?"

"When she called."

"Here?"

"Yes, to offer her sympathies upon Russell's death." She faltered, then said, "As well, she wished to let me know there was more to you than the emotionless martinet who blames everyone else for his own mistakes and shuts everyone out of his life. I had hoped she was right, that your ex-mistress knew you better than I did, but it is clear she is wrong. You have fought so hard to set aside every feeling you have that you have forgotten how to feel. You are so determined to govern your emotions that you have come to fear having them. You cannot even accept your due as a hero in the war against the French."

She pushed past him and out of the room. With a curse, he started to follow. Then he halted himself. If he gave chase now, he was certain to show her exactly how out of control his emotions were when he pulled her up against him and kissed her with every bit of his yearning for her.

That would be a mistake now. He reached under his

coat and pulled out the box. Tossing it back on the table, he cursed. Tess was right. He was determined to avoid his own feelings, especially the ones for her.

Thirteen

Eustace Knox poured himself another glass of wine, then faced Cameron, who was standing by a leather chair. Eustace's fingers clenched and unclenched on the glass, matching the nervous tic that had twitched Eustace's right eyelid since Cameron had come into the room.

Cameron had not intended to come to the club this morning, for he had hoped to pay a call on Pamela and find out whatever had possessed her to give Tess a look-in. Instead he was here in response to his friend's urgent request, which apparently was about to become another scold. Cameron was tempted to tell his tie-mate another dressing-down would just add to his ill humor.

"It is simple," Eustace said as he sat in another chair. "Even though *on dits* have been very clear that you returned to London with a bride almost four months ago, there are those who are questioning—very loudly and most rudely, if you wish to know the whole truth—why you and Tess have yet to be seen at a gathering."

"Do not lecture me, Eustace." Cameron set his glass on the table beside his chair and looked out the window to the street below. The rain had chased most of the pedestrians from the walkways, but the door to the club across the street was continually opening and closing. "I do not need more problems dropped onto my head."

"I am trying to halt a problem that has been brewing for the past fortnight."

"Do those same gossipmongers recall I have been in mourning for the recent death of my brother?"

Eustace shrugged. "Your father's death did not halt Russell from dancing at Lady Brigham's assembly a month later."

"I am not Russell."

"No, and so people are curious about the woman you chose to wed."

"Chose? You know the truth of that wedding."

In the reflection in the windowpane, Cameron could see Eustace set his glass on the table beside Cameron's and come to his feet. "Yes, but I thought, as you have made no motion in that direction, you had decided not to set Tess aside. You told me you did not fill out the papers from Paige." His eyes widened. "Or is it simply you have not filled them out *yet?*"

Cameron turned from the window. "I trust you had a genuine reason for sending me that frantic note asking for this meeting to discuss dire matters."

"Other than you should bring your wife to the assembly at Lord Peake's house next week?"

"Eustace, I have had enough of this skimble-skamble." When his friend seized Cameron's sleeve, Cameron shook off Eustace's hand. "Have you lost every bit of mind you had?"

"I am thinking of you and your wife. By remaining out of sight, you are the cause of too much poker-talk. You need make only a brief appearance at the assembly, and the Polite World will see nothing to interest them. Their attention, then, will turn to other matters."

Cameron had to agree his friend's suggestion made good sense. "I believe you are right, Eustace. Thank you."

"While you are in a grateful mood—"

"How much do you need?" Cameron shook his head and reached again for his glass. Taking a deep drink, he said, "I did not expect you to spend through your inheritance with this speed. 'Tis not like you to make pots and pans with me."

"I am not begging for alms from you." He grinned when Cameron arched a brow. "All right. I am, but I have had unforeseen expenses."

"Now you sound like Russell. He said that too often in the past year as well."

Eustace flinched.

"What is it?" Cameron asked.

For a long moment, Eustace did not answer. He drained his own glass, then said, "Disparaging your dead brother is bothersome to me."

"Sorry, but I have found lately that however difficult the truth may be, it is preferable to the alternatives." Those words echoed through Cameron's head as he agreed to lend his friend one thousand pounds and while he walked down the stairs toward the door to the street.

Did he truly prefer the truth? If so, why was he avoiding confronting it where Tess was concerned? He must either put an end to this marriage or accept it. He had been able to set aside that concern while dealing with Russell's estate, but he must make a decision soon. After all, as his mother had been eager to remind him, he was now the Duke of Hawkington, and it was fortunate he had a wife to give the family's title a legitimate heir.

"Hawksmoor?"

Cameron turned to see a door open to one of the card rooms. Inside, John Stedley was sitting with several other club members, playing cards. The viscount, a good-looking blond man with enough blunt to enjoy the flats whenever he took the notion—which, Cameron had heard, was often—was shuffling the cards for the next hand.

"Just the man I was hoping to see," Stedley said. With

his cigar, the viscount motioned for the other men at the table to leave. Cameron nodded to the others, who gathered up their winnings and moved away like well-trained soldiers. "Sit down, Hawksmoor."

"I see you are winning."

Stedley looked down at the pile of money and chuckled. Reaching into the box by his side, he pulled out a cheroot as thick as the one he was smoking and handed it to Cameron. "And Millsmere is buying, so you might as well enjoy raising a cloud at his expense." Without a pause, he said, "Pamela tells me I should, upon the very first opportunity I have, offer my congratulations to you on your bride, for she was much impressed with your new wife."

"Yes, Tess mentioned Pamela gave her a look-in to offer her condolences at Russell's untimely death." He lit the cigar as he recalled what else Tess had said to him about Pamela's comments.

"Untimely?" Stedley picked up his glass of wine and leaned back in his chair. "There are rumblings among those who should know better than to gossip that your brother may have chosen the exact time of his death."

"You believe Russell killed himself?" Cameron laughed tersely. "My brother was never fond of anything that did not bring him pleasure, and I doubt there is much pleasure in crashing one's carriage into a tree."

"My point exactly." Stedley sat straighter.

"I am afraid if that is your point, I do not comprehend it."

"Your brother was miserable just before he died. Dashed poor company, always down in the mouth about something or other, to the point there was a general feeling he was tired of life in London."

"When I last spoke with Russell, he was jubilant." His mouth twisted as he puffed on the cigar. Millsmere must have been losing badly, because this was a truly fine smoke. "He had a new mistress, and he, for once, was not asking me for a loan."

"He had regained his pleasure in life not because of his new incognita, but because he had decided not to pay hush money to whoever had a hank upon him."

Now Cameron sat bolt upright in his chair. "Had a hank upon him? Are you saying my brother was being blackmailed?"

Stedley shuffled the cards over and over. "I assumed you knew."

"No."

"It was not quite common knowledge, although I know he spoke of the disgusting matter to several friends one night when he was deep in his cups."

Cameron folded his arms over his chest. "Blackmailed for what? No matter what else my brother did, he showed good sense in not seducing another man's wife."

"That is not the only thing one can be blackmailed for."

"True, but Russell had no interest in politics, and he certainly was not interested in any sort of industry. No one could accuse him of taking another's ideas for his own profit." He put down his cigar, no longer interested in it. By the elevens, was it possible Russell had been blackmailed? That would explain the two hundred fifty pounds that monthly vanished from Russell's funds and was never accounted for.

"What about a duel?" Stedley continued.

"Russell?" Cameron laughed mirthlessly. "On that one subject, my brother showed the utmost common sense after his single encounter with an *affaire de honor*. He would ignore a gauntlet thrown down at his feet or slapped across his face. He enjoyed life too much to chance that some drunken beef-head might aim a pistol at his heart."

Stedley shrugged. "I have to own he never mentioned

why he was being blackmailed, only that it was costing him dear. Find out who was extorting money from him and why, and, I suspect, Cameron, you will discover what caused that carriage to crash."

"I know. 'Twas thieves chasing them."

"But who set those thieves upon them? That is the question you should be asking."

Cameron heard the shouts even over the clatter of horseshoes on the stones of the street. Drawing in the reins, he watched Russell's sons racing about the center of the square. A footman chased after them, adding to their giggles and excited cries. The younger boy ran up to where two women were talking. Throwing his arms around the waist of one for a quick hug, he then ran back to join his brother.

The perfect scene of domestic bliss . . . but one Cameron had no part in. He looked toward his door. When had his home become someone else's, so he felt like an outsider there?

He shivered, even though the air was warm. Blast it! Why was he acting as if he were jealous of those children? Marrying Tess would never have been his choice. Even so, he could not deny how her hands had gently enfolded Philip when the little boy flung his arms around her. Nor could he deny the thoughts of those fingers touching her husband in other, more intimate ways. This need was becoming more intense with the passing of each hour.

His wife.

Yet she was not his wife. Their marriage was a delusion. Thinking of other matters would be the best thing he could do. He should concentrate on finding out the truth about what had caused the carriage to crash, killing Russell and his mistress, and why. The muddled and often contradictory story the constable had shared with him had created only more questions in his mind.

"Cameron!" Tess's voice swept all dark thoughts from his head as his heart abruptly came to life as if it had been dormant too long. She waved to him, smiling.

He swung down from his horse and walked to where she stood by a woman who must be at least two decades older than Tess. The woman's hair was still an uncompromising brown, but her face bore the wrinkles of many years. She was plump and quite short. Her clothes were simple, but obviously well cared for. Over her arm, she carried a basket covered with a bright cloth. A pair of scissors stuck out of one side.

"Cameron, this is Mrs. Detloff, the new governess. Mrs. Detloff, Lord . . . I mean, the Duke of Hawkington." Tess's face flushed with her error. Then she smiled. "Forgive me, Cameron."

"It is a title both of us must still become accustomed to having connected with my name." He was astonished when she lowered her eyes, obviously not wanting him to guess her thoughts. What had unsettled her now?

Before he could ask that aloud, Mrs. Detloff said, " 'Tis a pleasure to have the chance to oversee your nephews, Your Grace. They are lively boys."

"Lively may be an understatement." He watched Donald pounce on his brother, and the two boys fell to the ground, wrestling like pups.

"I assure you I am equal to the task, Your Grace."

"I trust you will be."

"She has offered," Tess added, "to oversee the moving of the boys' things from their old house."

"Haven't they all been moved here already?"

"I thought it best for them to become used to this house before we brought in much that reminded them of their past."

"No doubt an excellent idea, and no doubt something

Mrs. Detloff and some of the footmen can handle with ease." He held out his arm. "Tess?"

Her fingers quivered when she put them on his sleeve. Leading her toward the house, he handed the reins to the lad who rushed to take them. He saw Tess's surprise when he continued along the walkway that edged the street around the green center of the square.

"The boys were collecting grubs and insects for Heddy," she said.

"Who?"

"My hedgehog." Tess started to add more, then saw the distant expression in Cameron's eyes. Not distant, but turned inward, warning he was wrestling with his own thoughts as fiercely the boys were on the grass.

While they continued to walk around the small square, he said, "I must tell you something that will distress you greatly."

She gulped. Had he found a way to end their marriage? That would explain his comment to Mrs. Detloff that he was unaccustomed to having the title of duke connected with his name. *His,* not hers. And she could not forget seeing that letter from Mr. Paige, the solicitor, in Cameron's book. A quaver slipped into her voice as she said, "All right."

"All right?" He looked at her and smiled. "Tess, your serenity makes it always a pleasure to speak with you."

"Always?"

He laughed, but the sound was taut. "Almost always, I should say more correctly." Without a pause, he added, "I was speaking with Lord Stedley at the club."

"Mrs. Livingstone's . . ." She knew her face was red again, because it burned like a flame.

"Yes," Cameron said with the gentleness he revealed so seldom. "Eventually you may become accustomed to Town ways and see it is not unusual that I can remain friends with my erstwhile mistress and her new para-mour."

"I doubt that."

"Again that honesty."

She put her other hand on his arm and stepped in front of him, forcing him to halt. "What is it, Cameron? What is wrong?"

"What is wrong is that Russell and his beloved Isabel's deaths may not have been as simple as a robbery."

Tess listened in growing horror as Cameron outlined what he had learned from speaking with Lord Stedley, the constable who had contacted Cameron with the news of his brother's death, and the office of the Bow Street Runners. "Blackmail?" she gasped.

"Yes. At least, that is what Stedley spoke of."

She tried to swallow past the clog in her throat. This was too much of a coincidence. Papa was having money extorted from him, and now it was possible Russell had been as well. By Mr. Knox, too? No, that made no sense, because Mr. Knox was Cameron's friend, and Papa had intimated Mr. Knox had been acting at the request of Russell Hawksmoor when he arranged for the special license for Cameron to marry her.

"But why?" she choked. "Why would anyone murder your brother? It makes no sense."

"I doubt if murder is the act of a sensible mind."

"Aren't you angry?"

"I am seething."

She stared up at him, searching his face for any sign of such a strong emotion. There was none, save in his narrowed eyes, which blazed. "How can you be so calm?"

He put his hand over hers on his arm. "I must be, Tess. So must you be. If the one who did this—"

"Assuming the *on dits* are right, and it was not simply

an unfortunate accident caused by a knight of the pad who took his booty and fled."

"I cannot assume that any longer." His lips tightened into a familiar straight line. "I do not know why I did not ask these questions right from the moment I heard of the accident."

"You may have been thinking solely of your loss." She knew she was being bold—even for a wife—in the midst of the walkway, but she put her hand up to his cheek and stroked it. "Cameron, do not curry your head. Self-flagellation is worthless at any time, especially now. I know you will do all you can to find the truth."

"For that, I will need your help."

"You need only ask."

He pressed his mouth to her hand, then whispered, "You have not asked what and how I need you to help."

"That does not matter." Looking at where the boys were down on their hands and knees searching through the grass for worms, she said, "An appalling crime may have been done against their father, and I will do what I can to help bring your brother's murderer to justice."

Tipping her face back toward his, he said, "Eustace told me—"

"What Eustace Knox has to say does not concern me."

"Tess, you must set aside your antipathy toward him. I do not understand why you hate him so much." He cupped her chin in his palm. "Do you blame him for this predicament we find ourselves in?"

"The predicament of our marriage? Yes, I do blame him for it."

"Blame your father as well, for none of us seemed to have a bit of sense that night." Again the inward expression filled his eyes. "So why did the vicar perform the ceremony? I should have asked that before."

"Mayhap you should have." She longed to blurt out the truth, but her pledge to Papa halted her.

Cameron lowered his hand and said, "Although you may hate the source of this counsel, I believe it is wise. You must join me in attending Lord Peake's assembly next week."

"How can you plan to attend a gathering when your brother is so recently deceased? Yes, we are out of first mourning, but to attend such a party? Certainly that will cause quite a hullabaloo among the *ton*."

He took her by the shoulders and held her gaze with his fervent one. "That is exactly what I hope. If there is enough babble about the most outrageous Duke and Duchess of Hawkington, people will focus on that instead of the questions I will be seeking answers to."

"Do you believe I wish to be part of another deception?"

"I believe you have no more interest in it than I do, but I know this is what we must do, Tess, if there is any chance in discovering the truth about who was blackmailing my brother and why." His jaw tightened. "And who killed him."

Fourteen

Tess eased the bedroom door closed behind her. Mrs. Detloff could not hide her conviction Tess was spoiling the boys by coming to tuck them in each night, but Tess did not want to have the children believe they had been abandoned again. Some days during the past week, the only time she had had with the boys was when they were on their way to bed. She had not guessed having a single dress made would be so complicated and take so much time. An uneasy sensation deep within her warned nothing would be simple now she was married to a duke.

Although the ceremony to invest him with the title of his father and brother had yet to be held, she knew it was little more than a formality. The modiste had fluttered about the shop as if she had no more weight than one of her glorious silks, so excited at the idea of making a dress for a duchess to wear to this large gathering. Tess wanted to ask why the seamstress was so determined to have every inch of the dress perfect when there would be more than a hundred other guests. She did not bother, because she knew the answer. No matter the number of guests, everyone would take note of what a duchess wore.

She leaned back against the door to the boys' rooms as she wondered if everyone would also take note of how this duchess's knees trembled at the very thought of going among the *beau monde*. Cameron was right. She was a country bumpkin, better suited to a church fair than an assembly. So why, if she was so anxious about this gathering, was she looking forward to it with eagerness?

Trying to tell herself she might be able to obtain answers about why both her father and Russell had been paying an extortionist was silly. She would help Cameron try to find the truth about his brother, because she hoped it would lead as well to the truth about Papa. But that was not why she trembled with anticipation whenever she thought of going to this gathering. It was the thought of dancing with Cameron, of being in his arms for the length of a waltz. The very thought sent shivers of delight coursing through her. Mayhap it was madness, but she could not help it. She was falling in love with this man she had every reason to hate.

"Tess?"

She shrank back against the door, then laughed nervously. Cameron could not read the thoughts of her wayward mind. She went to the door on the other side of the hall. It was slightly ajar, and it came open as she reached out for the latch.

The way her breath caught when she saw Cameron in the easy dishevelment he chose around the house was by now customary, but her heart pounded ardently within her. She could not keep from admiring how his collarless shirt accented his strength. With his waistcoat unbuttoned and hanging loosely, his shoulders seemed even wider. His fingers on the door were stained with green, and she knew he had been working with the samples delivered to him earlier today from a ship that had sailed back to England from the islands of the Pacific Ocean.

All of that she noticed before her gaze was caught by his bright eyes, which matched his cheerful smile. Oh, how she wished he would smile more often! It transformed his face, urging her to give into her craving and draw those upturned lips to her. Mayhap, she reminded herself, looking away, it was for the best that he usually wore an even expression, for then she was not so tempted to cede her common sense to this longing.

"I thought," he said, motioning her to come into this workroom, "you might be interested in seeing some of these samples. You asked many questions before."

"Where specifically did these come from?" She was proud of herself for asking a question that did not sound as if she desperately were seeking something to say other than to plead for him to kiss her.

"These are from the Philippines."

"The Philippines? Aren't they Spanish islands?"

He chuckled. "These samples have passed through many hands to reach me here, and they are in surprisingly good shape for their long journey." He held up a flower that once might have been almost any color. The wide petals were now a dried brown. "I know it does not look pretty, but this was once an orchid. Its scent would have been exquisitely sweet."

She touched the drooping petals. "Does it have a name?"

"A slipper orchid."

"That is such a lovely name," she said. "It sounds as if it should be part of lady's garments for a fancy assembly."

"Let me show you. Sit here." He pointed to one of a pair of chairs next to the table.

She sat while he pulled a book off the shelf. When he sat beside her and began paging through the book, she was treated to a view of his sharply sculptured profile. His hair fell into his eyes as he bent to read the pages.

With a laugh, she picked up the glasses that were folded on another shelf. She handed them to him. "I believe you need them, Cameron."

"Yes, I fear I do." He grimaced. "By the elevens, I despise these awkward things."

She ran her finger along the scar above his eyebrow. "If wearing barnacles is the worst you have to suffer when you were wounded here, you should be grateful."

"Tess, I do not want to talk of that." He drew her hand away.

"Then talk about your plants. Let me see a drawing of this orchid."

For a long minute, Cameron regarded her with astonishment. Had others pestered him with demands for tales of what had taken place on the day he was wounded? In the past few weeks, she had learned Cameron would divulge some experience only when he chose. She should be grateful he did not delve too deeply into her past, because then she might not have been able to hide the truth Papa had asked her not to reveal.

He paged through the book. When he pointed to a drawing, Tess smiled. The petals of the slipper orchid had once been a soft, deep green that was a dull sheen in comparison with grass.

"This type of orchid grows on the ground," he explained, "so it is easy to pass right by it without seeing it."

"It is beautiful." She looked at the plants placed in neat rows on the table. "You truly enjoy your study here."

"It shows that much?"

She nodded with a smile. "You describe these plants in the glowing terms most men save for the woman they love. It is the one time you do not hide your true feelings."

Leaning back on the hard chair, he closed the book and placed it on the shelf behind him. He stretched unself-consciously, giving her an excellent view of the rippling muscles shadowed beneath his lawn shirt. She made sure her eyes met his when he turned back to her. The agreement between them was so fragile, and she did not want to do anything to wreck it when she had this opportunity to hear him speaking with such candor.

"I have longed to sail away to the Pacific since I first read of Captain Cook's travels." He ran his fingers along one of the stems on the table. "I should say rather that I was fascinated by the studies conducted by Sir Joseph Banks, who discovered many new types of flora in those strange lands."

"I saw, on your map here in your workroom, you have many species marked from that region, so those must be the ones you have studied already."

"No, you have it quite in reverse, Tess. Those are the regions I planned to visit." He stood and sighed. Taking off his glasses, he said, "More accurately, I should say once upon a time I planned to visit them."

"Why didn't you go? When your father and brother were alive, there was nothing to prevent you from sailing to have your adventure."

He nodded. "You are right, as you are so irritatingly often. However, I chose a different sort of adventure."

"Fighting the French?"

"As the younger son, it was my duty." His mouth quirked into a reluctant smile. "Can you imagine Russell leaving the comforts and entertainments of London to march through the mud?"

"Many other younger sons did not go."

"But I did."

Tess came to her feet and around the table to stand beside him in front of the map. "And once you had done your duty to your family, you intended to sail here?" She touched the wide expanse of blue.

"That was my plan."

"All of which has come to naught."

"Plans do that." He set his glasses back on the shelf.

"I could not have imagined my life would be filled with more danger once I returned from the Continent."

"More danger? Do you think *you* are in danger from whoever was blackmailing your brother?"

"I think I am in danger, but not from that quarter."

"Then from what?"

"I believe you know quite well."

His lips tilted in a smile. It was her only warning before he pressed his mouth over hers. He pulled her to him, his arms enveloping her. Her skirt caught on the chair, but he simply tugged harder as his hands slid down along her back to hold her to his hard body. She gasped. Not at his action, but at her reaction to it. Every fiber of her delighted in his touch.

She met his mouth eagerly with her own. Her hands rose to curve along his nape. Moving the half step closer so her legs pressed against his, she sifted her fingers up through his hair as he traced a path of fire along her lips.

He lifted his mouth from hers to whisper, "You are what is most dangerous to me, Tess. You create a quandary within me."

"And what is that?"

"How can I want to kiss you when you are so contrary?"

"I am not the contrary one," she murmured as she traced the thick line of his right brow with her fingertip. "Nor am I the obstinate, obsessed, obnoxious, overbearing one."

With a grin, he caught her hand and laced his fingers through hers. " 'Tis about time you pay for all the insults you have heaped upon a man who enticed you into his workroom expressly to have you to himself for a few moments."

Her amazement at his words melted into his lips as he urged them to part beneath his gentle assault. While he sought pleasure within her mouth, she slipped her hands under his loose waistcoat. His strong sinews reacted to her touch even as his rapid breath mingled with hers before he bent to taste the skin along her neck. Waves of pleasure rippled through her, urging her to press even nearer.

His fiery fingers left scintillating sparks along her waist as his mouth covered hers once more. Rapture, stronger than anything she had ever known, soared through her. Her hands clenched on his back as she trembled, unable to govern the maelstrom within her. Was she out of her mind? She could not let him draw her into the insanity of making this marriage real. She tried to pull away, but his arm tightened around her waist.

"Cameron, we cannot be silly," she whispered as he swept her hair back from her face.

"What is silly about this?" His fingers twisted in her hair, sending pins flying about them in a silent storm.

She meant to give him a back-answer, to tell him she intended to leave this house and never to come back. She wanted to tell him she had been right. He was beastly to delight her like this when he still held on to the papers from the solicitor.

She had no chance as his lips slanted across hers. The sparks that had teased her when he touched her became a wildfire as his mouth dared hers to surrender to him. His fingers swept up her back, bringing her against him.

Turning her face away, she closed her eyes to keep the tears from leaking along her cheeks. She had depended on him to be sensible, but his fervor and her eager response warned this escalating desire could betray them more surely than Eustace Knox had. "Cameron, please stop." She slid out of his arms.

Cameron reached to pull Tess back to him, but his hands dropped back to his sides when he saw the tears jeweling her eyes. "Of course." Did she think he would force her into his bed? He never would do that. Or did she consider herself so irresistible to him that he could not control himself? Four months ago, he would have laughed at that question. Now it was no longer a hilarious idea. His gaze swept along her again, and the indisputable craving gripped him.

"Thank you for showing me your orchids," Tess said, her voice little more than a ragged breath. "Good night, Cameron." Her face bleached, and he knew even everyday words would be uneasy between them. She rushed out of the room, her footsteps echoing back to him until he heard her door shut at the front of the house.

He strode out of his workroom, closing the door behind him. By the elevens, what was wrong with him? He always had been able to keep his feelings firmly under control, just as his father had. His emotions would never dictate to him as Russell's had, for his brother seemed always at odds with himself in the battle between what he wished to do and what he knew he should do.

Having his coat, hat, and gloves brought, he went out of the house. Mayhap fresh air would bring some fresh ideas into his head and banish this unacceptable longing for his wife.

His wife!

There was the gist of the problem. She was his wife, to have and to hold. He had held her and now he wanted . . . her! He wanted her soft and willing in his arms as he watched her vibrant eyes burn with the passion that plagued him. Other relationships had been simpler, because the other women in his life had understood right from the onset what was to be between them. None of them had expected marriage, and it was the greatest irony that, now that he had a wife, he was denying himself the very pleasure he had enjoyed with those others.

This had to be resolved, one way or the other. But to make Tess his wife in more than name chanced opening himself up to someone as he never had, because he knew she would settle for nothing less than the very honesty she offered him.

"Cameron, you know you do not wish me to help you solve this problem." Pamela Livingstone watched as Cameron paced the floor of her pretty parlor, which was the perfect complement for her own loveliness.

"If I had not wanted that, do you think I would have demeaned myself to come to beg for your assistance?"

She laughed. "You do not play the petitioner well."

Cameron scowled, for her words were too reminiscent of ones Tess had spoken to him not so long ago. "I did not give you a call so you could ridicule me."

"Ridicule? You know that is not my intention. As well, we both know I cannot undo whatever contretemps you have created now with Tess, so you must have come here for another reason."

"Pamela, I am quite aware you are with Stedley now. I would never suggest you and I resume what we once shared."

Again she laughed. "Dear Cameron, even more poorly than you play the petitioner, you take on the role of the gallant ex-lover." Holding out the plate of cakes, she waited until he had sat and chosen one. "It was by mutual consent, as you recall, that we ended our *affaire de coeur.*"

"I do recall that."

"We both know I am very happy with the viscount, and we both know you should be very happy with your charming wife."

"Charming?"

"You sound surprised."

"I am not, but I had not expected you to speak so of Tess."

"If you are in such a pelter you cannot own to that

obvious truth, mayhap you should not have come calling."

He set himself on his feet once again and strode toward the door. There, he paused. Looking back, he saw Pamela was still smiling.

"Well?" she asked.

"It is true." He clasped his hands behind his back. "Tess is very charming. Too charming, if you must know the truth."

"Aha!"

"Aha?" He knew that self-satisfied tone. It meant Pamela believed she had gotten the better of him, something that had not happened often in their year together. Something that had happened already many more times with Tess in the short time she had been in his life.

"Do sit for more than a half second, Cameron, and tell me why you seem to be distressed that your wife is so charming she sends you fleeing from the comfort of her arms to my side."

He walked to the chair where he had been sitting and leaned his hands on the back. "I do not wish to speak of Tess."

"Oh?" Her eyebrows rose, and she smiled. "I had no idea you were developing such a *tendre* for your wife."

"What gives you cause to say that?"

"You have always been frank with me." She picked up her cup and sipped her tea. "As frank as you are with anyone, but now you are being even more reticent than usual. It would seem you have more reason than usual to keep your counsel, and that suggests to me there are feelings growing between you and your wife. Cameron, I am so pleased for you."

"Tess is not the reason I called."

"No?"

Picking up his own cup, he said, "You always know

all the rumors that flutter through the *ton,* Pamela. What have you heard of the cause of my brother's death?"

"Cause?" She put her hand to her chest as her voice caught on the single word. "Other than that the carriage accident was a terrible tragedy, I have heard nothing more than the usual supposition when someone is killed suddenly."

"You need not try to protect Stedley. I have already spoken with him, and he has offered information that adds to the questions that have been bothering me about the incident." Cameron did not add that the viscount was the one who had given credence to the questions swirling through the back of his mind.

Pamela relaxed, her studied smile vanishing. "I had hoped John would tell you what he knew."

"And what else do you know?"

"I know Russell was rumored to be in a great deal of trouble."

"Do you know what sort of trouble?"

She shook her head. "From what I heard from Major Carey, it began more than a year ago."

"It? You mean the blackmail?"

"Yes. Russell was involved in something that must have been so horrible he did not want anyone to learn of it. Your friend Eustace Knox is as well, I fear." She hesitated, then said, "Take care you do not get mixed up in whatever it is, too. You have the opportunity to have a happy life with your wife. Do not keep asking questions that might bring you information to ruin that."

"I am not sure I can stop without knowing the truth."

She lowered her eyes. When she did not reply, Cameron walked out of the room and out of her house. Pamela had not told him anything he already had not known, either about his brother and his friend or about what he risked.

Fifteen

It was everything Tess had ever dreamed of. Much more, truthfully, because she had never imagined she would be part of such a glittering assembly. The room was grand, from the marble floors polished until they shone like porcelain to the ceiling decorated with friezes highlighted with the same light green as the walls. The draperies at the windows, which must have been more than fifteen feet tall, had been pulled back to fall in elegant folds of a deeper green toward the floor. In the very center of the ceiling, a chandelier with more crystal drops than she could count lit the guests who thronged in glorious white silks and perfectly cut evening coats.

With one hand tucked into Cameron's elbow and the other holding the ivory and silk fan that had been delivered along with her dress, which was a darker shade of emerald than the draperies, Tess took a bolstering breath as he led her into the room. She had not recognized herself when Jenette completed her ministrations, for never had she worn her hair in such ornate curls or had pearls strung through her hair.

Cameron's hand covered hers, and she looked up at him. He was dressed de rigueur in his black coat which was free of any lint, and his white breeches. Yet, she had to own—if only to herself—he looked far more handsome when he was dressed casually while working with his plant samples.

"You have faced worse than this," he said in a hushed voice.

"Have I?"

"You faced me on the morning after our impromptu wedding." He chuckled. "If you can endure that temper, my dear, you can endure this evening, when everyone will be eager to lavish you with compliments."

Startled by the endearment, she blurted, "I do know the difference between Spanish coin and the truth."

" 'Twill be the truth that you are the loveliest woman here tonight."

"A compliment from you, Your Grace?" That was the wrong thing to say she realized when his smile vanished. Quickly she added, "Cameron, you must not flinch each time someone calls you that."

"Nor must you."

"I shall try not to."

His thumb brushed her chin, tipping it up to see he was once again smiling. "I have seen how hard you try, Tess. Tonight, while you bewitch those around us, I hope to find information on the very devil who was involved in my brother's death."

Tess quickly discovered Cameron meant just what he had said. He wandered about the room, introducing her to so many people she could not sort out the litany of names. His conversation always focused on those who were owed money by his brother. Amazed at how many among the *ton* had lent funds to the duke, she worked to keep a smile in place. This was not the evening she had dreamed of, when she would be dancing in Cameron's arms, but she was fascinated to listen to how he allowed the other men to bring up the subject of his brother and his brother's debts.

When she heard a familiar laugh behind her, Tess could

not keep from tensing. She heard Cameron greet Eustace Knox with obvious enthusiasm. Wishing she could devise a way to excuse herself from this conversation, she was dismayed to hear Cameron say, "Do me a favor, old chap, and bring Tess something to drink. I fear we have both talked ourselves quite dry."

"Cameron—"

He silenced her by squeezing her hand, which he withdrew from his arm. "Pardon me, my dear, while I speak to a gentleman who has been anxiously awaiting the chance to talk with me all evening." He pushed his way through the crowd ringing the floor, where some of the guests were dancing to the music provided by the orchestra set in an alcove to one side of the room.

Eustace halted a passing servant and handed Tess a glass of wine from the tray the man carried. "You look lovely this evening, Your Grace."

"Thank you." She knew she had no choice but to be friendly to Cameron's tie-mate.

And Cameron was right. How could she place all the blame at Mr. Knox's feet? Her father could have halted the wedding, too, if he had not been as drunk as the other men. Her fingers closed tightly on the stem of the crystal glass. Now that she knew Cameron better, she realized being drunk as an emperor was not customary for him. She wondered why he had drunk himself nearly into oblivion that night. Another question that seemed to have no answer, because he could not tell her. Could Mr. Knox?

Her smile became more sincere. "I suppose it would not be proper to reply that you look quite well yourself."

He laughed. "With comments like that, you are certain to win the attention of every man in this room."

"That is not my intention."

" 'Tis only one man's attention you wish to garner, I collect."

Tess knew she should be circumspect. "It is a wife's place to think only of her husband's attentions."

"That does not sound like you."

"What? I am his wife, and I should not—"

Taking her arm, Eustace drew her toward the back corner of the room. "Do not mistake my observation for something it was not meant to be. I simply am amazed you would be so docile in the pursuit of what you want. You are your father's daughter, after all."

"That sounds like an insult."

"Quite the contrary. I admire your father's determination to get what he believes is his due, Tess. I trust I may address you so informally now that you are my friend's wife." He rested his elbow on a mantel above an unlit hearth. "We might as well call each other by our given names, as we shall be seeing much of each other in the years to come."

"Yes."

"So Cameron has given up the silly idea of trying to put an end to your marriage?"

Making her face a mask to hide her true reaction, she said, "It is not a matter of which we speak any longer." She hoped Eustace would continue the conversation in such a way that she could be honest and still not embarrass her husband.

Her hope was dashed when he chuckled. "Does that mean we shall soon be hearing an announcement of an heir to his title?"

"That will happen when it happens."

He smiled and leaned toward her. "There is a wager among many of us at the club that the first will be born before the year's end."

"But that would have meant that before the wedding I—" She raised her fan as a shield between them. Looking at him over it as she wafted it gently, she said, "I collect you have put an end to such absurd gossip."

"Why should I when I can take wagers they have no chance of winning?" He laughed, then choking, began to cough.

Tess pressed her glass into his hand, but he continued to cough as if something was jammed in his throat. She held up the glass to him, tipping it so he could drink without any wine spilling down his waistcoat.

"Are you all right?" she asked when he ceased coughing.

"More," he whispered.

She complied, again holding the glass to his lips. She saw heads turning toward them, but she concentrated on helping him drink enough to ease the cough. "Mayhap, Eustace," she said as she drew it back, "you should take care with what you are prattling about. Your own sense of fair play may have made it impossible for you to swallow your words about a bet you cannot help but win."

"I am doing the wise thing." He tapped her nose and smiled when she pulled back, shocked, at his outrageous motion, which suggested she was no older than Donald. "You should consider doing the same thing, Tess."

"Thank you. I shall." Shoving the glass into his hand, she crossed the ballroom. What an obnoxious man! Even being loyal to a friend was not reason enough for Cameron to insist on her enduring Eustace Knox's company.

Where was Cameron? In the press of the guests in the huge room she had not guessed would become so crowded, she could not see him. She paused, knowing she could wander about for the rest of the evening and not find him in this ballroom. Closing her eyes, she tried to listen for his voice. Other conversations pummeled her, but she sifted through them.

"Your Grace, I do hope I am not intruding."

She affixed a smile in place as she turned to see a dark-haired woman she did not know. "No, you are not."

"I have so wanted to meet you. I am—"

A man grasped Tess's hand and bowed over it, tearing her attention from the woman as he began to gush compliments. Before Tess could even reply, another man pushed forward to kiss her hand—rather too warmly, she thought as she extracted it from his grip. His name went unheard as well when a second woman, wearing even more jewelry than the first, began to prattle.

She knew each of them hoped to make a favorable impression on the newest Duchess of Hawkington, and she could not ease away when she was surrounded. It was, she decided, going to be a long evening.

Tess sighed with relief when she tossed her shawl onto a chair in the parlor. "Why didn't you warn me, Cameron?"

"About what?"

"About how tiring a soirée could be."

He drew off his coat and put it atop her shawl on the chair. "You would not have heeded me."

"If—"

"Do not lather me with nothing-sayings, Tess. Have you ever heeded anything I have said to you?"

She was taken aback by his tone. The only word she could think to describe it was surly. Mayhap he was as exhausted as she was, because she had not had a moment to herself the whole evening. Nor, she realized thinking back on it, had she had more than a few minutes with Cameron.

"I have tried to listen to any good counsel you have offered me," she retorted, knowing she should hold her tongue, but too fatigued to care just now. "The only thing you said to me was to bewitch—yes, that was your exact word—the guests so you might find out more about what had happened to Russell."

"Which you succeeded in doing."

"Thank you."

"*That* I did not mean as a compliment." He walked across the room as if he could not bear to be close to her. "Mayhap you do not know, because you were so busy chatting, but many of the guests were discussing why you and my best friend were whispering so close together in a corner when we are so newly married."

"What?" She searched her mind, then said, "Oh, you must mean when Eustace was coughing, and I offered him my wine."

"Was that all you offered him?"

She abruptly despised his unemotional voice. He was angry. Why didn't he just show it? Determined he would not best her at this game of wills, she said, "You denied once that you would be a jealous husband, Cameron. It seems you were wrong."

"Pointing a finger at me does not lessen your unthinking actions."

"Would you have rather I let your friend choke to death?" She shook her head. "Cameron, what is wrong with you? This is not like you. After all, you asked Eustace to get me something to drink while you spoke with someone about your brother."

"True. I have allowed your flirtations to unsettle me far more than I should."

"I was not flirting with Eustace Knox!"

"Mayhap not, but it appeared to too many of the guests that you were. Whether you were or not is now irrelevant." He combed his fingers back through his hair. "By the elevens, Tess, I thought you said you were aware of the vagaries of the *ton* and what you must do to avoid creating gossip about yourself—and your husband by association—that tarnishes your reputation."

"Reputation? Worrying about my reputation led to this catastrophe. If I had not cared so much about my reputation and feared I would be ruined, destroying any chance for a happy life, I would have tossed you out of my father's house as well as my bed."

"Tess," he said in a low growl, "take care what you say."

"Why? What worse can befall us than has already?" She swallowed, hard. This was not the way her first night among the *ton* was supposed to end. She had imagined them coming back here and sitting and laughing together about the odd things the guests had said and done. And then she would have slipped into his arms and . . . she choked back a sob. "I wish I had remained in the country with Papa."

"You are free to leave." He gestured toward the door. "Hurry yourself back to your father's house, if you wish."

"And?"

"Stay there until you can speak without such hysteria."

Tess scowled and muttered an oath that would have earned her a reprimand from Papa if he had chanced to hear it, although she had heard him speak it more than once. She was not hysterical. She was the one who was remaining calm through this brangle. Cameron may not have raised his voice, but he was being irrational.

"That is kind of you, Cameron," she said, fighting to keep her voice even. "However, who will tend to the children if I leave?"

"You have hired Mrs. Detloff."

"You cannot mean that! You were displeased your brother left his children with only servants to supervise their upbringing." She frowned. "I did not think you would be as selfish as Russell."

"Are you going to resort to name-calling now?"

"No." She shoved his coat aside and picked up her shawl. "I am going to put an end to this conversation now before I say something that will only add to your childish fury."

"Childish?"

"Yes." She should not have said that, but she would not retract it.

Cameron bit back the words he wanted to speak, both the angry ones and the hurt ones. He longed to believe Tess when she said her actions had been misconstrued, for she had never given him cause to distrust her.

She is her father's daughter. How many times had he heard that tonight? He had not guessed how many people abhorred Bernard Masterson. More than one had expressed curiosity about how Masterson had persuaded Cameron to wed his daughter. Others had looked hastily away at the question, clearly uncomfortable.

"If you have nothing more to say," Tess said primly, "then I bid you good night."

"Tess . . ."

She gazed at him with a warmth in her eyes that belied the venom in her voice. If he raised his arms, would she walk into them? And then what? Surrendering to his craving for her would complicate the situation even further.

"Good night," he replied.

He listened to her steps flying up the stairs and cursed himself. He had seen the tears in her eyes. Blast it! He did not want to hurt her, either, but she was no longer satisfied with this mockery of a marriage.

Neither was he. He wanted more. He wanted *her!* Every inch of him ached with the need for this beautiful, passionate woman who dared him to unleash his own passions.

Angrily, he reached for the bottle of wine on the sideboard and emptied what was left into a glass. He swallowed it in one gulp, then asked himself for what must be the hundredth time why he baited her when he wanted to enjoy her company. Honesty told him he feared if he let her too close, he would lose his self-control. Then all the emotions he kept restrained would break free. And then . . .

He reached for the bellpull and jerked it so hard it nearly ripped from the wall. Too much of him had urged him to go to her and to tell her of the dreams that woke him at night with the longing to have her in his arms.

Only one thing would dissolve thoughts of her from his mind. When Harbour entered the parlor, Cameron snapped a series of orders. The butler stared before nodding and walking out of the room, and Cameron knew his majordomo was amazed at what had been ordered.

Cameron shrugged and went to sit by the window that overlooked the street. It was going to be a long night.

It was not sunshine that awoke Tess, for the draperies remained drawn. The room was bathed in a soft, golden glow that filtered through the heavy bed curtains. Its warmth was like a gentle caress against her. Not enough to bring her fully awake, but enough to warn that a sunny day waited on the other side of the window.

Lost in the twilight between night and the morning, she wished she could return to sleep. There, in her dreams, she could be dancing with Cameron and could pretend her heart's hopes would not be dashed. He had been everything she had longed for in a suitor last night . . . until they had separated at the gathering. If she concentrated on his kindness, she did not have to think of his sarcasm. Nestling the remnants of her loving fantasies around her, she snuggled under the covers.

The need to sneeze intruded. She willed the irritation to vanish. Anything she did might sever the thread holding her to that oh-so-fleeting happiness. When the itch became unbearable, she reached up to rub her nose. Her fingers touched skin . . . that was not hers.

Her eyes flew open. Only her hand over her mouth muted her gasp.

Cameron!

What was he doing *here?*

His head was on the pillow. His eyes were closed, and he breathed slowly, deep in sleep. A night's growth of beard outlined his strong jaw, which rested against her head. Her own cheek was lying on his shoulder.

His naked shoulder!

She stared across the breadth of his chest and the muscles that had been hinted at beneath his shirt. Her fingers splayed across that strong warmth before she could halt herself. He mumbled something in his sleep, and she froze.

How could he say what he had last night and then come here like this? If he had intended to seduce her, why hadn't he awakened her instead of falling asleep at her side? If she did not know better, she would swear he was insane.

She tried to edge away so she could think more clearly. The masculine scent of his skin unsettled her more than she wanted to own. Her nightgown cut into her neck. A quick tug revealed the distressing truth. Cameron was lying atop one side of her nightgown, securing it to the bed.

Gently she shook his shoulder. "Cameron, wake up!"

He opened one eye a meager slit. His arm encircled her shoulders and drew her against his enticing chest. "Hush, sweetheart. Have sympathy for a man who drank too much last night." He tilted her face toward him.

She gasped in astonishment and undeniable pleasure as his lips traveled along her cheek to nibble on her earlobe. She stiffened for the shortest second, but her longings betrayed her, and her arms slid up his back to enjoy each sinew. He claimed her lips, and his tongue darted between them to explore anew the pleasure within her mouth. The brush of his skin against hers created a yearning that ached to the very center of her soul. She wanted his lips on her, and his body firm against her, softening her with the heated fire of his kisses.

Her fingers sifted up through his hair as his mouth moved away from hers, down over her chin and along the lace on her nightgown. His kisses seared away the linen as if it did not exist. The hard line of his body pinned her to the bed as he pressed her more deeply into the pillows. Each motion brushed her against him, burnishing her with desire. She grasped his face and brought his lips back to hers.

The bed bounced once, then a second time. A finger tapped her shoulder as a young voice asked, "Can we see Heddy now?"

Tess turned her face to see Philip's eager smile. The little boy was kneeling beside her. Donald was tugging on his brother's shirt, but the younger boy paid him no attention.

"Can we see Heddy now?" Philip asked again as Cameron was turning her face toward his.

"Yes," she whispered, edging away as far as she could from Cameron and taking care not to look back at him. Realizing that the top buttons of her nightgown were undone, she grasped the loosened bodice close to her. "Quiet now, and do not wake her if she is already asleep."

"If she isn't?" Philip asked.

"You can take her cage out into the other room and give her something to eat from the container by her cage. Just take care you do not let her out."

With a whoop, the two boys ran to the table and looked under the cloth. Heddy must have been awake, because they carried the cage and the glass jar into the sitting room.

"Tess?" Cameron croaked in disbelief, as if seeing her for the first time.

"You must leave! Please!" She tried to slide farther away, but could not. "You have to move off my night-gown."

"What are you doing here?" His bewilderment was evident.

"Me?" she squeaked. As he frowned, she lowered her voice to a whisper. She did not want to chance calling the boys back in here. "Cameron, why are *you* here? The door to the hall—"

"I know. You lock it every night."

"You have tried before this to . . ." She could only stare at him.

"Do not be absurd! I do not sneak about in my own house like a thief." He leaned back into the pillows and closed his eyes. "Harbour thought I would want to know."

"So how did you get in here?"

"The only other way is through the connecting door in the dressing room between these rooms and the ones I have been using." He put his hands over his eyes and groaned. "I had a lot, a very lot, to drink with Eustace after you stormed out."

"Eustace was here?"

"Yes. He thought I might want to be reassured my wife was not a coquette dallying with him last night. He brought a bottle of his best brandy to share. I remember only wanting to get to bed and sleep it off. I do not remember seeing you here."

"Is this a habit with you?"

"No." Looking out from beneath his hands, he said, "I know you have no reason to believe that, but I can assure you it is true. I am customarily very prudent about the amount I drink. I had planned to be last night, for I asked Harbour to bring me coffee, enough for the whole night, if necessary." His forehead furrowed. "Odd, I do not recall having more than a glass or two with Eustace last night after you stormed out."

Tess reached for her wrapper, but her hand was captured by Cameron's broad fingers. Stretching out her other hand, she grabbed her wrapper and flung it over her shoulders. He yelped, and she knew it must have struck him in the face. She started to slide out of bed, but his arm encircled her waist, pulling her back.

"Stop!" she gasped. "This is the time to keep all such thoughts under your girdle."

He laughed without humor. "An odd choice of words, Tess." He released her as if he abruptly could not tolerate being near her.

She wanted to take back the words that had been aimed at his most vulnerable spot. Those words had been the very best way to guarantee she would drive him away.

And she had succeeded, for he sat and stretched, showing off far more of his muscular body than she had ever seen. Although she should have looked away, she could not help admiring his virile lines.

"Will you please go?" she whispered, unsure how long she could govern her longing and keep from touching him.

"Are you sure that is what you want?" he asked, leaning toward her.

She shrank back into the pillows, suddenly overwhelmed by his strength so close to her. "What I want? How can you ask that? If—"

Donald ran back into the room and cried, "Aunt Tess, come and tell Philip he should not be trying to touch Heddy."

"You tell him to do as he should," Cameron replied.

The little boy nodded, wide-eyed.

"And I should do the same," Cameron continued, standing and reaching for his shirt to tuck into his breeches.

Tess sat, drawing up her knees. She folded her arms on top of them. Was Cameron waiting for her to say something? If she told him the truth, that she loved him, she wondered if he would rush away or draw her near.

The delighted shouts from the boys in the other room filled the silence before Cameron said, "We need to speak, Tess."

"At breakfast might be wiser."

"Yes."

She hated when they spoke like polite strangers, but she only nodded. He held her gaze, then left. Hearing him talking to the boys, who were laughing with delight, she knew she should be pleased. She had hoped Donald and Philip would get over their awe of their uncle, and Cameron would come to see them as something other than a burden.

With a wry smile, she slid off the bed. She must not become so dreary that she ignored the serendipitous joys. She rang for Jenette.

As her abigail came into the room, Tess's eyes alighted on a man's dress collar by the bed. Cameron must have dropped it there last night. She forced an innocuous expression onto her face as she kicked the collar beneath the bed. Mayhap Jenette had not noticed it. Now was not the time for her abigail's questions when she had so many of her own.

She had no need to worry, because Jenette could not keep from talking about how Park had taken her for a walk last evening. Although Tess should caution her abigail about being alone with Cameron's valet, she simply listened until Jenette had finished brushing her hair and tying it back with a ribbon that matched Tess's light green gown.

Tess had Donald bring Heddy's cage back into her room, then took the boys to a second breakfast-parlor, which had been set up for the children soon after the boys' arrival. It was a sunny room decorated in yellow. A small table was adorned with flowers and waiting dishes. On the sideboard, breakfast steamed, announcing its recent arrival from the kitchen.

Harbour greeted them with his usual smile as he motioned to the footmen to serve them a generous portion of the eggs, sausage, and muffins. Yet when she glanced at him when he thought she was not, she could see his smile waver. How much did the servants know of what had happened less than an hour ago?

While the boys talked, Tess sipped her coffee. Her thoughts were confused and contradictory. Her breakfast went untouched. Her accusation to Cameron could have been aimed at herself. His touch had teased her to lose control. It scared her she had been so ready to succumb to his seduction when he still spoke of their marriage as something that would not last. She had let herself be trapped in his embrace, where he smothered her with sweet words and honeyed caresses. She should have tried to escape, but she did not want to and now it might be too late to salvage her heart without damaging it.

She had fallen in love with this man who had made every effort to make her despise him. He might be cantankerous and as set in his ways as an old tough, but she could not deny Pamela Livingstone had been correct. Within him beat a kind heart that had prevented him from doing the sensible thing and denouncing her in a divorce petition.

She glanced at the boys who were now giggling over a joke. Cameron had opened his home to two little boys who complicated his life even more. Others would have turned away these children, who had no legitimate claim on the Hawksmoor name, but he had not.

Hands settled on her shoulders, and a sensation like a bolt of lightning cut through her, bringing her upright in her chair. She fought her desire to respond to the sensuality Cameron wrought in her with even such a chaste motion. Her fingers curled into fists as she struggled to rule her recalcitrant body.

Her dismay deepened when she saw Eustace come into the breakfast-parlor. She had not guessed he had stayed in the house overnight. If he had gone to Cameron's rooms, he would have known Cameron was not in them early this morning. She took a sip of her coffee and told herself not to panic. Eustace's eyes were droopy, suggesting he had just gotten out of bed.

"Good morning . . . again," Cameron said in a near whisper as Eustace lumbered to where the newspaper was set on the table. "I would have been down sooner, but I had to send Park to retrieve my missing collar, and I believe he took advantage of the opportunity to flirt with your abigail."

"I am glad someone has benefitted from . . ." She glanced at Eustace.

The footmen waited until Cameron sat. Then one placed a cup of coffee in front of him. He did not seem to hear when a maid asked what he would like for breakfast.

"You must be hungry, Cameron," Tess said. "Can I have them fix you a plate of breakfast?" Her words sounded foolish, but she had to say something.

He looked up, startled. "Yes, thank you. Eustace, do not lurk over there. Sit and eat with us."

"You are still in an atrocious mood this morning," his friend replied. "I had not thought you could be in a worse one than you were last night."

Cameron waved aside his words as he stirred cream into his cup. "Forget last night. It is over." He glanced at Tess as he added, "I want to forget everything about it."

Eustace seemed to take the order to heart, because he began to read the newspaper, aloud when he found what he clearly considered an interesting tidbit of poker-talk. If he noticed Tess said nothing, not even chiding him for his inappropriate comments when the boys were eagerly listening, he did not let it show.

Cameron had told her they would talk at breakfast, but there was no need. He had already made up his mind to pretend nothing unusual had happened. Mayhap he could. She feared she could not any longer.

Sixteen

The tavern was in a section of London where the *ton* did not openly venture. That was why Cameron had disguised himself in clothes he had had his valet obtain from a cart not far from this place. If Park had been curious why Cameron wanted this ragged wool coat and the breeches with no buttons at the knees, the valet kept his questions to himself.

Cameron ignored the odors that reeked in every direction. The narrow street was shadowed by the buildings, which leaned over it as if they intended to meet. A single cart was being pulled along the street by a horse so thin every bone was revealed.

Ducking into the tavern marked by a sign stripped of any color by years of fog and smoke, he sat on a bench close to the door. Another man was perched on the bench and eyed him with a derisive grin.

"Fine day fer a glass of ale, eh?" asked the man.

Cameron motioned to the barman. Two mugs of ale were brought. Setting his on the thick windowsill, he watched the other man take an appreciative drink. His own head still recalled the thud left by the brandy he had used to ease his unhappiness two nights ago with Eustace. This cheap ale might bring that pain right back.

"Ye be wantin' t'talk to someone?" asked the man.

Cameron nodded. Just opening his mouth would betray his origins. He could try to ape this man's vulgar speech, but the ears of this section of London would note any error he made.

"I 'ear ye be lookin' for me, Yer Grace."

Cameron looked over his shoulder and saw another man. Rising, he went to a table and gestured toward the bench across from him. The man who slipped around the table with the grace of an alley cat appeared as out of place in this low tavern as Cameron did. His clothes were clean and free of patches. No beard hid his face, and a pair of glasses perched on the very edge of his nose.

"If you have the information I am seeking," Cameron said quietly, "then you are the man I am looking for."

"Ye be a mutton'ead to be pokin' yer nose where it don't belong." He rubbed his chin, and Cameron noted the man was missing two fingers on his hand. The man glanced at his hand and grinned, revealing ragged teeth. "Could spin ye a tale of wot 'appens to them that pokes their noses into other's business."

"I know about that already. What I wish to know is any information you have about the carriage accident that killed my brother."

"And m'sister."

"Isabel van der Falloon was your sister?"

"Jes said so, didn't I?" He pulled a cigar from beneath his dark waistcoat and lit it with an ember from the fireplace. "Isa always 'ad plans to raise 'erself above 'er station. She got 'er chance when 'Is Grace lit eyes on 'er. She was a fine-looking woman."

"And generous."

"To 'er family, yes."

"And you expect the van der Falloon family—"

The man laughed around his cigar.

Cameron gave him a wry grin. He had known van der Falloon must be a name concocted by Russell's last mistress, but he had become accustomed to thinking of her by that name. Picking up his ale, he said, "You expect *your* family to be given some sort of settlement that will ease your grief at losing her and the income she would have obtained from my brother when he set her aside."

"Thought ye'd understand."

"I do." He dropped the small purse on the table. "Five crowns in there, my good man. Yours to ease your grief when you have eased my curiosity."

" 'Bout the so-called accident?"

"Yes. What you told my friends at Bow Street suggested you had some knowledge of who might have been involved in the so-called accident."

"I do."

"So why are you seeking me out instead of telling the Runner? Other than for the money, of course."

"Of course." The man grinned through the rancid clouds of cheap cigar smoke.

"Why haven't you dealt with these chaps yourself? This loss of your sister has cost you dearly."

" 'Cause it ain't wise fer a man to put 'is nose where it don't belong."

"So you have said."

"And my nose don't belong in the Polite World."

Cameron sat straighter. "Polite World? Are you saying there was more to this than a botched robbery?"

"Aye." He rubbed his chin again, and Cameron wondered if the man had shaved just for this meeting. Not an unwise move, for the man could regrow his beard, and Cameron would never be able to find him again. Many men along the docks were missing fingers.

"Go on."

"Five crowns ain't a lot, Yer Grace."

"It will be double that, if you have proof of your extraordinary claim."

"I do."

Cameron listened, growing more amazed with every word the man spoke. The man did not embroider the tale. The simple recitation of the facts were even more horrific. Two men he knew had been paid well—"by a gentleman"—to make certain the duke and his mistress never reached his town house that afternoon.

It was, he realized, going to be far more complicated than he had guessed.

The house was so quiet Tess could hear the servants speaking in the kitchen as she passed the stairs. Mrs. Detloff had taken the boys to Green Park for an outing, as always with her brightly colored basket filled with toys and tidbits to make all sorts of paper toys. Harbour was overseeing the polishing of the silver. He had told Tess that Cameron would be returning in time for dinner. No other explanation, which told Tess that Cameron must be in pursuit of the truth about his brother's death.

She kneaded her hands. What would he do if he found proof of treachery? Or if he found none and had to accept that it was simply a horrendous accident? Then he would have to turn his attention to his obligations as the Duke of Hawkington, and that included obtaining an heir.

A quiver rushed through her, but she shook it aside when she noticed a motion in the parlor. Was Cameron back? She paused in the open door. Her voice came out in a squeak as she recognized the woman rising from a chair. "Mrs. Livingstone?"

The lovely blonde turned and smiled. "Your butler is very efficient to find you so quickly, Your Grace."

"Yes." She did not want to own she had stumbled upon Mrs. Livingstone.

"Forgive me for calling again, but I thought it imperative we speak."

"Is something amiss?" She bit back her ironic laugh.

It would be more accurate to ask if anything *else* was amiss.

"I assume you know Cameron called at my house recently."

Tess's hands clenched at her sides. "No, I was not aware of that, but he has assured me, as you have, that you remain friends." She forced her fingers to unbend so she could motion for the other woman to sit.

Mrs. Livingstone's face lightened with relief as she sat next to Tess on a settee. Grasping Tess's hand, she said, "He called on me because he was upset about some words you had exchanged."

"He told you of that?"

"Not outright, but I know him well enough to know what is distressing him."

"Me!"

"Yes, you." Mrs. Livingstone smiled. "Do not look so grim. You are not directly the cause of his distress. *He* is creating it by refusing to acknowledge the truth—that he is falling in love with you."

"Absurd!" Tess surged to her feet, unable to sit when her heart was leaping with joy. Silly joy, for the very idea Cameron would fall in love with a woman he had married by mistake was ludicrous.

"Is it? You are in love with him, aren't you?"

"I don't know."

Mrs. Livingstone chuckled softly. "No wonder the two of you are upsetting each other so. You are very much alike." She held up her hands as Tess started to retort. "You may argue with me as much as you like, but you cannot deny the truth. You are as stubborn as Cameron, and you are as intelligent, save about the matters of your hearts. Like him, you will not own when you have made a mistake, even when conceding you have would bring you great joy."

"I should not be speaking of this with you."

"Quite true, and I did not come here to discuss this with you. I came here to urge you to speak honestly to Cameron. He is, as you said, someone I consider a friend. I believe you and I could have been friends, too, if circumstances had been different."

Threading her fingers together, Tess said, "That may be true, but as someone who knows Cameron well, you must know he will do everything he can to avoid acknowledging his emotions."

"That was never an issue between us. Cameron asked for no emotional connection with me." She put her hands on Tess's. "But he has fashioned one with you. I can see you have reached a part of him he has not shared with anyone." Her smile became sad. "Not even with me, to own the truth."

"Yes, I have infuriated him beyond anyone else."

"You are helping him to stop being afraid."

Tess stared at her. "Afraid? Cameron is not afraid. I have seen the medal he was awarded for bravery at Waterloo."

"I am not speaking of bravery on the battlefield, but the courage to dare to feel what is in one's heart. Cameron so longs to be the man he believes his father was, always in control of himself and never making a misstep." She smiled as she folded her hands in her lap. "Then he makes the greatest one a man like him can make. He not only marries, but he marries a woman who refuses to let him hide behind the delusion he can leash his emotions, a woman who so revels in every emotion that she cannot curb her feelings, a woman who challenges him to be as open."

"Cameron does not wish to change."

"What man does?" Mrs. Livingstone laughed lightly. "But you *have* changed him by making him question his assumption his father's way is the best one for him." Coming to her feet, she said, "Promise me that you will continue in this direction, Your Grace. Cameron deserves that."

"I will consider what you have said."

"Consider it well, for it may be your only route to making your marriage a success."

When she heard familiar footfalls, Tess looked up to see Cameron by her sitting room door. He motioned toward where she was sitting and asked, "May I?"

"Please come in." She hoped he did not hear how her heart started beating like a wild bird trying to escape from a snare. When he closed the door behind him, her breath seemed unwilling to move out of her chest.

Her fantasy that he would rush to her and sweep her up into his arms and carry her to the privacy of her bed-chamber was dashed when he said, "Sir Walter Long has sent this invitation to enjoy some musical selections this evening." He offered the slip of ivory paper to her. "I thought you would find it amusing."

"You wish me to go to this musicale with you?" she asked as she merely glanced at the invitation. If she had met Sir Walter Long at the assembly, she could not recall either his name or his face.

"Yes."

She could not halt the question that burst from her lips. "But why? After what happened when we went out among the Polite World last time—"

"It is because of that mix-up that it is imperative you join me tonight. We must assure everyone you are not having an *affaire* with my good friend."

"I will not speak with him unless you are present." She came to her feet. "Even if he is choking in front of me, I shall not offer him my glass without your permission."

She thought she saw his lips twitch, but she must have

been wrong because he said, "I have learned you cannot keep your emotions in check."

"You have no idea how many I do!"

"Mayhap, but that could mean you are hiding your true feelings for Eustace."

"You think I have a *tendre* for Eustace Knox?" she gasped. "Are you mad?"

"It might be the most brilliant solution I can imagine, save that there must be no question the heir to my father's title is my son, not someone else's."

"You *are* mad!" She stared at him. "Or is this your attempt to drive me into another man's arms so you can return to the arms of your mistress?"

"Both Pamela and I have told you that our *affaire* is over."

"She is not the only woman in London. If you have found another—"

"Tess, you know I am searching only for the answers to Russell's death."

"Then why are you pelting me with questions about your friend and me?"

"Because I want you to know what you will be facing tonight."

Tess's shoulders eased from their angry tension. Knowing she might be risking seeing his face lose all emotion as he shut her out again, she stepped closer to him and put her hand on his shoulder. He placed his own hand on hers.

"I will be able to handle any comments fired at me tonight," she said softly, "if I know you do not believe any of them."

"Are you asking if I trust you?"

She wanted to argue that she was asking if he loved her, but she said, "Yes."

"My answer is the same as yours, Tess. Yes, I do trust you." He lifted her hand from his shoulder and pressed his mouth to it. When her breath sifted past her parted lips, he smiled. "You need never ask that again, for I would not reveal to you all I have learned today if I did not trust you completely."

As he shared what he had found out in the tavern, Pamela Livingstone's comments echoed in Tess's head. Should Tess believe what her husband's former mistress had told her? Was it possible Cameron was more intrigued with Tess than he had been with any woman? His trust in her seemed to confirm that, but she must not allow her eager heart to betwattle her. He was speaking of camaraderie while she longed to hear him speak of love. As well, he was speaking of a duplicity she had not suspected could exist.

"If you ask questions," she said, giving voice to her fears, "you could be refocusing upon you the fury of whoever had your brother murdered."

"I cannot let the mastermind behind this evil plot go unpunished. I must know the truth, and for that I need your help." He folded her hands between his. "You have been more than patient with me, Tess."

"Patient?"

"With my ignoring how I would find a way to end our marriage as I had promised you."

She could not answer. She had not guessed that he would speak of this *now*. Despite his words to Eustace, she had hoped Cameron would have changed his mind about their marriage. She recalled again, as she had not in days, the slip of Mr. Paige's letterhead that Cameron had had in his account book. Had he been figuring how to pay for a divorce? The cost would be high, even for a duke.

"First I must discover what really happened when Russell died," Cameron continued, and she guessed he had not taken note of her despair. "Once I have done that, then we shall take a look at the future. Is that agreeable?"

"Yes," she said, although she wanted to shout *no!* "You need not worry about me tonight, Cam."

"What did you call me?" he asked, astonishment filling his voice.

"Cam. It is what the boys call you, and I fear I have let their habit become mine." Again she did not add the whole truth. It was simple to think of him as Cameron when he kept that wall between them. When he lowered it, even a single brick, this name had seemed so natural on her lips. "I apologize if you find it distasteful."

"Quite to the contrary, for it is the way my father always addressed me. I had forgotten that until just now." He squeezed her hands gently. "Thank you for reminding me of that, Tess."

She smiled for only a moment, then said, "You can trust me tonight, Cam. I will not heed any insinuations about me and Eustace," she said as she watched his finger glide along hers.

"Made by others?"

"Will *you* be making insinuations?"

"Not about you."

"Only in search of the truth about Russell?" she asked.

"Yes."

"Cam, tell me if there is any way I can help."

"There is." He tugged her against him, his lips on hers. Sweeping her fingers up through his hair, she savored the firm lines of his body . . . for as long as she could. The questions he would ask tonight might be as dangerous as anything he had faced at Waterloo, because he had no idea who his enemy was.

Seventeen

Cameron pulled his gaze away from his wife, who was listening to the music with an enrapt expression. He had planned to look around the room while he considered which one of the guests might be an appropriate one to speak to. The man who had arranged for his brother's death could be among the guests, but Cameron must not tip his hand before he had some information to point him toward his prey.

Tonight could be the night that would bring him the answers he sought, but he was unable to concentrate on his hunt for the truth. Instead he kept watching Tess. He had not guessed she had such an appreciation for music.

When she glanced at him and smiled, his lips rose to return her warm expression. He had been congratulated again and again tonight on his good fortune in marrying such a pretty woman, even though he had seen some brittle smiles when he mentioned her maiden name.

"Isn't that lovely?" she whispered as the orchestra paused before the next part of the selection.

"Very."

"Whom do you plan to speak to first?"

"Our host." He could not add more as the conductor raised his baton and set the percussionist to a flurry of drumming.

When her fingers brushed his arm, he put his hand over them, holding them to his sleeve. He wished this program could last for the rest of the evening so he could sit here with Tess close as the music enveloped them.

Cameron silenced his sigh as he applauded when the conductor lowered his baton for the last time. He came to his feet. Tess looked up at him and smiled before turning back to listen to Lady Peake, who was expounding on each piece of music they had heard. From experience, he knew the white-haired lady would keep Tess busy long enough for him to ask Sir Walter Long the questions that might get him the information he needed.

Tess wanted to wish Cameron good luck in his search for answers, but she listened to Lady Peake, who was disappointed that her favorite music from Mozart had not been played. The performance tonight had been more wonderful than Tess had imagined. The melodies had been sweet and Cameron's touch even more so.

"You two ladies seem to have enjoyed this evening's entertainment." Eustace bowed over Lady Peake's hand. "You are looking quite enthralled, my lady." His smile broadened as he took Tess's hand and raised it to his lips. "And you look absolutely luminous, my dear Tess."

"Thank you." She pulled her hand away. Surely Cameron had spoken to him about the perils of flirting like this. If not, she must set him straight with all speed.

"Can I hope it is because you soon will have excellent news to share with all of us?"

"That, sir, is none of your bread-and-butter."

"Listen to the Town cant," he said with a broad smile. "Yet you are being a country bumpkin, Tess. Such matters of heirs are spoken of candidly among the *ton.*"

"Mayhap, but not by me. It is no one's business but Cam's and mine what takes place within the private regions of our house."

She heard Lady Peake's sharp intake of breath. Curse Eustace!

Standing, she said, "I think you—" A motion beyond him caught her eye. "Papa!" Tess hated how her voice came out in a squeak. "What are you doing here? You should have let us know you were coming to Town."

He gave her a kiss on the cheek. He was dressed in perfect style, looking as if he often called upon friends among the Polite World. "My dear daughter, it would appear marriage is a happy state for you. Knox is correct. You are positively glowing."

"Thank you." She smiled. "Do you know Lady Peake, Papa?"

"Papa?" Lady Peake extended only the tips of her fingers, surprising Tess, because the lady had been more than welcoming to her. "I did not realize the duchess is *your* daughter, Mr. Masterson."

"Yes," he said, "my daughter is now a duchess. It is amazing how the fates unfold, is it not?" He clapped Eustace on the shoulder. "Knox, you are just the man I had hoped to see here tonight. If the duchess and Lady Peake will kindly excuse us . . ."

Tess nodded, fighting the uneasiness in her center at how her father grinned with triumph each time he spoke of the title she had gained when Cameron's brother died. "Papa, how long will you be in Town?"

"Don't worry, Tess," he said, giving her another kiss on the cheek. "We will have plenty of time to enjoy my visit, but for now, I have some business with Mr. Knox."

She clamped her lips closed. Of course Papa had business with Eustace. How could she have forgotten how Cameron's friend was blackmailing her father? She wanted to grasp her father's arms and cry out that he must let her help him. Cameron had such a strong sense of duty to what was right that surely he would help. As a duke, Cameron would have allies to assist Papa in resolving quietly whatever matter Eustace Knox was using to extort money.

Pardoning herself as well, Tess sought Cameron through the crowd discussing the evening's music and the day's gossip. She saw him at the far side of the room. Rushing up to his side, she said, "Cam, I must speak with you at once."

He looked from her to the man he was conversing with. The man was tall and frightfully thin, and she could not recall being introduced to him. With a bow of his head, he said, "I will leave you to your wife, Hawksmoor."

"What is it, Tess?" Cameron asked, tight-lipped. "I thought you understood nothing must get in the way of my conversations this evening."

"My father is here."

"Is that so?" He frowned. "Then why are you not chatting with him while I seek the information I need?"

"Something is not right." The words sounded silly when she could not explain the truth of how Mr. Knox— she could not think of him by his given name, which implied some sort of friendship—was blackmailing Papa.

"You are quite correct about that. Now I see someone I must speak with, so I beg your indulgence to be patient a while longer."

She did not move aside. "Cam, please, there is something you must know."

"What is it? Does it have some impact on the search for answers on my brother's death?"

"No."

"Then it must wait." He added in a gentler voice, "I know it is difficult for you to be patient, Tess, but I promise you it shall not be much longer."

"Promises! I am sick to death of promises!"

"What?" Puzzlement widened his eyes even as his brows lowered.

"You should be, too! How many more promises are you going to make to me that you cannot keep?"

"I have never—"

"To love, honor, and cherish is what you must have promised."

He glanced past her. "Tess, I must speak to Williams before he leaves for the club. I have told you we will resolve this after I have uncovered the truth about Russell." He walked away, catching up with a man who was standing by the door.

She sighed. Why was she trying to rush them into having this discussion? Cameron might be able to learn what had happened with his brother, but she doubted he would come to discover the truth about how much she wished they had met under other circumstances and could have had a chance at a true marriage.

Tess saw her father's eyebrows rise nearly to his hair when she was announced by the butler who had opened the door. She wanted to ask when Papa had hired a butler for a house in Town. She was curious when he had purchased this house on Soho Square, for they had always stayed at her grandmother's house when they came to London. Even more, she longed to know how he could afford the luxury of obviously new furniture and rugs and even artwork when they had been watching every farthing in the country.

Now was not the time for those questions when she had another, far more important one to ask him.

Her father rose from a chair by a white marble hearth and smiled. Taking his pipe from his mouth, he said, "Now it is my turn to be surprised at your call."

Tess ran to his side. "Papa, I am coming to seek your advice. Please help me."

"Help you?" He laughed. "My dear daughter, I cannot

imagine what more you could want. You have a wealthy husband, a lovely home here in London, a fine estate at Peregrine Hall, and you are a duchess."

"Mayhap."

"Mayhap?" He frowned. "What do you mean?"

"I mean I may or may not be a duchess, because the title might not be rightfully Cameron's."

He seized her arm and sat her, rather roughly, on the closest chair. "Are you mad, Tess? Of course the title is his. Once Russell Hawksmoor was dead, your husband assumed the title. There is no one else."

"But there may be."

"Will you explain instead of hinting at the source of this trouble? You have always been so uncommonly concerned with not hurting someone's feelings that you avoid speaking directly."

Tess winced as her father's voice rose to a shout. In the months since she had left his house, she had forgotten how volatile he was. She had not realized it, but she had become accustomed to Cameron's reserve, and she had come to appreciate it.

"Russell left two sons," she said, watching his face closely. She had seen Papa fly off into a pelter over having milk for his tea instead of cream, and she wanted to be prepared for any explosion that might come now. "We believed they were illegitimate."

"He had many mistresses."

"Yes, but he may have had a wife."

"What?" he roared.

She wanted to put her hands over her ears, but she came to her feet. "Papa, I have heard that the mother of the older boy, Donald, may have been Russell's legal wife."

"Nonsense!"

"It is possible. I have sent my abigail to the church where they were supposedly wed to find out if their signatures are in the register there. If they are, Donald may be the legitimate duke."

"Legitimate?" He puffed vehemently on his pipe. "It may be no more than a rumor started by someone who wishes to discredit your husband."

"I trust the one who told me this."

"Who spoke to you of this?"

"One of the servants in the house." She would not tell her father how Jenette had come to her with the information that the servants had been whispering about this since they had talked to people who lived near the house where the boys had been kept until their father's death.

He laughed. "Then it is clearly just poker-talk. I had thought you were wise enough to discount the gossip servants enjoy at the cost of their betters."

"I am, but this has the ring of truth about it. That is why I came to you to ask your advice."

"My advice is to say nothing to your husband about this."

"But, Papa, Cam must be told of the rumors that are being spread."

"No doubt he already knows of them."

"He has said nothing to me."

Her father patted her check as if she were no older than Philip. "My dear child, it is a man's place to keep his family from becoming upset."

Tess bristled in spite of herself. "He has not failed to tell me of other matters I found quite upsetting." Pushing aside her own vexation, she added, "Papa, I cannot fail to tell Cameron about this. If he has *not* heard of it, the ones behind these stories may be working to cause him more trouble. If it is the truth, he must know of it now rather than in the future, when it could be humiliating for him."

"And what if he has heard it and intends to squash this rumor so the title remains his?"

"Then I should help him find out who has started this malicious story that is sure to hurt him and the boys."

"Even if the rumor is true?"

"Yes."

"Ah, I see," her father said with a grimace, "that Town has not changed you. You still are as honest as a parson." He took her elbow and turned her toward the door. "Go home, Tess. I will tend to this."

"How?"

He frowned, clearly vexed she would continue to question him. "I will tend to this, I said, and tend to it I will. You must vow to say nothing to your husband of this."

"I cannot vow that."

"You must!" he shouted. "You may stir up a beehive if you speak out of hand now. You have no idea how many plans you will be upsetting if you prattle."

She almost asked whose plans. Then she halted herself. Papa and Cameron had spoken briefly at the musicale. Mayhap Cameron had told her father of his intention of finding out the truth about the carriage accident. Cameron had learned to trust her, so he could be trusting Papa, too.

"Promise me, Tess," he ordered, his fingers tightening on her arm.

"Yes, Papa." She pulled her arm out of his grasp and went toward the door. Another promise! She had too many of them restraining her as tightly as Cameron held in his feelings, but none of them had felt as wrong as this one.

"Where is Uncle Cam?" asked Donald as he rocked with excitement from one foot to the other.

Tess smiled. It was amazing to think they were becoming a family in spite of themselves.

"I believe," she replied, "he is upstairs in his workroom. He received more plants. Some of them are still living, and he is making sure they are properly watered and getting the right amount of sun."

Philip's nose wrinkled. "That sounds boring."

"It is not for your uncle." She squatted down and adjusted the front of his coat. "Do you have your extra spool of string in case you can get the kite to go extra high today?"

"I will get it," both boys shouted as they ran up the stairs, nearly plowing Mrs. Detloff down. They slowed only a bit when she chided them as her scissors bounced out of her ubiquitous basket.

"They are so excited," Tess said as the governess tied her bonnet securely under her chin. With a steady wind swirling through the square and the sun shining brightly, it was the perfect day for Mrs. Detloff to take them to Hyde Park so they could fly the kites she had had them working on for the past two days.

Mrs. Detloff chuckled. "I hope they will be just as excited if a string breaks and their kite lands in the Serpentine."

"You will have a difficult time keeping them from jumping in after it."

"That is why I am taking a footman with me. Matthew is having the carriage brought around." She paused before adding, "It would be a wise decision to have His Grace purchase a pony cart for the use of the children and me. It is more appropriate than a closed carriage."

"I shall speak to him of it this very afternoon."

"Thank you. I—" She did not get a chance to say more as the boys swooped down the stairs.

Tess laughed as the governess herded them out the door. When she heard a deeper laugh behind her, she turned to face Cameron. Her greeting vanished, unspoken, when she saw how his eyes twinkled. She recognized that expression and exulted in her own delight when his fingers stroked her cheek with fleeting fire. She yearned to grasp them and draw his hand along her in an endless caress.

She stepped away before she could cede herself to the longing to be in his arms. Now, more than ever before, she must resist her desire to delve the depths of the passion they could share. If the rumors about Donald were true, Cameron would no longer be in need of an heir. He might find this marriage very convenient—a wife at home with whom he could discuss his scientific work and a mistress elsewhere with whom he could share his love.

If the rumors about Donald were not true, then—a scream came from the street just outside the door. The shriek from a horse was even louder, but was drowned out by a woman's screech of terror.

"The boys!" Tess cried.

Eighteen

Cameron reached the door before Tess and flung it open. She rushed out past Mrs. Detloff, who was dropping to the steps, senseless. A horse and rider were pausing to look back at a crumpled form in the street.

"Tess, wait!" Cameron shouted.

She ignored him as she raced to the tiny body in the street. Donald! It was Donald! Was he alive or . . . no, she could not even complete the thought. As she knelt beside him, the rider shouted to his mount and was fleeing around the corner. Three footmen gave chase, but they had no chance of catching him.

As Tess knelt by Donald, she put her hand on his back, for he was curled into a ball. "Donald?" she asked, her voice almost breaking on his name.

A hand against her own back told her Cameron was beside her. She did not take her eyes from the little boy, who was slowly raising his head.

"My leg. It hurts," Donald whimpered.

Cameron ran his hands along the little boy's leg. "I do not think it is broken, but a doctor will be able to tell us for certain." He put his arms carefully under the little boy and lifted him off the ground. "You must be more cautious," he said. "Some neck-or-nothing riders will not halt. You must look—"

Donald scowled a youthful version of Cameron's most irritating expression. "I *did* look before I stepped into the street. I am not a baby. I know to be careful."

"Later," Tess said, hushing Philip, who was bouncing from one step to the next, torn between seeing what had happened to his brother and getting help for the most definitely swooned governess. Tears were racing down his cheeks, and there was blood on his right elbow. "Cam, take Donald upstairs please. Harbour, send for a doctor and have someone bring the *sal volatile* to wake Mrs. Detloff." Taking Philip by the hand, she watched as they all went to do as she had requested.

Only then did she look over her shoulder to see the footmen returning. They wore disgusted frowns. When she motioned to the taller one, he walked toward her as the other man hurried to the carriage.

"You are Matthew, correct?" she asked.

"Yes, Yer Grace."

"Mrs. Detloff had you bring the carriage to the front door?"

"Yes, Yer Grace."

Glancing down at Philip, she hesitated. Then, knowing anything Matthew might say could not be worse than what the little boy had witnessed, she said, "Tell me what you saw."

"I didn't see anythin', Yer Grace. That is," he hurried to add when she frowned, "I didn't see anythin' while I was bringin' the carriage 'round. Then, all a sudden, 'e was there."

"Donald?"

"No, Yer Grace. That addle cove came out of nowhere and rode Donald down." He muttered something under his breath, and she guessed she would be wise not to ask him to repeat it. "A brave youngster, Yer Grace. Master Donald got hurt 'cause 'e jumped out to push this cunnin' shaver—" He gave Philip a wink. " 'E pushed Master Philip right away from that crazy rider."

Tess's stomach twisted with fear. Mayhap it was simply a coincidence, but had someone else heard of the rumors that one of these children might be the true heir? "Would you know the rider if you saw him again?"

He shook his head, his smile disappearing. " 'Appened so fast, and I was thinkin' of the lads."

"I am glad to hear that. Thank you, Matthew, for trying to catch that Newgate saint."

"Wish I'd caught 'im. Time 'e learned a thing or two." As she turned, he said, "Yer Grace, 'e was ridin' a gray horse."

"A gray? Are you certain?"

"Aye. Good-lookin' 'orse it was."

Carrying Philip into the house, Tess smiled when she saw Harbour assisting Mrs. Detloff up the stairs. Tess calmed the governess's fears that she would be turned off with a bad character for failing to protect her charges and told Harbour to have some tea and some sweet cakes sent both to Mrs. Detloff's bedchamber and to the room that had become the nursery.

More quickly than Tess would have guessed possible, the doctor had arrived, cleaned the scratches and bruises on Donald's leg, put on a bandage of which the little boy seemed inordinately proud, and taken his leave. Cook must have taken the time to make new chocolate frosting for the cakes for the boys, because there were signs that other frosting had been scraped off before this thick, dark layer was applied.

"You must sit still, Donald," Tess said for what she suspected was the twelfth time as Cameron held his finger to his lip to try to calm Philip. "Even though your leg is not broken, you need to rest."

"Did you see me?" asked Donald, still excited by his

adventure. "I copied Heddy and curled right up into a ball."

Cameron laughed, but the sound was tight, and she knew he was as furious as she was at the careless rider. "But a hedgehog who curls up in the middle of the street is sure to be run down."

"Do not tease him," she said, faking a smile. "You were a very brave boy, Donald. You chose the right thing to do when you tried to protect your brother from harm. Now you must choose the right thing again and sit quietly."

"I will." He gave her a sly smile. "I will if you will let Heddy come in here. I can watch her until she wakes up. Then I can feed her while I sit here on my bed."

This time, Cameron's laugh was a bit more genuine. "The lad has the Hawksmoor charm, I must say."

"Charm?" she returned with a grin. "I would say rather he has the Hawksmoor determination to get what he wants, no matter what." Turning to Philip, she said, "If you will be very, very, very careful, you can bring Heddy from my room. Do not wake her, because she becomes quite testy if she is disturbed." She tapped his thumb which still bore the imprint from the hedgehog's teeth from when he had stuck his fingers into the cage to jostle Heddy.

"I will be very careful," Philip said with every inch of his childish pride.

"Very, very, very careful," corrected his brother.

Tess looked back at Cameron. "I would like to speak with you for a moment." She had held in for too long the appalling thoughts that the rumor of Donald's legitimacy and this incident were somehow connected. Yet who had anything to gain by making sure there was no reason for those rumors to continue? Cameron had become a duke with his brother's death. Although he had protested it was a title he did not want, he might have changed his mind.

No! She could not believe that. Cameron might be tight-lipped and unwilling to express his emotions, but his distress on the street when they had not known if Donald was alive could not have been feigned by even the greatest thespian.

Following Philip out of the room, Tess was not surprised when Cameron led her down the hall and into his sitting room. Unlike the day when she had been here before, the draperies were thrown back and sunshine filled the room. She let her shoulders droop from the tension left by her fear as she took the cup of tea Cameron held out to her. Sitting in the closest chair, she sipped.

"The doctor seems to think the injury will not cause him to limp," Cameron said as he sat beside her.

"That is good. He may have nightmares for a while, because he is frightened, despite his brave words. While the doctor was examining him, Donald kept saying he could not believe that nice gray horse would try to hurt him."

Cameron arched his brow. "Donald is very much his father's son. Russell adored horses when he was a child. He had spoken of breeding a fine line of race horses when he became a man. Grays were what he planned to breed, but he had only the one, which he apparently lost in some card game while I was on the Continent."

"My father likes grays, too. He bought one in Town almost a year ago."

Continuing as if he had not heard her, Cameron said, "When Russell was old enough to invest his money in a line of grays, Father believed it was a waste of money and that Russell would end up owing even more money on bets than he already did."

"Mayhap if he had allowed Russell to follow his

dream, your brother would not have gotten himself into the trouble that brought his death." She put her fingers to her lips as he scowled. "Cam, I am sorry. I should not have said such a thing about your father."

"I have said worse."

"You have? I thought you admired your father."

"I did, but he was a hard-hearted, narrow-thinking man." He stood and placed his cup on the mantel. "You look shocked, Tess."

"I am." She came to her feet, too, for the pulse of fear still pumped through her. "You have struggled to be so like him."

"Yes, but not because I admired him." He walked to the other side of the room and to the window which overlooked the spot where Donald had been injured.

"I do not understand."

"Mayhap it is better that you do not."

She bit her lip, not wanting to let the sob bubbling up through her escape and show him how it hurt when he raised this barrier between them. Placing her cup back on the tray, she said, "I should go and make certain Philip does not mishandle Heddy." She went to the door.

When it would not open, she looked up to see Cameron's broad hand, stained green from where he had been working with the living samples that had been delivered to the house earlier today, pressed against the door.

"Don't go, Tess." The soft whisper of her name wafted through her hair, setting each strand to dancing.

Looking over her shoulder, she stared at his lips, which were at the exact level of her eyes. Her gaze rose to his eyes, but she did not turn as she met the question displayed so vividly there. Ideas of how she should answer it, but unsure if she should even attempt to answer it, drifted within her head. She was caught by the sapphire fervor in his eyes. His yearning swept over and through her, becoming her own. For so many months, they had been man and wife, but strangers. Their cooperation while he sought answers about Russell's death had made them reluctant partners.

As his gaze moving along her enthralled her until she found each breath matched his, she faced him. Her arms slipped up his back to savor the warmth of his skin through his shirt. Lightly he brushed her hair back from her forehead. At his touch, her fingers quivered with a need she could not name, but which urged her to bring his mouth to hers and sweep away everything save her longing for him.

She flung her arms around his shoulders, which were broad enough to bear her despair as well as his own. Pressing her face to Cameron's shirt, she closed her eyes and listened to the sound of his heartbeat. The steady pulse helped her hold on to her senses, which seemed determined to vanish into a black void of horror. When his arms slowly rose to encircle her, she savored the warmth she had enjoyed so seldom. He might kiss her and hold her when he wanted to lure her into his bed, but she needed this gentle compassion which asked nothing from her.

Then she drew back. She must not lose herself in this exquisite pleasure when the boys might still be in great danger. She took a shuddering breath as she fought her own desire. First . . . "There is something I need to tell you."

He ran his finger along her lips, inciting the hunger for his lips. "Yes?"

"What happened to Donald may not have been an accident."

Cameron was sure some invisible force had struck him in the gut. *May not have been an accident.* He had heard those words too often lately. First Russell and his mistress, now Donald. "That is a strong accusation."

"I know." Tess's face became colorless, and her hands were shaking even more than they had been when she was in the children's room. "I want to tell you, but—"

"But what?"

"I promised I would not." She closed her eyes. "I made that promise before Donald was hurt."

He held out his hand. When she put her fingers on it, he watched her face as he drew her closer. By the elevens, he hated seeing her eyes dim with dismay. He wanted to see them sparkling with delight. Even more, he longed to watch them close as she held her mouth up for his kiss.

"Tell me," he ordered quietly.

She looked past him when a shout sounded in the hallway, but he tipped her face back toward his and repeated his command.

"There is," she whispered, "a rumor that one of Russell's sons may not be illegitimate. Your brother may have been married to a Mrs. Baum."

He released her, but only so he could step back an arm's length. Holding her so near kept him from concentrating on her words, and her fearful expression warned him that he would be very wise to heed them. "Mrs. Baum? Who is that?"

"Pamela Livingstone told me that she believes a Mrs. Baum was the boys' mother because of their hair color. You should ask her."

"Mrs. Baum?"

"No, for she is dead. You should speak with Mrs. Livingstone."

He chuckled. "You are an exceptional wife, for few would bid their husband to go and call on a woman who was once his mistress."

"This has nothing to do with you and me. This is about Donald and Philip."

"If one or both are legitimate, you will no longer be

a duchess." His finger stroked her cheek. "You need not say you care nothing for titles."

"That is true."

"It is possible Russell married in secret." He stroked her hair, but drew his fingers away. He must focus on the danger to Donald, not forget all about the children and everything else as he lost himself in the wonder of her kisses.

"I have sent Jenette to several of the nearby churches to discover if there is any record of such a wedding."

"It could have been held anywhere in Town."

"Anywhere? There are scores of churches."

"That is true. I shall share this with my contact at Bow Street right away. Russell could have married while I was out of the country."

"But your mother surely would have heard of it. A duke's wedding is not something that goes unnoticed."

"It is possible to keep any secret if one is willing to pay highly enough for it."

"Do you think that is why your brother was being blackmailed?"

"No, for Russell never cared a rap what other folks thought of him and his decisions, no matter how foolish they might be. He always knew someone would come along and help him clear away the mess."

"Like his younger brother?"

Cameron nodded.

"And now you are again." She squeezed his hands in a touch meant to offer a connection where he had tried to make sure none was forged. "Everyone should have someone like you, Cam, who is always there. Few other men would be willing to consider there might be truth in a rumor that could deny them the title of duke." Her lips quivered as she said, "I doubt my father would. He did not want me to tell you about this rumor."

"I am not your father—nor mine, either."

"I think I understand that now."

"Thank you, Tess."

"Thank you for shaking up your life *again?*" The gentleness in her smile threatened to undo his resolve to think only of how to protect the children.

"No." He cupped her cheek and tipped her face toward his. "Thank you for trusting me enough to tell me this even when your father asked you to say nothing and stay out of what could be very messy."

She edged away from him. "It is not a matter of trust. It is a matter of love."

"Love?"

"I have seen how you have come to love those boys as much as I do."

"They are good children," he somehow replied. His stomach had lurched and his heart had thudded against his ribs when she had spoken of love, but now his heart had fallen silent. The ache in his middle was not dread that she might be speaking of loving him, but regret she had not.

"They are naughty little boys," she said with a smile. "Much as you and Russell were, I suspect."

"You would be right."

"You must miss your brother."

He sighed. "He has been gone from my life for so many years that he seemed like a stranger."

"But he trusted you to raise his children."

"That trust has been tested now, when I nearly allowed one of them to be killed."

She gripped the back of the chair. "Cam, you must not fault yourself for that."

"I cannot bear to lose one of these children." He sank to the chair by the window. Looking down at the street where Donald had been, he said, "I have lost too many."

"Your brother and your father in such a short time." Tess knelt beside Cameron's chair and gazed up at his face that was more open than she had ever seen it. "I don't know how you endure it."

He stroked her cheek. "Tess, you are kind to think of those losses, but I am thinking of others." His gaze seemed to turn inward, and she put her hand on his arm. She must not let him slip away into his memories as he had too often before.

"Who?" she whispered.

"The names would mean nothing to you, for they were the men who served under my command during the battles against the French. They were more than comrades. They were friends, and I, as their officer, had to choose which one would have a chance at life and which one would risk dying."

"So you cut yourself off from all feeling in order to make that choice?"

By the elevens! Cameron did not want to answer that question, for he had spent his life striving to be like his father, who had made no secret he believed only fools gave in to melancholy and exultation. A man, his father averred, should keep his thoughts away from the seduction of emotion so every decision made was done so with clear thought.

Mayhap Cameron had learned the lesson well, for it had saved his sanity when he faced the insanity of the battlefield. He had learned to watch a friend die and still keep his mind on his duty. Upon returning to England, he had rebuilt his life with the same common sense.

Only here, where he had clung to the boyish dream of learning more about exotic plants, had he failed to banish emotion from his life. Even so, he had pursued his studies in a methodical manner . . . until Tess became part of his life.

"Now you understand. I am becoming ever deeper in debt to you, Tess," he said as he stood. Bringing her to her feet, he let his fingers sweep upward through her hair to tilt her mouth closer.

"Aunt Tess!"

As Cameron released her with a curse, Tess turned to see Philip race into the room. She started to chide him, but the little boy held up the cover that went over the hedgehog's cage and cried, "Heddy is gone!"

"Where?" she gasped.

"I don't know." Tears rushed down his round face. "I carried the cage very, very, very carefully to the table by Donald's bed. Just like you said, Aunt Tess. When I peeked under the cover, Heddy was gone."

"She could not have gotten far." She put her hands on his shoulders and turned him toward the door. "She must still be in my room. It has only been a few minutes."

Philip dragged his feet and muttered, "It may have been more than an hour."

"What?"

In a burst of words, Philip said, "Donald and I took Heddy to our room earlier. We wanted to show her our kites that we made with Mrs. Detloff." He choked back a sob. "She is not in our room. I looked everywhere."

"She will be looking for a place to hide. Somewhere under a shady leaf or—" In horror, she looked up at Cameron. "Your samples!"

Gathering up her skirt, she ran after Cameron, but his curse as he went into his workroom warned her he had found the hedgehog already. She went in and stared as he picked up a broken pot. The leaves were scattered in pieces across the floor. Although Heddy would not have eaten them, she had shredded them to build a hiding place behind the door.

Tess took the cloth from Philip and lifted the irritated hedgehog, which promptly rolled into a ball, out of the ruined plant. "Cam, I am so sorry."

"Get that beast out of here." His clipped words warned

how he was fighting to hold back his fury. "If it comes in here again, I will feed it to the closest fox."

"No!" cried Philip as he came in with the cage. "You can't do that!"

"Get both of them out of here." His voice was colder than she had ever heard it, as if every bit of life had been frozen out of him.

"Cam—"

"All of you, leave now."

"If you are angry," she said, placing the frightened hedgehog in its cage and latching the door, "be angry, Cam. Do not shut us out again."

He picked up the torn leaves, then dropped them on the table. "Being angry will gain me nothing now. Weeks of work is destroyed. Flying up to the boughs will not repair it."

She gave the little boy a gentle shove out the door. "No, it will not, but, Cam, if you—"

Clearing his throat by the door, Harbour could not hide his discomfort in intruding on this brangle. "Your Grace," he said, looking at Cameron, "this was delivered for you."

Cameron took the page held out to him. Reading it swiftly, he placed it under his coat. "Harbour, have my horse brought around." He did not look at Tess as he added, "I must go out and attend to this matter. Stay close to the house. I shall be back within an hour or two."

She took one step to follow him, but he was gone, the door closing behind him. Her shoulders sagged. So much she had hoped—had dared to believe—that he was changing. She had almost persuaded herself he cared about her and no longer viewed her as a tiresome burden. What an air-dreamer she had been to hope that he would care about her feelings and opinions.

Nineteen

The coffeehouse was far more respectable than the tavern where Cameron had gone to meet Russell's mistress's brother. Nodding to several men he knew, he walked to a clean table by a window that gave an excellent view of the street. Anyone who passed by and saw him talking to Todd would know that the Duke of Hawkington had engaged the services of the Bow Street Runners. He did not, at this point, care.

Blast that creature! He should have banished the hedgehog from his house as soon as he had learned it was there. If he had half the wit he claimed to possess, he would have sent Tess back to the country with it. How dare she challenge him to unleash his anger simply because she believed it would make him feel better? Blast that woman!

Forcing his exasperation into submission, he turned his attention to the man seated at the small table. Todd epitomized the word nondescript. His face was unremarkable and his hair a common brown. Of a middling height, he wore clothes that would have made him appear at home in a fine house or in a more impoverished one.

Taking the chair facing the representative from Bow Street, Cameron said, "I understand from your message you have uncovered something I should know about immediately."

"Yes." The man's accent gave no hint of his origins or his station. He pushed another piece of paper across the table. "You may want to read this, Your Grace. Mr. Knox is a friend of yours, I believe."

"Yes." He was abruptly irritated. If all the Bow Street Runners had managed to uncover was that he and Eustace Knox were friends, as they had been since their youth when they were a trio with Russell, terrorizing the countryside with their antics, then this was a waste of his time and his money. "What does that have to do with my brother's death?"

"Read this please, Your Grace." The man's expression did not alter from its practiced smile.

Cameron took the page and scanned it. He read it a second time, wanting to be certain he was not mistaken. Lowering it to the table, he asked, "Why do you believe Eustace is being blackmailed?"

"We have spoken with his solicitor. There has been a regular disbursement of two hundred fifty pounds each month."

That was the same amount unaccounted for in Russell's books. As he did not believe in coincidences, there must be some connection, but that was not the issue now. "Why have you gone to speak to my friend's solicitor? I asked you to find out who was involved in my brother's death. Surely you do not believe it is Eustace Knox."

"No, we do not." Todd folded the page and put it back under his coat.

"Then why are you delving into his private matters?"

"Because it appears he is being blackmailed for the same reason your brother was."

"Russell?" He leaned forward and lowered his voice. "Tell me what you have discovered."

Todd stood. Withdrawing a sheaf of papers sealed with wax, he said, "You should find everything you need to know in here. I urge you to read them with all due speed, Your Grace. Contact us once you decide what you wish to do."

Cameron broke the seal and began to read. He was only partway down the first page when he jumped to his feet. Racing through the door, he shouted an apology over his shoulder to the man he had struck in the doorway. Looking both ways along the street, he knew he had no time to lose . . . or he could lose everything.

Donald fingered the tail of his kite and whined, "But, Aunt Tess, today is the day we are supposed to play with Ned Wainger at his house."

"I know."

"He is leaving by the week's end for his father's estate somewhere in the country." Donald folded his short arms over his chest. His frown made him resemble his uncle more than ever. "You promised I could show him my kite before he left."

"That was before you were knocked off your feet by that horse." She looked out the door of the nursery again, although she had not heard any footfalls. How long would it take Cameron to complete this errand? With each passing minute, the wounds between them festered. She wanted to apologize for Heddy's misdeeds, and she longed to hear him say he was sorry, too. She dared to believe he would give her a chance to speak of the love she could no longer push out of her mind or her heart.

Donald slid from the bed to the floor, struggling to hide his grimace as he brushed his injured leg against the covers. "Please, Aunt Tess. I will not be wild-acting."

"Wild-acting?"

"That is what Mrs. Detloff says," interjected Philip, "when we are ramb—ramb—"

"Rambunctious?" she asked, smiling. These little boys somehow had found their way into her heart, as well, and they soothed its anguish. She held out her hands to them. "Very well. We shall make a brief call on your friend." When Donald opened his mouth to cheer, she raised her hands to her lips. "No wild-acting, remember?"

As the boys pulled on their shoes, Tess asked for the carriage to be brought around. She went to tell Mrs. Detloff she was taking the boys out. The governess offered to come along, but Tess urged her to remain in bed for the rest of the afternoon. A lump on the side of Mrs. Detloff's head showed where she had struck it on a step when she had suffered her *crise de nerfs* and fainted.

Tess listened to the boys chattering like two blackbirds while she tied her bonnet under her chin. They did not pause even as they gathered up their brightly colored kites and went down the stairs.

"Harbour," she said when the butler held the door for them, "let His Grace know, if he returns before we do, that we are visiting the Waingers' household. We shall not be long."

The butler was scowling. "Your Grace, I heard His Grace say—"

"We shall not be long," Tess repeated, not wanting to be scolded by the butler for not remaining here as Cameron had asked.

With the tiger's help, she assisted the little boys into the closed carriage. She handed the two kites to the boys. When Philip let out a cry when the tail of his caught on the edge of the step and tore, Tess told him to wait while she went in and got some material to fix it.

"By the time we get to Ned's house," she said, "it will be as good as new."

She hurried into the house. Waving aside Harbour's

offer to get the small basket of supplies Mrs. Detloff always carried with her whenever she took the boys out, Tess retrieved it from the nursery. She was rushing too quickly down the steps, and several wooden spools fell out. With the tiger's help, she gathered them up and put them back into the basket.

When she was sitting beside the boys in the carriage, Tess helped Philip mend his kite. Her fingers trembled, and she knew it had not been only the need to hurry that had made her so clumsy on the steps and now here in the carriage. Unlike Cameron, penting up her emotions made her shake as if with a fever. This trip to Mr. Wainger's house must be brief, because she wanted to return to her rooms and let the heat of her tears scorch away this pain in the very center of her heart.

"Are you all right?" Donald asked.

"Yes. Why do you ask?"

He reached up and touched her cheek. "You are crying, Aunt Tess."

"Something must have gotten in my eye." She wiped away the tears. She must conceal any sign of them. Weeping could cause Cameron to withdraw even further from her. "I will be fine."

Donald started to ask another question, but the carriage suddenly rocked to the side. Both boys grabbed her arms. She pulled them close as she looked out the window. She could not see anything at first. Then a gray horse raced too close to the carriage, cutting it off.

The coachee shouted as he tried to turn the carriage before it struck the horse and rider. It lurched again, out of control.

Pulling Donald into the crook of one arm, Tess reached for Philip with the other. He slid out away from her outstretched fingers as the carriage tipped. wildly, then bounced like a child's ball. The wheels struck something. Wood splintered, and the carriage tilted again. This time, it did not right itself.

"Philip!" she screamed as she slanted over Donald, trying to protect him as a wheel snapped and the back left corner of the carriage slammed into the ground. Everything in the basket flew. Mrs. Detloff's scissors! Would they strike one of the boys? She ducked her head as she shouted Philip's name again.

The door was torn open before Tess realized the carriage had come to a stop. The coachman peered in. "Your Grace, are you unharmed?"

"Donald and I are. Philip?" she called.

A shadow moved at the far side of the almost upended carriage. Philip let out a screech when she reached for him, and she saw his arm was hanging at an odd angle.

"Help me get him out," Tess said.

The tiger assisted the coachee, who lifted Donald out of the wobbly carriage. Tess stood to one side, comforting Donald. As soon as Philip was out of the carriage, she sent the tiger running back toward the house to have a doctor waiting.

Coughing as dust swirled up from where the carriage had hit the walkway, Tess picked up Philip. He wept softly against her shoulder as he cradled his right arm in his left hand.

"Can I call for a chair for you?" the coachman said, anxiously glancing over his shoulder. She knew he wanted to tend to his horses, checking for injuries and calming them before a crowd could gather.

"Yes, thank you."

As the coachman went to tend to his horses, a form came from the other direction through the dust. She was about to open her mouth to cry out in fear when she heard a familiar voice ask, "Tess, whatever were you doing in *this* carriage?"

Tess was relieved to see that the man stepping from

the clouds of dust was her father. What was he doing here? It did not matter. He was here when she needed help. "Papa! Did you see the rider who . . . ?"

Sickness sifted through her stomach when she saw the horse her father was leading. It was the gray that had been ridden with neck-or-nothing speed toward the carriage.

"Tess, I did not mean to put *you* in danger," her father said, his face the same shade as his horse.

"Then whom did you intend to put in danger?" She answered her own question before he could. "You were trying to drive the carriage off the road because you believed Cam was in it?"

"Of course not. Do not be silly." He flicked dust from his coat. "I worked hard to make sure you wed Hawksmoor and became a duchess, Tess. I would have been a fool to let all my hard work go for naught because of—"

When he reached for Donald, Tess stepped between him and the boy. "Do not touch him!"

The coachee came around the carriage and choked, "It was you! You cut us off and drove us into that tree."

"Your head is addled, my good man. I am the duchess's father. I would not risk my dear daughter's life."

Tess ignored her father's smooth answer. Mayhap her head was the one that had been struck hardest on the side of the carriage, but it seemed to have given her a clarity of vision she had not had since she woke with Cameron in her bed.

"Not *my* life," she said. "You were trying to kill Donald and Philip."

"Tess, you are becoming hysterical."

She backed away from him as she saw him reach under his coat. When he withdrew a dueling pistol, the coachman drew in his breath with a hiss.

"Papa, what are you doing?" she cried.

"Finishing what I started when I learned your husband's father was dead." He spat on the ground. "Finally he was on his way to burn in hell."

"But the duke was your friend!"

"Once." Her father's mouth grew straight. "Until the night he belittled me at our club by suggesting I was a leech preying on my betters. Doors that had been open to me before were instantly closed, and I was utterly humiliated. I vowed he would pay and pay me well. When he died before the debt could be evened, his heir inherited the debt. I found a way for him to repay it when I chanced upon a carriage accident much like this one."

"When Russell died?"

He laughed. "No, he escaped the other one. He and Knox both escaped, but the ladies they were with—ladies of quality who were married to very powerful men—were not so lucky. It became imperative that it not be known either the new duke or Knox was involved in the accident. They paid me well to keep my mouth shut."

"Paid?" She drew Donald away from her father one step, then another. "You lied to me. You said Eustace Knox was blackmailing you."

"It was actually quite the reverse." Cameron came around the side of the coach. Tess barely recognized him. His face was taut with rage, and his hands were fisted at his sides. "You were extorting money from both my brother and Eustace, Masterson, bleeding every penny from them until they were forced to do your abominable bidding. Otherwise you would have spilled the truth. First, you took my brother's dream along with his gray stallion. Then you forced Eustace to bring me to your house along with some drugged wine so you could have me married to your daughter."

Tess gasped. It all fit so well, but she did not want to believe it. Papa had done all this? Just to even an insult?

When Cameron moved closer to her father, she wanted

to cry out a warning. Didn't he see the gun her father was holding? She did not dare to speak, fearing anything she said might be the impetus for Papa to fire that gun.

Cameron did not look at her as he said, "Eustace became tired of your greed and your determination to have your grandson obtain my father's title. After he came to my house—upon your orders—with doctored wine after Lord Peake's party, he was sickened by his own part in your scheme. That was when he devised the rumor that my brother married Donald's mother. He decided to force your hand."

"There will be no need to prove or disprove any rumors when there are no competitors for your title." He raised the gun, pointing it at Donald.

"No!" Tess cried, stepping in front of the little boy.

Her voice was lost beneath a shout—not hers, nor the boys'. Cameron's!

He launched himself at her father. He knocked the gun from her father's hand, then slammed her father up against the carriage, striking him once, then again. Only the coachman running up to him halted him from hitting Papa a third time.

Cameron shoved the coachee away and whirled back to her father, who had slumped to the ground. Grasping Papa by the lapels, he lifted him and shoved him against the carriage.

"No!" Tess shouted again. She handed Philip to the coachman, who was staring at Cameron in disbelief. She ran to Cameron and seized his arm. "Don't! You will kill him."

"And save the hangman his prize," he snarled.

"No," she cried. "If you kill him, you will hang, too."

"I don't care."

She put her hands on either side of his face and turned it toward her. His eyes were wild with unfettered fury.

She quailed before it, for she had never seen its like. *This* was the wild anger Cameron had fought to hide.

But it was part of the man she loved, and she would not be frightened by anything about him again. She took his face in her hands again as she whispered, "Cam, I love you. I want you with me, not at the end of a hempen noose."

He shook her off, but she refused to be pushed aside. Again she turned his face toward her.

"I love you, Cam. Let the hate go, and tell me you love me, too."

He released her father and pulled her into his arms. His kiss was as untamed as the fire in his eyes. She reveled in the passions she had known were deep within him—awesome, overmastering passions she wanted to share.

Shouts came from every direction, and Cameron stepped back. He kept his arm around her waist as a trio of men she did not know surrounded her father. When Cameron whispered they were Bow Street Runners, she hid her face on his shoulder, not wanting to see the end to this debacle.

"Tess!" shouted her father.

She knew she could not let her own delusions keep her from confronting the truth. Looking up, she said, "Papa, I thought you loved me, but you used me."

"I did this for you. You are now a duchess."

"No, Papa, you did this for yourself. You left me living frugally and all alone in the country, watching my beloved home fall into ruins, while you enjoyed your ill-gotten money here in Town. You did not do any of this for me." She walked to where the boys were watching, wide-eyed, as people paused to gawk at the broken carriage.

A chair appeared, and the coachman put Philip and

Donald into it. Cameron waved for them to leave for Grosvenor Square. "I will bring Her Grace."

The coachee, leading the horses, followed the chair.

Ignoring the crowd, Cameron steered Tess to where his own horse waited. He stopped and sighed, the incredible fury gone from his voice. "Tess, I am sorry it had to end like this."

"Sorry? You saved me from my own father's treachery." She shivered, then whispered, "I hated your father for persuading you, you should never let anyone get under your skin and anger you or let someone's kindness touch you. I thought he had destroyed your life. 'Twas my own father who was out to destroy not just my life, but yours, too."

"Tess, forget that."

"Forget it?"

He gripped her shoulders. "Tess, I am so sorry I lost my temper."

"You had every cause." She smiled. "Now that you have unleashed your feelings, Cam, do not put them away again. They are fearsome, but they are *you*. And I want to love every part of you, not just the man who controls all his emotions with such ease."

"As you can see, it is not with such ease." He stroked her shoulders. "The first day we were wed, you said something to your father I wished you would say to me now."

"What?"

"That one forgives those one loves. I could not forget that."

"Why would that remain in your mind when you hated me?"

He shook his head as he framed her face with gentle hands. "Sweetheart, I have never hated *you*, even though I must own I hated the idea of being married to you."

"Honest as always." She smiled, sure her heart would burst with joy.

"Honest as always."

"I will be glad to forgive you anything." She chuckled.

"Anything?"

"Almost anything." She curved her hand along his cheek. "And will you be as honest with me about one other thing?"

"Yes."

"Do you hate being married to me?"

He drew her closer. "No, I have not hated being married to you for a long time."

"But you kept the papers that Mr. Paige gave you."

"Papers?"

"I saw them in the account book in your room the day you told me about your brother's death."

He thought for a moment, then laughed. "I was using that folded letter from Paige for a marker as I went through Russell's accounts, trying to figure them out. The rest of his papers were thrown away the day after he had them delivered to me in hopes I would change my mind about divorcing you."

"So you don't want to divorce me?"

With a growl, he tugged her up against him. "Why would I want to divorce you? I love you, and I will never give you cause to divorce me." He chuckled. "Nor shall I let you give me cause to seek a divorce from you."

"And just how do you intend to do that?"

He answered her with his lips over hers. The gentleness vanished into the desire that had waited so long and now would be so sweet.

AUTHOR'S NOTE

I'm glad you picked up *His Unexpected Bride*. I hope you enjoyed it.

My next Zebra Regency will be *A Rather Necessay End,* available in September 2002. This is the beginning of a romantic mystery series about Lady Priscilla Flanders and Sir Neville Hathaway. Priscilla Flanders is recently out of mourning for her husband, the Reverend Dr. Flanders. She has three children, the eldest who is badgering Priscilla to be fired-off into the Season, and the youngest who has inherited the title of earl. The last thing she needs is to find a duke's corpse in her garden. Her only ally is Sir Neville Hathaway—a rogue who is a dear friend. Together, they must find the murderer before more elderly men in the village die, and Priscilla is accused of the crime.

I like hearing from my readers. You can contact me by email at: jaferg@mediaone.net, or by mail at: Jo Ann Ferguson, P.O. Box 575, Rehoboth, MA 02769. Check out my web site at: www.joannferguson.com

Happy reading!

Put a Little Romance in Your Life With
Constance O'Day-Flannery

Discover the Romances of
Hannah Howell

Celebrate Romance with one of Today's Hottest Authors
Meagan McKinney

More Zebra Regency Romances